First Bitten
(The Alexandra Jones Series #1)

Samantha Towle

Copyright 2012 Samantha Towle

All rights reserved. No part of this book may be reproduced, stored in a retrieval system, or transmitted in any form or by any means without the prior written permission of the publisher, except by a reviewer who may quote brief passages in a review to be printed by a newspaper, magazine, or journal.

Second edition

All characters appearing in this work are fictitious. Any resemblance to real persons, living or dead, is purely coincidental.

Mum, this one's for you. Thank you, for everything.

Contents

Chapter 1: The End of Me

Chapter 2: The Transition

Chapter 3: The Morning After

Chapter 4: Scarred

Chapter 5: Existing

Chapter 6: Blood Drinker

Chapter 7: Shifters

Chapter 8: Brothers

Chapter 9: Headlines

Chapter 10: Hope

Chapter 11: Knee Deep

Chapter 12: Stripped Bare

Chapter 13: Over and Over

Chapter 14: Instinct

Chapter 15: In His Hands

Chapter 16: The Beginning

Chapter 17: Surprise

Chapter 18: Nathan

Chapter 19: Spiders Web

Chapter 20: Hold Your Breath

Chapter 21: Who Knew

Chapter 22: The Lost One

Chapter 23: I Am Not There

Chapter 24: The Unknown

Chapter 25: Ipseity

Chapter 26: Imputed

Chapter 27: You and I

Chapter 28: Without You

Chapter 1

The End of Me

"Arggh! Just leave me alone, Eddie! I can't believe a word that comes out of your mouth! You're a lying, cheating … scumbag and I don't ever want to speak to, or see you, ever again, you … you wanker!" I disconnect the call and angrily loft my mobile toward the mass of trees standing tall before me.

Turning sharply, I catch my heel in a crack in the paving. "Shit!" I cry out as I fall backwards, losing my shoe in the process. I land hard my bum. "Oww!"

"You alright?" Carrie gets up from the bench she was sitting on and drunkenly totters over to me. I can tell she's trying not to laugh, the grin she's not so gallantly suppressing saying it all.

"No," I grumble. Tears sting my eyes. I take a deep breath and force them back.

I will not cry. I will not cry.

A giggle escapes Carrie as she plonks herself down on the concrete floor beside me.

I glare at her.

"Sorry, babe." She throws her arm around my shoulder, hugging me to her. "Eddie is a complete twat. Twat with a capital T. And you, my gorgeous friend, are far too good for him, always have been. You deserve so much better than him." She twists a lock of my hair around her finger, tugging on it good-naturedly. "You know I'm right. I've said this to you a million times before. You're far too good to waste your life on a ... twatting wanker like him."

Through my misery, I glance sideways at her. "Twatting wanker?"

She grins mischievously, her green eyes sparkling, and I can't help but laugh. Carrie always manages to make me laugh, even when I'm at my lowest, which is where I am right now, literally.

I lean forward, releasing myself from Carrie's caring hold and pick my shoe up. "Ahh no, I've scuffed the heel!" I groan as I inspect it. "My beautiful, two month old Jimmy Choos and they're bloody ruined! These were my treat from my bonus." That dismal feelings seeps back into me.

"Here, let me have a look." Carrie takes the shoe from my hand and puts it close to her face, examining it. "It's not that bad," she says dismissively, handing it back to me. "It'll glue back down."

I turn and look at her with disgust. "Glue! I'm not gluing a pair of Jimmy Choos. Bloody hell, Carrie, that's sacrilegious!" I clutch the shoe to my chest. "Arggh! This is all Eddie's fault. I bloody hate him, the bastard!"

Well I don't hate him, yet, but I will very soon, I'm sure of it. I'm just currently stuck in the 'I should hate him' phase, but struggling to because I still love him.

Eddie, my lying, cheating, scumbag, arsehole of a boyfriend, or, as I should now say, ex-boyfriend. Eddie, the cheating bastard, whom I've wasted three years of my life on.

That all too familiar pain stabs straight into my heart. Tears swell my eyes again. I run my fingers under them to catch the tears before they fall. The last thing I need right now is mascara-stained cheeks.

I found out about Eddie's extra-curricular activities yesterday morning while we were eating breakfast together. I'd received a text from his slutty new squeeze the night before, but only realised I had a message that morning. Accompanying said text was a very graphic photo of Eddie in a 'compromising' position for added effect. Classy, I know. Really I should have learnt my lesson from the last time.

It will never happen again, Alex, I swear to you ... I love you ... I'm so sorry ... I can't live without you ... I made a terrible, stupid mistake ...

But really it was me who made the mistake when I believed he wouldn't do it again.

So, after chucking my breakfast at him, coffee included and a few other choice items, I headed to our bedroom, called Carrie and asked her to come and pick me up. I packed my bags, ignoring Eddie's pathetic pleas for me to stay, while I waited the twenty minutes it took Carrie to drive from her parents' house in Hackness, where she still lives, to my house in Scarborough.

When she arrived, honking her horn, I rushed out the front door in a flurry of tears, threw my bags in the car boot and didn't look back, even though I knew Eddie was standing in the doorway watching me leave.

Carrie and I have been best friends for fifteen years. The first time I met her was on introductory day at our old senior school, Scarborough High, and I just knew I'd know her my whole life. She was all fiery red curly hair and braces, but as confident as hell. Smart, vivacious and sassy, she takes no shit, unlike me. She's all the parts I'm missing, my other half really and that's when I knew I'd met my soul mate. Carrie is always there for me, no matter what, and vice-versa.

Both my parents were killed in a road accident when I was sixteen, a drunk driver overtaking them on a country road with an upcoming bend, an oncoming car; there were no survivors.

I fell apart and Carrie put me back together. Legally an adult, I had absolutely no clue how to take care of myself, let alone do things adults have to take care of. That's when Carrie's family became mine. Her parents, Angie and Tom, stepped in and sorted everything for me. They took me into their huge home and spoilt me like I was one of their own, which now, nine years later, I still am.

Carrie's been on hand with Kleenex and Ben and Jerry's for all my boyfriend disasters, well mainly Eddie the boyfriend disaster from hell. She sat patiently with me yesterday while I cried the whole day and night away. Then, when I woke up this morning feeling very angry, Carrie suggested we should get dressed up and go out to the only pub in Hackness tonight, The Grange, and get drunk.

I was completely on board with the idea - anything to numb the pain - but then the pain was still there when they were calling last orders at the bar and I didn't want to wait the forty minutes it would take for the taxi to arrive, so we decided to walk home, which we've done hundreds of times before. It takes about half an hour and, to be honest, it's not the nicest of walks, even in the daylight. It's all country roads and forests but it's also as safe as houses around here. The last time there was a crime here was – well never.

All I wanted to do was get home as fast as possible and continue on drinking myself into oblivion, well, just until I passed out. And I was well on my way to achieving that goal until I, for some ungodly reason, made the fatal error of answering Eddie's call. And here I am, right back to square one. I've let Eddie and his lies into my head again. This is what happens when I drink; I lose all common sense. Or is it just when it comes to Eddie that I lose my common sense?

I drop my heavy head into my hands. "I'm such an idiot, Care."

"No you're not. Eddie's the idiot." She rubs a soothing hand on my back. I glance up at her. "He just doesn't seem to realise when he's got a great thing," she affirms. "The guy's a loser. L-O-S-E-R." She spells the word out for dramatic effect, putting her thumb and forefinger into the L shape and resting it against her forehead.

Yep, she's definitely drunk – she'd never do that sober. I giggle through my haze of tears and make a mental note to remind her of that in the morning so I can take the piss.

"You were the best thing that ever happened to him," she adds sincerely, taking hold of my hand and patting it with her other. "He'll know this soon enough when you're not there taking care of him anymore."

I stare into the black dense forest before me. "Mmm ... "

She grabs hold of my shoulder, forcing me round to look at her. "Alex, please tell me you're not actually considering going back to him. You know he'll do it again."

"No I'm not," I say, sounding way too defensive.

"Alex ... " She arches her eyebrow at me in that knowing way she does. She knows me better than anyone.

"No," I repeat, my voice quieter now, "I'm not going back. I promise. But it's hard. I can't just stop loving him in a day. We've been together for three years. We have a home together. Okay, so it's his house and the mortgage is still in his name, but we have other stuff together, like ... like ... CDs and DVDs ... and well, other stuff."

Actually now that I think about it, after three years together we really don't have a lot to show for our relationship, except for a lot of broken promises and betrayals.

"I know it's hard, Alex, but Eddie didn't care about the last three years when he was messing around behind your back. Just keep reminding yourself of what he's done to you, twice, now. It'll get easier, babe, I promise, and you know I'm here for you, no matter what. I've always got your back."

"I know." I look gratefully at her. "Ditto."

"Anyway, I was thinking we should get my dad to sack him," she says out of the blue, very nonchalantly.

Eddie works for Tom. He's a sales manager at Tom's car dealership in Scarborough. Tom has ten altogether across the region. That's how I met Eddie. It was at the dealership's annual Christmas party three years ago. He was so handsome, smart and funny, and I was hooked from the word go. Little did I know.

I shake my head, tempting as it is, and say, "No, Care, we can't ask Tom to do that. It'd be wrong to put him in that position."

"He'd do it for you though." She nudges my shoulder with hers. "You know he would. He loves you to death."

I turn and give her a firm look. "I know, and that's why I won't ask him ... and neither will you."

She grins wickedly and winks. "No promises."

"Care ... !" I warn.

"Okay, okay." She rolls her eyes. "Whatever you want. Is twat-face Eddie at work tomorrow?"

I scrunch my nose up in thought. "What day is it?"

"Er ... " she pulls her mobile out of her bag and lights the screen up, checking the date and time, "it's Saturday now."

"He's not back in work till Monday."

"Okay, well I'll go round to your house on Monday while he's at work and pick up the rest of your stuff, if you want? Get you out of there and moved back home properly. Start as you mean to go on."

"Would you mind?" I look hopefully at her. The last thing I want to do is go back to the house. I'm worried if I do, I might end up never leaving.

"Wouldn't offer if I did." She smiles warmly and gets to her feet. "Come on, let's go home." She holds her hand out to me.

I take a lingering, woeful glance at my shoe and slip it back on my foot. Eddie the bastard, he's ruined my life, and now my beautiful shoes.

I take Carrie's hand and get unsteadily to my feet. I wrap my arm around her waist, resting my head onto her shoulder. "Thanks, Care," I mumble into her red hair. "I don't know what I'd do without you. I love you, you know."

"You'd do fine," she says, "and I love you too. Now come on, you soppy git, let's get you home." She wraps her arm around my shoulder and we start to walk on, supporting each other.

"Ahh shit!" I sigh dramatically, coming to a halt.

"What?"

"I chucked my phone in there." I gesture dramatically toward the forest laid out to the side of us. "My whole life is on that phone," I whine. "I can't lose it."

Bloody Eddie. He doesn't even have to be here and he causes me problems. Maybe it's the essence of him that's still lingering over me, continuing to make my life shit.

I walk over to the edge of the pavement, teetering between it and the slope down into woodland.

"Whereabouts did you throw it?" Carrie asks, following me over and standing beside me.

"I dunno." I shrug. "Around there ... somewhere." I point at the bracken.

Carrie peers forward. "Well, it can't have landed that far away. You're not that good a thrower. I remember your weak arm from netball at school." She nudges me with her shoulder, grinning. "Tell you what, I'll ring your phone and we'll follow the sound to it."

"Good thinking Batman." I nudge her back.

"Er, more like Catwoman, if you don't mind," she says dramatically, sweeping a hand down herself. "Does this body look in any way masculine to you?"

"Shut up and get your bloody phone out, will you." I laugh.

She smirks and gets her mobile out of her bag again. It takes her a good minute to dial my number, which I know for a fact, she has on speed dial. She really is drunk.

"It's ringing," she sings, phone clamped to her ear.

I immediately hear my phone start to blast out Adele's 'Someone Like You'. I changed it to that ring tone yesterday. Okay, I know I'm being maudlin, but it's not every day you find out your boyfriend's been cheating on you. Well, okay, for me it's the second time in a year, but that's not the point.

Carrie pulls the phone away from her ear and leaves it ringing in her hand. Holding hands, we both clumsily make our way down the incline into the woods as we begin our search, following the sound of the music into the trees.

"I can't see it anywhere," Carrie says looking around. "Mind, I can hardly see shite-all in here. It's pitch black!"

I squint into the darkness. She's right, it is pitch black. Nerves creep over me. I quickly quash them. I need to find my phone.

The ringing stops. It must have diverted to answerphone.

"Ring it again, Care, will you."

Adele resumes her singing. I can hear it clear over to my right. Breaking away from Carrie, I head that way. The music's getting louder. I'm getting close. A few more steps and I spot it nestled in a bush, flashing prettily away at me. Not a good thrower, eh, Carrie?

"Got it!" I cheer, staggering toward it. I lean down and pluck it out of the prickly bush. I snag my hand on a prickle. "Ouch!" I suck the wound on my hand and get an instant taste of metallic ... blood.

"You alright?" Carrie asks concerned, heading toward me.

"Yeah, fine. Just cut my hand on the bush. Nothing serious. Got my phone, though." I grin, waving it about.

"Good. Now can we get out here?"

"Yep, let's go." I make to move and get nowhere. I'm stuck in some soft mud. "Bloody hell," I grumble, looking down. "My heels are stuck in the mud."

"You and them feckin' shoes!" Carrie laughs loudly. It echoes all around. "Here." She holds her hands out for me to take. "I'll pull you out."

I take hold of her hands. She starts to pull me forward while I try to wriggle my shoes free from the sticky mud. I get one free, step forward and suddenly the other comes free. I fall forward onto Carrie.

"Bloody hell!" she chuckles, somehow keeping us both up. I have no clue how she's managing to stay vertical.

I glance down at my shoes. They're all covered in mud. "Ahh crap!" I groan, lifting my feet up in turn. "I've knackered the heel and covered them in mud in the space of five minutes. I bloody love these shoes as well." My lips turn down at the corners.

"Really, I would never have guessed," she skits.

"Piss off," I mutter in a light-hearted tone, but inside the gloom has clamped itself steadfastly around my heart.

She grins at me in the darkness and links her arm through mine. "We'll clean them up when we get home."

"I don't think anything is gonna save these babies now, well nothing short of a miracle."

"Come on, drama queen. We'll pray for their salvation on the way home."

"Ha, ha, funny! You ever thought about becoming a comedi–"

"Wait." She grips hold of my arm with her fingers. "Did you hear that?"

"What, the sound of my heart breaking for the second time in two days?" I glance down longingly at my ruined shoes.

"No ... that."

I strain to listen. "I can't hear anything." Now I think about it, it's actually eerily silent in here. No rustling leaves, no animal sounds. Nothing.

I start to move, but Carrie stays put, pulling me back to a standstill. "No seriously," she whispers, "I definitely heard something ... it was like, I dunno, like ... someone's chopping wood or something."

"Shurrup, Carrie, you div," I say at normal volume, laughing. "Who the hell would be out here at this time chopping ... ?" Then I hear it. It's not loud but Carrie's wrong, it doesn't sound like wood being chopped, it sounds more like something's being sharpened on wood, kind of like when our cat used to run its claws down the doorframe.

"You hear it," she whispers.

"Yes," I breathe out. The hairs on the back of my neck prickle. I hear movement behind me. My stomach drops hollow. Swallowing hard, I loosen my arm from Carrie's grip and we both, very slowly, turn around.

It's standing about ten feet away. Its yellow eyes are protruding like beacons in the dark night, and they're fixed onto me.

It's obvious why it's here. You would think I would have tried to make a run for it by now or screamed, or done something. I don't know why I haven't. All I do know is I can't seem to tear my eyes away from its penetrating stare. It tilts its head, almost as if contemplating me, chilling me to the bone.

Then I feel Carrie's hand search for mine. She grabs hold, interlocking our fingers. I can feel her fear almost like it's pouring out of her skin and sinking straight into mine. A silent communication passes between us, and in the same instant we both turn and run.

I don't get far.

I'm hit in the back. The air is knocked out of me. I'm going down. I'm pinned to the floor. I can't move. My face is pressed into the mud. I can't catch a breath. I'm suffocating. I feel a searing pain tear down my right side. I cry out but no sound comes. I manage to move my head slightly. I get a glimpse of Carrie's red hair. The pain intensifies. I feel like I'm being ripped open...

The last thing I hear is screaming. An ear-piercing scream. And I can't tell if it's coming from Carrie or me.

Chapter 2

The Transition

Saturday, 1:03am

"You got her? Careful, she's bleeding out pretty bad. She's lost a lot of blood already. Nathan, press down hard on her wound. Sol, get the first aid kit. I'll stitch her up for all the good it'll do her. Poor lass ... What the hell happened? ... Was it one of them? ... I didn't know there was any in the area ... Is he dead? ... He won't have been alone, there'll be others ... Hey, she's coming round...

"Can you tell me your name, honey?"

I blink up at the blurry figure hovering above me. "Where's Carrie ... ?"

Saturday, 2.55am

"Sorted?"

"Yeah."

"Do you think anyone could have seen you move the bodies?"

"Nope, there wasn't a soul around for miles."

Saturday, 4:15am

"It hurts..."

"Ssh, don't try to talk. Just sleep."

"Where's Carrie?"

"Sleep."

"But it hurts..."

"I know it does. Sleep."

Saturday, 10:30am

"How's she doing, Nate?"

"She's sleeping at the moment."

"You wanna get some rest? I'll take over watching her."

"Nah, Dad, I'll stay with her. I brought her here. I feel like I should be the one to be with her when she passes."

Saturday, 16:44pm

"She still alive, Nate?"

"Yes, she's still alive, Sol."

"You look knackered, son. Why don't you go get some sleep? Sol can stay with her."

"No. I'm alright."

"Mind, it shouldn't be much longer now. I'm surprised she's lasted this long, to be honest."

"Maybe we should just put her out of her misery."

"Christ almighty, Sol!"

"I'm just saying! I mean, look at her."

"I know, but I didn't raise you to say things like that."

"What, so we're just gonna sit by and watch while she dies an agonising death?"

"No, son, but we're not playing God either."

Sunday, 12:02am

"Arggh!! What's happening to me? It hurts! Help me, please help me!"

"It's okay, honey, we're here. Sol, go get some more of those painkillers. Nathan, fetch a bowl of cold water and some towels, will you? She's really burning up."

"The pain ... you've got to make it stop ... "

"I know, honey, it's gonna be okay ... Nate, soak that towel and lay it over her stomach where the wound is."

"God, Dad, look at her. Maybe I shouldn't have saved her. Maybe I should have let that bastard kill her and have been done with it, instead of putting her through all of this agony."

"You did the right thing."

"I'm not so sure anymore. I'm starting to think maybe Sol's right, maybe we should just, you know, end it for her."

"Sol talks shit."

"I am still here, you know."

"Well you shouldn't be. Go get those bloody painkillers! Nate, I know you, there's no way you could have lived with yourself if you'd walked away and let him kill her."

"I know, but I just didn't know it'd be like this, and it's been a day now.

Shouldn't the infection have killed her? I didn't think they lasted this long once infected."

"Neither did I but–"

"Arggh! Help me! Please! Help me!"

"I'm here, honey. Sol, where the bloody hell are you with those painkillers?!"

Sunday, 06:30am

I want to go home. Carrie, is that you? I'm so sorry, Care. Help me, please ... help me ... I can't take the pain anymore ...

Sunday, 13:05pm

"You've gotta make it stop! My body's on fire, I'm burning. Help me, please!" I grab hold of the blurry figure beside me. "You've got to make it stop!" A strong hand untangles mine from their clothing, and encompasses it. "Don't leave me, please."

"I'm not going anywhere, Alexandra. I'm staying right here." A hand brushes over my clammy forehead. "Just try and relax. I'm going to get something to make you feel better."

"Dad, that morphine..."

"I'm getting it now."

"I don't understand how she's still alive."

"Me neither, son. Me neither."

"She's going through the transition, though, isn't she?"

"Seems that way, Nate."

"Do you think she's gonna survive?"

"If you'd have asked me yesterday, I'd of said no, but now I'm not so sure. The girl's a fighter, I'll give her that."

"She's human, though. I just don't get it, but it's bad though, isn't it, if she makes it through?"

"Well, it's not great, son, no."

A large shadow hovers over me. "Here, sweetheart, this'll take the pain away." I feel the needle pierce my skin. "Thank y–"

Sunday, 23:55pm

"She's asleep?"

"Yep."

"So she survived, then."

"Looks that way."

"And the bite?"

"Healed. She has the trademark scar."

"She's changed, then. She's one of them."

"The only one. She's in trouble, isn't she, Dad?"

"We all are son ... we all are."

Chapter 3

The Morning After

Ooh my whole body's stiff. I must have slept in the same position all night. I feel like I've been run over by a bus. My head hurts – a lot. Painkillers needed ASAP. I run my tongue around my dry mouth. Urgh, it tastes like the inside of a toilet, not that I know what the inside of a toilet tastes like, but, well, you know what I mean.

Great idea Alex. Drink copious amounts of alcohol to numb the pain. Downside, I'm now going to pay for it today with the mother of all hangovers. And, of course, the hurt of Eddie's betrayal is back with a vengeance.

"Ugh," I groan, blinking open heavy eyes, rubbing my sore head and stretching my achy limbs out. It takes a few seconds before my eyes come into focus and, when they do, I find myself staring across at cream walls, cream walls I don't recognise.

Where am I?

I skim my eyes over the room on my journey, catching sight of the time on the wall clock - 7:03am. Then I see sitting in a chair over by the window, not far from the end of the bed I'm currently laid in, a man, a man I most certainly do not know. From my quick appraisal, I see he looks to be in his late twenties, early thirties, is fairly good looking, tanned skin, dirty blonde hair which hangs messily in his eyes and skims the collar of his plain black T-shirt, which looks like it's seen better days. So do his jeans, for that matter. One leg is crossed up onto the other one, his bare foot resting up on his thigh. He looks a bit rough and tired, and is rocking some serious stubble on his face.

"Hi," I say. My voice comes out scratchy. I push the dark blue duvet cover back and slowly sit up. My head is so woozy. It's practically wobbling on my neck.

"How are you feeling?" he asks me. His voice is deep and gruff. It sends an unexpected, but pleasurable, shiver over my skin.

I look at him again, this time more closely. His eyes meet with mine and I notice what an extraordinary shade of green they are. Really bright, like the colour of the first leaves in spring. Actually, looking at him properly, I see that he is very good-looking – my first appraisal really didn't do him justice at all. Must have been my initial alcohol haze blurring my judgement.

"Hungover," I finally answer with a sheepish grin.

He doesn't smile back. Mine very quickly falls from my face.

I run a self-conscious hand over my blonde hair. Then I notice I'm not wearing my outfit from last night. I went out in my grey skinny jeans and Rock and Republic top. I'm currently wearing a grey T-shirt which is way too big for me. A man's T-shirt judging by the size of it.

Ahh crap! I didn't get that drunk last night that I did the deed with a complete stranger, did I, a very good looking stranger, but a stranger, nevertheless? Funny though, I don't recall seeing anyone as good-looking as him in The Grange. I mean, I'd definitely remember him, I think. Oh God, I hope we used a condom.

"Erm ... " I wrap my arms around my chest. "This is gonna sound like a really shitty thing to say but ... who are you and where am I?" I cast a glance around the room, quickly taking in my surroundings.

The guy's certainly tidy, I'll give him that. This room is the epitome of cleanliness. There are no clothes lying around, no photos, no mementos – nothing. There's a stack of books over on the desk by the window but even they look tidy. It seems like everything has its place here, except for me that is.

He puts his foot down to the floor, leans forward, rests his elbows on his knees and clasps his hands together. "Who are you?" he throws back at me.

What? Okay, this is getting weird. He doesn't remember me and I don't remember him. Maybe he was just drunk as I apparently was. I reach back into my memories but nothing is there, just a foggy haze covering last night's events. It sets off an uncomfortable feeling rolling around my stomach.

"I'm, erm ... Alex – Alexandra." I pat a hand to my chest, a nervous laugh escaping me.

"I know what your name is," he states bluntly, brushing his hair out of his eyes, his stare on me unwavering. "What I want to know is, what are you?"

Eh? What does he mean – 'what am I?' Jeez, this guy is really rude, and also quite weird, and I have no clue how to answer that. So, well, I won't.

The silence is heavy. I've never been great with silences. They make me all nervous and fidgety. "Look, erm ... " I stare at him, willing him to fill the gap and tell me his name. He doesn't. I envisage banging my head against a wall. I rub my nose. "I'm sorry but you're gonna have to help me out here as I seem to have ... misplaced your name."

Misplaced? Is that the best I can come up with? Well I suppose it sounds better than saying 'forgotten'. That would sound way, way worse when addressing the man I quite possibly have recently had sex with.

"Nathan Hargreaves," he says, and that's when I notice just how intense his voice actually sounds, clear and precise, like every word he says really, really matters. I know he's a bit odd - well, a lot odd - but I can certainly see why I fancied him in my drunken state. The guy is hot. And I'm talking Matthew McConaughey hot.

Maybe I'm being too hard on him; he might not be rude at all. He's probably just feeling as awkward and uncomfortable in this 'morning after' situation as I am and this is how he deals with it.

One thing I do know for sure is that I would really like to get out of here as quickly as possible, taking with me whatever scrap of dignity I have left. Drunken-vengeance-on-your-cheating-ex-sex is obviously never a good idea.

Mental note to self – I, Alexandra Jones, do solemnly swear to never, ever drink again, or to ever again have sex with a complete stranger, regardless of how insanely good-looking he may be.

I shuffle myself forward, perching on the edge of the double bed, and let my toes sink into the thick shag pile carpet. "Well, Nathan Hargreaves, if you wouldn't mind pointing me in the direction of my clothes, I'll get changed and get out of your way."

"Your clothes are gone."

"What?"

"Your. Clothes. Are. Gone."

"Gone. Where?"

"They were burnt."

"Burnt?" My voice shoots out with a high-pitched incredulous tone to it.

"Yep, burnt." He nods.

It takes a few seconds for that to actually register. Then it does. "And can you tell me just why the bloody hell my clothes have been burnt?!" My voice has hitched up a good couple of notches further, now bordering on hysterical.

"They were ruined."

"Ruined?!"

"Yep." He nods again, resting back in his chair, folding his arms across his chest.

I stare at him, bewildered. Just exactly what kind of sex did I participate in that would have resulted in my clothes getting ruined? Possibly the kind I don't want to remember. I've got this really bad feeling creeping across my brain. I'm actually completely and utterly speechless. I really have no clue what to say. That happens rarely, if ever. I massage my aching temples with my fingers, trying to grasp a hold of all of this.

So overnight I've somehow turned into a woman who has sex with a complete stranger, a slightly weird stranger might I add, that results in my clothes getting ruined to the point of incineration and I have no memory of said sex. Which I suppose in a way is kind of shame because he is really fit. But still, it's all just too frigging bizarre. This is not me at all. I don't do stuff like this. I feel I've woken up in bizarro land. Maybe I had some form of bad reaction to the alcohol I was drinking last night which is why I can't remember anything ... or I could have had a seizure, or something. I could have even had a stroke. I mean it is possible. You hear about these weird things happening to young, healthy people, or ...

Oh God. A cold feeling creeps down my spine.

He could have slipped a roofie in my drink last night. I might have been date raped.

I swallow hard and let a careful eye roam over him. He doesn't look like the kind of guy who would need to slip a girl a roofie to get her to sleep with him, but then you just don't know anybody, and he did burn my clothes. He might have been burning the evidence.

Okay, just calm down. You don't know that's what happened. Keep rational and try to get out of here, as quickly as possible.

I clear my thick throat. "Look, Nathan, burning my clothes seems ... erm – a tad extreme, but it's okay, it doesn't matter, if you can just lend me some trousers to wear to go home in," I gesture to my bare legs, "I'll get off."

"You can't go home."

A hollow feeling drops in my stomach. I gulp down. "Why not?" My voice wobbles.

"Because there are thing we need to discuss."

I'm starting to sweat. My palms are clammy. "Look Nathan, I won't tell anybody you raped me, I swear!" My voice comes out all breathy and high-pitched. *So much for the calm approach, Alex.*

"I didn't rape you!" His face is incredulous.

"You didn't slip me a roofie?"

"No! ... Well I did give you some morphine but–"

"WHAT?!" I jump up to my feet.

He leans forward. "Purely for medicinal purposes."

This guy is mental. "Why the bloody hell would you give me morphine?!" *Jesus Christ, I know I was in pain over Eddie – but morphine!*

He pauses eyeing me curiously. Lines of concentration form on his forehead. "Alexandra, do you really not remember a thing about what has happened to you?"

"Obviously not!" I scowl. My heart is beating out of my chest. "But I'll put that down to the fact you've being feeding me drugs ... oh God, you're one of those pimps that takes girls off the streets and gets them addicted to drugs and turns them into prostitutes, aren't you?!" My future suddenly maps out in front of me. I can see myself all greasy hair, short skirts and ripped tights, getting into strangers cars ...

Oh God. I can't breathe. I'm going to pass out. I start to hyperventilate.

"Just calm down for fuck's sake, will you," Nathan says irritably. "You're completely safe here with me. I haven't, and am not planning to, hurt you."

Putting my hand to my chest, clutching it, trying to calm my breathing, I raise a suspicious eyebrow at him.

"Seriously, Alexandra, I haven't raped you, I'm not planning to rape you, and I'm not a drug baron or a pimp. Okay?"

My breathing slows and I start to relax a bit. "Okay ... " I say after a pause. I fidget uncomfortably on my feet. " ... but why did you give me morphine?"

He starts muttering under his breath, too quiet for me to make out.

"What?" I say.

He looks past me, ignoring me. "Fine," I hear him utter.

"Fine? What are you on about, fine? What's fine?"

"Okay," he says, voice still lowered but his tone sterner.

"Okay? Have you gone mad? Are you actually talking to yourself?!"

Great, he is bonkers, and here was me actually starting to believe he was normal.

Trust me to end up with the lunatic. *Thanks Carrie.* Talking of Carrie, where the bloody hell is she? Oh God, I hope she's okay and not stuck with a deranged future cell mate of his. I need to go and find her.

I make for the door. Nathan's there holding it shut before I even get the chance to turn the handle.

"What the bloody hell do you think you're doing?!" Angry, I turn to face him, but come face-to-face with his chest instead. Wow, he's tall. He's towering over my five-six frame. He's what … six-two, six-three?

Resisting the urge to step back, I straighten myself up, trying to exude confidence I most certainly aren't feeling and look him straight in the eye. "Nathan, let me out of here – now!" I try to sound firm but my voice betrays me and shakes ever so slightly. I'm hoping he doesn't notice.

He looks down at me with a stony expression on his face and takes a step closer to me. He's way too close now for my liking. "I can't." His voice is measured, controlled. "Well, not yet anyway."

Okay, so those words have done nothing to appease me.

He pinches the bridge of his nose, closing his eyes briefly. "Alexandra–"

"Alex, my name is Alex!" I say, irate.

He gives me a look. I can see frustration etched all over his face. "Fine, Alex." He sighs. "Look, there are things you need to hear before I can let you leave here."

I wrap my arms protectively around myself. "And what if I don't want to hear these things you've got to say?"

He frowns. "You won't but you need to hear them nonetheless."

I swallow hard at that less-than-cheerful thought. I feel all confused. I want out of here but he's obviously not going to let me go until I listen to whatever it is he wants to say.

Slowly, I step back away from him, his eyes stay trained on me as I back up across the room and sit down on the edge of the bed.

"Fine, I'll listen to what you've got to say," I gesture a hand in his direction, "but the second you're done, I'm leaving."

"Okay," he agrees, leaning his back against the door, "but you're probably not gonna want to leave when you've heard what I've got to say."

This guy is deranged. On what planet would I ever want to stay here with him?

I eye him up and down. "You really are weird, you know that?"

"Yeah, well you're kind of an anomaly yourself." He shrugs, leaving his words hanging in the air.

Anomaly – what does he mean anomaly? Cheeky git. "Well you're just an arse." *Great come-back, Alex. Really, well done.*

He purses his lips and nods. "You're not the first to say that, and I'm fairly sure you won't be the last."

"Do you have a bloody answer for everything?"

His mouth creeps up into an almost smile and he pushes his hands into his pockets. "Pretty much."

I tuck my hands under my legs. "Well, smartarse, you've got two minutes," my eyes flick to the clock on the wall, "starting ... now, so you better make good use of them."

Chapter 4

Scarred

Nathan doesn't say anything for a long moment. You'd think for someone so desperate to tell me whatever it is he wants to tell me, he'd speed this up.

I sigh impatiently, tapping my foot loudly against the floor.

He pulls his hands from his pockets and pushes his hands through his hair, scraping it back away from his face, revealing a pretty good set of cheekbones and a jaw that looks like it was chiselled by the man himself. Then he releases his hold on his hair, letting it fall back messily around his face, folds his arms across his chest and starts speaking, "A few days ago, in the early hours of Saturday morning, you were attacked ... "

"Whoa!" I lift my hand up, halting him. "I was attacked? By who?" I suddenly have this clutching pain in my stomach and a sense of familiarity that for the life of me I can't place.

"If you'll stop interrupting me, I'll tell you." He frowns.

I frown back, giving him a look that lets him know just exactly what I think of his crappy attitude.

Nathan's face clears and he begins tapping his fingertips rhythmically against his solid thigh. "You were attacked by a Vârcolac. They're a vampire-werewolf hybrid. He was in his wolf form when he attacked you." He takes a quick breath. "I saved you, killed him, and brought you back here to my home. You'd been bitten and were infected. You were in a really bad way, hence the need for the morphine, you know, to kill the pain, and we've - me, my dad and my brother - have been caring for you for the last few days while you went through the transition, but the thing is, though, Alex," he pauses momentarily and puts his hand to his head, scratching his temple, "well, basically, you shouldn't have gone through the transition. You should have died from the infection, but for some ungodly reason you didn't. And you have to understand a woman has never survived the change before. Only men do. But, well, like I said, you did and now I'm sorry to tell you this, but you're one of them, a Vârcolac, the only female one of their kind." He takes a deep breath, obviously done, his eyes intent on me, assumedly waiting, gauging my reaction.

I stare at him agape. An awkward sounding laugh escapes me. "Okay..."

"I know this is hard to believe," he quickly interjects, "but it is the truth." He adds a firm look for good measure.

I cast my eyes over him, from his head down to his bare feet and back up again, trying to read him. I'm no body language expert but he seems to actually believe what he's saying is the truth, which can only mean one thing – he's completely insane. Like 'needs to be in a straight jacket' insane. And this is clearly the moment I should run screaming for the door but he's still blocking it. My only other option – humour him.

"So you're saying I was attacked by a–"

"Vârcolac."

"Vârcolac – right." I nod. "And you're saying I'm now one of these Vârcolac things."

"Yes."

"And they're a vampire-werewolf thingy?"

"Hybrid," he corrects.

"Right, vampire–werewolf hybrid." I nod again.

I clamp my lips together and count to ten in my mind, while I decide what to do next. I make it to three before hysterical laughter bursts from me.

"This isn't a fucking joke!" Nathan snaps, banging his fist against the door. The whole back wall trembles slightly.

My laughter quickly dies out, overtaken by anger. "I don't have to sit here and listen to this shit! You ... " I jab a finger at him, " ... are obviously completely out of your tree and I highly recommend that you see someone, you know, for psychiatric help, so they can give some medication - well lots of medication - to make you normal, well as normal as you could be. Or maybe you just need committing or something - whatever, I don't know!" I mentally shake myself, stopping the incoherent babbling that often plagues me. "Look, Nathan, I've heard enough and I've had enough. I'm leaving now, so just move yourself away from the door." I waggle my fingers at him in a patronizing manner as I once again get to my feet, prepping to leave.

He doesn't move. Instead he makes a noise of anger that can only be described as a growl. It sends a shiver running over my skin, and not in a good way.

"Did you just ... growl at me?!" I say appalled.

He raises his frustrated eyebrows. "Alex, I'm not some lunatic who makes up crazy stories. Do you think I even want to be having this conversation with you? Do you think I want you here in my home? Seriously, you have no idea how much danger I have put my family in by saving your life."

"Well, I didn't bloody ask you to, did I?" I stare back at him angrily.

"That your idea of a thanks?" he smarts. There's not a trace of humour in him.

"I'm not thanking you when you just insulted me!" Okay, so I'm not actually sure if he did insult me, but it sounds like a good thing to say, and it's the only thing I've got.

"Insulted you?" His look is incredulous. "Insulted you?!" He starts to pace the room before me, a storm brewing on his face. "So far you've accused me of being a rapist, a drug dealer, a pimp, and have just told me that I'm clinically insane." He stops his pacing and gives me a cynical look. "I'd say the only one being insulted here is me."

"I was only stating the obvious," I reply with a wry smile.

"Jesus Christ, you're impossible to talk to!" He shakes his head roughly and his dirty blonde hair falls into his eyes. He pushes it back out. I can see his jaw working angrily as he sets his hard eyes on me. "Do you have to work hard to be this annoying or does it just come naturally?"

"Piss off!" I snap. It's weak but it's all I've got left.

We glare angrily at each other across the room for a long moment. If someone tried to walk between us they would walk career bang into the wall of tension, it's that thick.

Then, surprisingly, Nathan looks away, staring out of the window. "We done?" His voice is calmer now.

I snag my lower lip with my teeth. "Yes."

He looks back at me and spreads his hands out, palms down, in a placating manner. "I know all of this I've told you will seem very unreal. I get that, honestly I do, but think about it seriously. What have I got to gain from telling you this if it wasn't the truth? What do I benefit from it?"

And I don't know what it is. Maybe it's the calm tone of his voice, or the reflective look in his eyes, or maybe it's the actual sense in some of his words, and the resonating effect they're having on me. Well, whatever it is, a teeny-tiny part of me is actually starting to take him seriously. It's only a microscopic part but still it's there, and I suppose I've got nothing to lose by hearing the rest of his crazy tale.

"Look, Alex." He pauses and rubs his hand across his stubbly jaw, his expression torn. "I didn't want to show you this yet as I thought it would probably freak you out, but it will go some way in proving to you that what I've been saying is true."

I don't get a chance to respond before he's walking toward me and standing before me, reaching his hand out, taking hold of the hem of the T-shirt I'm wearing, lifting it up, exposing my knickers ...

I slam my hand down on his, stopping him. "What the hell do you think you're doing?!" I exclaim. My body starts to tremble.

"I'm not going to hurt you." His tone is soft, gentle. "Trust me." He speaks the rest with his eyes.

I hesitate, and for some reason I can't explain, I move my hand away from his.

Nathan continues to lift the T-shirt up. "Look," he says, his eyes cast down, focussed on my stomach.

I follow his stare. My breath catches in my throat.

There's a huge scar on the right-hand side of my stomach, practically spanning the whole of my waist. It looks like a bite mark. A very large bite mark. Like a 'lion bit me' sized bite mark.

Nathan lets go of the T-shirt, but I catch hold, keeping it up. He moves away and sits back in his chair, leaving me standing here feeling dazed and bewildered.

I lean my face down closer, examining it. It looks old, like it's been here for months. How is this even possible? Maybe it's a trick? Maybe it's that fake make-up. I rub hard at it with my finger. It's still there. I wet my finger in my mouth and try again.

"It's real," Nathan says from across the room. His voice is like an echo in my vacant mind.

I know it's real. I knew the instant I touched it. But my memory's telling me that yesterday there was smooth skin where this hideous scar now is. Bite marks don't heal that quickly. Skin just doesn't heal that quickly. What did Nathan say before - that it was few days ago I was attacked - so right now it should just be a scabby, sore wound.

No, this can't be right.

I look up at Nathan with helpless eyes, searching his for an answer.

"They ... you heal quickly but that is the only scar you'll ever have again. All Vârcolacs have them. It's their mark, their brand, so to say."

I know I'm freaking out because my brain's finally gone hyper-active and currently feels like it's short-circuiting, but I just can't seem to convey it. It's like my body is lost in translation.

I let go of the T-shirt covering the evidence I'm not ready to face, suddenly feeling dizzy and off-balance. I slump myself down onto the edge of the bed. I curl my fingers around the edge of the bed, grip the carpet with my toes, take a deep breath and look up at Nathan. "Tell me everything."

Chapter 5

Existing

"I was out running in Hackness woods when I heard your screams. I got to you as quickly as I could but that bastard was already feeding on you ... and your friend, well, she was ... "

"Carrie was attacked as well?! Oh my God!" I clutch a hand to my suddenly tight chest. "Where is she? Is she okay?" He's shaking his head. *Why is he shaking his head?* "Why are you shaking your head?"

"I'm so sorry, Alex."

Oh God no.

The room suddenly feels incredibly small. The walls are closing in on me. I swallow down past the dryness in my throat. "Wh–why are you sorry? What do you have to be sorry about?" I twist my hands in my lap.

He leans forward, forearms on thighs, hands clasped together, and looks at me with sympathetic eyes. "Alex, your friend Carrie, she's dead."

A pain so fierce shoots though me I'm sure it stops my heart beating for a moment.

Dead? Carrie's dead? But ... she can't be ...

Silence rings in my ears. "No ... no that's not possible," I stammer, "because I was only with her last night. I mean ... " I can hear my mumbling voice but it doesn't feel like it's me talking anymore. It's almost as if I've taken a back seat and someone else is driving for me. "Carrie can't be de- ... gone, because ... because ... we're going to Leah's birthday party next Saturday and I'm lending her my black dress to wear ... and ...

and ... " My lips have gone numb. My head's started to buzz. "She can't be ... you've got it wrong."

He's shaking his head again. "I'm not wrong. I'm sorry."

My hands are trembling. I clasp them together, trying to control the tremor. My eyes have filled with tears but I can't blink. If do, if I cry, it makes it real, it makes what he's saying real. It means Carrie gone. And she can't be.

He must be lying.

I fix my eyes to Nathan's face, looking for anything to tell me he's lying, that this is some awful, sick thing he's making up. I stare hard through the thick wall of my tears.

"Alex, are you okay?"

I can't see anything, not a flicker of deceit. Oh God he's telling the truth. Carrie's dead.

I blink and the tears wash down my face in a torrent. And my world comes crashing in all around me.

"Bu ... but I don't understand. The last thing I remember is ... " I close my eyes and force my mind to work, to bring me back my last memories of Carrie. "We ... we were walking home from The Grange," I begin, "and ... and I was on the phone with Eddie." Salty tears are trickling into my mouth. "I was arguing with him on the phone and I got so angry with him ... my phone, I threw it. It landed in the woods." I squeeze tighter on my memory. "And we went to look for it, Carrie and me, and ... " I stop cold as the sickening realisation thuds into me. I open my eyes. "The woods. That's where you said we were attacked. That's where you found us."

He nods. It's almost imperceptible but I see it.

The pain I feel is so immense ... so intense that momentarily I can't move.

Then suddenly it bursts out of me, so fiercely there should be a hole left in my chest where it exited. "Oh God!" I sob, clutching my hands to my head, "it's my fault! Carrie's dead because of me! If I hadn't thrown my phone in there, we would never have gone in and she'd still be alive!"

Nathan shifts forward in his seat urgently. "You don't know that." He speaks quickly, trying to reassure me. "He'd probably been watching you both for a while, and if he wanted you it wouldn't have mattered if you'd gone into the woods or not, he'd have got you at some point. Alex, this is not your fault." He continues to stare at me, trying to stress his point, but his words have just bounced off me. Nothing he can say will change the fact that it is my fault.

Then, without warning, something starts to burn inside of me, something the likes of nothing I've ever felt before. It's like white hot rage. It starts in the pit of my stomach and quickly spreads through me, heating my blood up so it's practically bubbling up underneath my skin. I feel like my skin is lifting up off my bones from the sheer force of it.

"NO!" I cry out, leaping to my feet. Nathan looks up at me surprised. "Carrie can't be dead! She can't be! And all of this," I throw an arm around the room, my movement jerky, frantic, "what you're saying happened to me, what I am, it can't be real, it can't be! I can't deal with it!"

Panic is raging a storm through me, searing into my veins, taking control. I back up across the room away from Nathan until my back meets with the wall. "Carrie can't be dead," I whimper, burying my face in my hands. "She can't be." I let my body slide down the wall until I'm sitting on the floor.

Why did this have to happen? If only I hadn't taken Eddie's call. If only I hadn't thrown my phone in the woods.

A thought suddenly flickers through my mind and it halts all others.

I move my hands away from my face. "Why are you only telling me about Carrie now?" I sound oddly composed.

I see a look of discomfort flicker over Nathan's face. "What do you mean?"

"I mean why didn't you tell me the moment I woke up that my best friend was dead?!" I bang my fists against the floor. I'm so angry. I've never felt anger like this before. I've gone from cold to hot in less than five seconds and I have no idea what to do with it.

I watch Nathan's chest expand under his T-shirt as he inhales for a breath. "I needed to find out what you were," he exhales, "before the infection, I mean, before you changed. I thought you were human, but like I said, women don't survive the change and I needed to make sure you weren't something else, something I didn't know about, something that was potentially a danger to me and my family."

"Of course I'm human!" I cry. "I don't know anything about those bloody vampire things you've been going on about!"

"Vârcolac," he corrects, and has the audacity to sound irritated. "And I know that now but I didn't at the time. For all I knew you could have been lying just to get yourself out of here and I couldn't risk it. If the Vârcolacs find out what I did … " he rubs his face roughly with his hand, " … if they find out it was me that killed him, I'm basically fucked."

But right now I don't care about his problems, even if they do involve me. "I couldn't give a toss how it affects you! Carrie is dead and you kept it from me!" I'm breathing so hard I have to clutch my hand to my chest to keep myself steady. It's like my grief and pain have been coated by the anger, and that's all I can feel now - complete and utter anger.

Nathan's brow creases into a tight line. He looks angry, which only manages to incense me further. What right does he have to be angry?

"I was going to tell you," he says through gritted teeth.

"When exactly?! When I passed all your bloody tests! You should have told me the second you opened your mouth, instead of keeping me here talking about this shit. And Carrie's been dead all this time and I ... I didn't know and ... " The grief floods back and sobs well in my throat. I struggle to choke them back.

"I know you're in pain ... "

"I'm torn apart!" I scream.

Nathan gets up from his seat and takes a step toward me.

"Don't come near me." I put my trembling hand out, stopping him.

"I wasn't trying to be callous." He begins speaking quickly. "When I realised you weren't lying about not knowing anything, I thought I should explain everything that had happened to you before I told you about her, about Carrie, and honestly, I really didn't know how to tell you. It's not something I do every day, you know, tell people that ... " He stops and looks at me helplessly. "I'm sorry."

I bite my quivering lip. "You're sorry you kept it from me or that Carrie's dead?"

"Both."

Even though deep down I know none of this is his fault, I want it to be.

I want to blame him. I need to be angry with him. I need him to feel this excruciating pain I'm feeling because I can't be alone in this.

I rub my eyes roughly and look up at him through my tangled lashes. "I want to see Carrie." My voice carries barely a whisper across the room.

There's a beat of silence. His eyes flicker in my direction but he doesn't actually look at me. "We'll talk about it later," he says, walking toward the door.

My insides take a step dive. I'm up and on my feet. Moving quickly, I grab hold of his arm, stopping him. "Where is Carrie?" I can't stop the tremor in my voice.

Nathan glances down at my hand on his arm, then back up at my face. There's a threat in his eyes but I don't move it. I keep my grip firm.

"You really don't want to hear this," he says, not a shred of emotion in his voice.

He's right, I don't want to hear it, but I have to.

"Tell me." My chin trembles and even I don't believe the tone of my voice.

He presses his lips together. He looks as if he's considering his words, or maybe mine. My heart is pumping so hard against my chest it's all I can hear.

After what seems like an infinite amount of time, he looks me in the eye and says, "My dad and brother went back for the bodies - Carrie's and the Vârcolac's. I stayed here with you. They brought them back here and ... well, they burned the bodies."

"Arggh!" I bang my fists hard against his chest, utter wretchedness taking me over. He barely moves. I grip hold of his T-shirt, my fingers digging into his chest which is so hard It barely gives. "Why?"

He sighs. "We had to get rid of any evidence linking me to killing the Vârcolac. Soon enough the others will notice he's missing and will come looking. If we'd left them both there to be found, the Vârcolacs would have smelt my scent on them, and that would have led them straight here to me, to you." His large hands encircle my wrists, his touch gentle. "I really am sorry."

I close my eyes, but all I can see behind my lids is Carrie. Carrie burning ...

I open my eyes and yank my arms free from his hold, staggering backwards. "I ... I have to go ... go," I stammer. "I have to see Carrie's mum and dad."

"And tell them what?" he retorts, his voice suddenly harsher, "that you were attacked by a Vârcolac, that I managed to save you, but Carrie was already dead when I got there? You've been gone for almost three days, Alex, three days. The police are at the stage now where they're looking for your bodies. They don't expect you to be alive, and if you turn up fit and well - without Carrie - with the truth as your only explanation, you know they wouldn't believe you. You know what they'd think."

I look at him through a haze of confusion and tears. "What?"

"They'd think you killed her and that I helped you, or the other way around."

"I could never have hurt Carrie," I whimper, dismayed.

"But the police don't know that. They don't know you. They'd just look at the surrounding evidence and facts, and that would make us their prime suspects."

His words ring painfully true in my ears.

"And by going home you'd only be exposing yourself to the Vârcolacs," he continues, his voice hardening with each word spoken. "If they find out about your survival ... " He pauses, shaking his head as if to highlight the point. "If you let people know you're alive, you're giving the Vârcolacs an open pass to you. And who's gonna protect you from them - the police?" He gives a curt laugh, minus the humour.

And that laugh runs abrasively against my skin. I feel my hackles rise. "And you will?" I glare at him. "I get the distinct impression you couldn't give a flying fuck about me, so why are you so keen on protecting me?"

He glares right back, his green eyes slicing into me. "I'm not. I'm keen on protecting my family."

I break eye contact. Looking at the floor, I wrap my arms around myself. "Why is your family in danger?"

He shifts his weight and a sound of exasperation escapes him. "Because of you, Alex. Because I saved you. If the Vârcolacs find out about you, well then God help us all." He exhales. "But they're gonna wanna know how you survived the attack, who it was that saved you, and that's when the finger points at me, and that's when my family's in danger. There's a line I crossed when I killed him and without a doubt they'd come after me and my family."

I rub my runny nose with my hand. "I wouldn't tell them it was you that saved me," I utter meekly. "If they found me, I wouldn't tell them."

He lets out a sharp laugh. "Trust me when I say this, you really don't want them to find you. And yes you would because you wouldn't have a choice. They are evil motherfuckers and can be very, let's say ...

persuasive when they want to be, and I don't want my family put in harm's way because of a rash decision I made when I saved your life. So for now, you need to stay here and out of view, until I can figure out what to do with you. I know this is the last thing you want, and honestly I don't want you here either, but we don't have a choice. I know it's hard to hear, but to your old life ... you're dead. You can't go back, ever."

Everything closes in on me. It's like I'm free-falling into a cavern of darkness and I'm never going to hit the bottom. It's never going to stop. And I know unequivocally, from this moment on, I'm never going to know peace again.

My legs give out on me and I slump down to the floor. I pull my knees up to my chest. My eyes are blurring up with a fresh batch of tears.

"I ... I just can't believe Carrie's g ... gone," I choke out, "and all of this that's happened ... it's too much ... I can't c-cope."

"You're gonna have to find a way to," he says stonily, sitting down beside me, "because you don't have any other choice."

The grief returns to hit me with the force of a tsunami hitting land. I drop my head onto my knees, bury my face, and cry.

I have no idea how long we sit here for, side by side. Nathan doesn't move. He doesn't touch me. He just sits here silently with me while I attempt to cry this ache from out of me.

Eventually, when the tears begin to dry up, I lift my head.

"You okay?" He glances sideways at me.

I push my hair off my damp face and shake my head. The tears may have momentarily subsided but the pain will never go away.

Nathan gets to his feet and swiftly exits the room, returning a moment later with a handful of tissues. He crouches down in front of me and hands them over. "Probably should have got you these a while ago."

He smiles a weak smile. I can't muster anything up to return it.

"Thanks." I take the tissues, wipe my face and blow my nose. I scrunch them up in my hand knowing I'll need them again soon.

"Do you feel hungry?" Nathan asks.

I shake my head. I don't think I'll ever be able to eat again.

He looks at me for a moment longer than necessary. It makes me uncomfortable. I look away.

"Why don't you try and get some rest," he suggests. "We can talk more later."

I nod my assent.

Standing, he holds his hands out for me. I take them and let him pull me to my feet. Exhaustion suddenly burns through me. The room spins, black dots dance before my eyes and my knees buckle.

"Hey, take it easy." Nathan scoops me up into his arms and carries me over to the bed. I rest my head against his shoulder. He smells earthy and something about it momentarily fills the hollow places inside of me. He lays me down and pulls the cover over me. The moment he lets me go, the hollow coldness creeps back into me.

"Nathan?" I utter when he's at the door.

He turns back, giving me a questioning stare.

I roll onto my side, facing him. "Thank you for saving my life." I realised I haven't said that, and all things aside, he at least deserves my thanks.

He shrugs. "No problem."

"How do you know all this stuff, about these ... Vârcolac things?"

I see something flicker behind his light eyes. "We'll talk about it later. Just rest now." He turns away and pulls open the door.

"Nathan?"

He doesn't attempt to disguise the sigh and he doesn't turn around, he just stands there, back to me, a foot out of the room. "Yes?"

"What will happen to me ... if the Vârcolacs find me?"

His back stiffens. "Let's hope you never find out." Then he's gone, the door gently banging in his wake.

I roll onto my back and stare blankly up at the ceiling.

Carrie's gone.

My heart compresses, squeezing tightly in on itself, the agony unbearable, and sobs break from me. I bury my face into the pillow, trying to muffle the cries coming from me.

It's my fault. I ended her life, both our lives, the moment I made the decision to step into those woods. It should have been me that died in there, not Carrie. I'm going to have to live with that knowledge for the rest of my existence. Because existing is all I'm doing now. What I'm left with isn't anything resembling a life.

And it's nothing less than I deserve.

Chapter 6

Blood Drinker

"Alex?"

"Hmm."

"Wake up." A strong hand gently shakes my shoulder.

"Go away, Eddie. I'm tired." I roll away from his hand, stretching my stiff legs out.

"Alex?"

I sigh loudly and roll back over, forcing my sleep-laden eyes open. "Eddie, for God's sake–" My words catch in my throat because it's not Eddie my eyes meet with, it's Nathan. Of course it is. I'm not at home; I don't have a home anymore. I'm not me any more, and Carrie's gone, forever.

The present slams back into me with all its ferocity. The relief sleep offered is no more and the loss of Carrie consumes me all over again. Tears insistently spring to my eyes.

Nathan looks down at me curiously, his green eyes almost luminous in the dusk light. "You okay?" he asks.

I manage a nod as I press my lips together and attempt to swallow down my grief. I've cried enough in front of him already. I don't want to cry again.

But it's not working. My eyes are swollen with the tears, top lip quivering, chin wobbling. I hold my breath. But a stray tear trickles out from the corner of my eye, snaking its way down my cheekbone, and the feel of that one single tear breaks down all my defences and the grief engulfs me, and there's not a single thing I can do to stop it. The pain is so intense I feel like my chest is being crushed.

I can't breathe.

Clutching a hand to my chest, panicked, I sit bolt upright and crash straight into Nathan.

"Whoa, take it easy," he says, taking hold of me by my shoulders, but I can't focus on him, or anything. My whole body is shaking, tears streaming down my face.

Carrie's dead. How can she be dead? It just doesn't make sense, any of it. And I miss her so much it hurts.

"Alex, you need to calm down." Nathan takes a firm hold of my chin between his thumb and forefinger, forcing me to look at him.

My eyes flicker back to the now, and when they meet with his, I'm surprised by the intensity I find there.

"Take slow, deep breaths," he says. It's not a request.

Knowing he's got my attention, Nathan slides his hand from my face but stays sitting where he is, which is mere inches from me, so close I can smell his aftershave.

I know he's only trying to help me but his nearness and fixed gaze are making me uncomfortable for reasons I can't explain.

I break away from our stare and look out through the window behind him. Red is commanding the sky tonight. It disappears under the remaining clouds, drifting into a soft shade of pink. What is it they say: red sky at night shepherds delight? It really is a beautiful sight. I know it is. I just can't even begin to appreciate it. How can I ever allow myself to appreciate something when I shouldn't be the one here to see it? There's a blackness inside me now coating everything. I already had a gaping, hollow place where my heart should have been - my parents dying saw to that - but now Carrie's gone, well, whatever was left went with her.

I shut my eyes and take a deep calming breath, forcing my frantic mind and body to still. "I'm sorry," I utter, as my breathing slows to something close to normal.

"Don't be." He moves up the bed putting space between us.

I watch him with interest as he pushes his hair off his forehead and lets out a light sigh. "I'm sorry I had to wake you but it's time you fed. You should have fed earlier but I didn't think it was wise to suggest it with the state you were in, and I know you're far from great now, obviously, but it's been far too long and you need to feed."

I tilt my head and stare at him confused. "What do you mean, 'I need to feed?'."

He frowns for a fleeting moment. "Feed, you know, on blood."

A chill runs through me, cutting into my bones. I wrap my arms protectively around myself. "Blood? What are you talking about?" The words practically dribble out of my mouth.

Nathan mirrors me, folding his arms across his chest. I see the muscles flex in his forearms. "You're a Vârcolac now, Alex. You're part vampire, therefore a blood drinker. I thought you would have realised … " He peters off, and I'm assuming it's because of the look of absolute horror on my face.

My mouth forms the words to speak but nothing comes out.

He unfolds his arms and shakes his head. "You didn't realise?"

My brain is failing. I'm half expecting it to start trickling out of my ears.

"You need blood," Nathan says in a careful voice. "Well, you'll crave it. I'm surprised you've lasted this long already without feeling any urges. You can still eat food, Alex, but basically blood is your sustenance, for want of a word."

My body's gone numb. I dig my nails into the skin on my arms, just to try and feel something. Taking in a big gulp of air, I attempt to still my erratic heart. My mouth's gone dry, and the words are gloopy as they leave my mouth. "You're saying I need to drink blood to stay alive?"

He nods. And I feel sick.

"That can't be right," I stammer, holding back the fast rising bile. "You must be wrong. You've gotta be wrong."

As I clutch at straws, Nathan shakes his head empathetically. "For your sake I wish I was, but I'm not."

Something inside me clicks and then I know what's happened here. I get it. I almost laugh out loud with relief. I've finally cracked and have had a nervous breakdown. With everything I've been through over the years it makes sense. I've stepped out of reality and into a dream world that I've created. That's it. I'm currently in a dream world, just like Alice in Wonderland, except I'm not in Wonderland, I'm in Horrorland. Actually it's more like I'm trapped in a Freddie Kruger film. Now all I need to do is find a way to get myself out of this never-ending horror story and back to normal.

"If you don't feed," Nathans continues, snapping me back to the now, "it'll make you do things you wouldn't normally do to satisfy your hunger."

The sound of his continuing voice against my ears is abrasive. I feel like nails are been driven into my skull.

This isn't real. I don't want him here. I don't want to be here anymore. I want him to stop talking. I don't want to hear any of this anymore.

I cover my eyes with my hands, thumbs pressing over my ears, blocking out the sound of his voice.

This isn't real. This isn't real.

It's just a figment of my over-active imagination. I've always had wild thoughts, usually ideas of grandeur, not sick and twisted scenarios like this but ...

Nathan grabs hold of my arm, yanking my hand away from my face, polluting my ears with his words again. "Have you been listening to a fucking a word I've said to you?"

Anger quickly takes me over. I peel my other hand away from my face. "I heard enough." I scowl at him.

"You haven't heard the fucking half of it," he chastises me. "You think I'm telling you this for my health? I'm trying to help you, Alex, and you need to pay attention to every single fucking thing I tell you from now on because I'm telling you these things for your own good, to give you a fighting chance of staying as near to human as you possibly fucking can."

"You swear too much," I observe, coolly.

A smile ghosts his face. "Yeah, and you're impossible to talk to."

I look down at my hands. Deep down I know this is real and what he's saying is true, and not just that I'm impossible to talk to, but that he's only trying to help me.

Also, knowing I have no way out of this horror that is now my life, I tilt my chin up and force myself to ask, "What will I happen if I don't have ...

blood?"

"You'll turn on people to feed. You'll kill, without meaning too."

My stomach drops through the bed. "And ... how long before that would happen?" The words shiver out of me.

"Not would, *will*. It'll be about another day max. Soon the hunger will start to take over and you'll turn into someone you would never wish to meet, worse than the fucker that did this to you because it'll be your first feed and you'll be hungry. You'll be like a junkie searching for a fix who will do anything to sate that need. But unlike the average junkie, you'll be stronger, quicker, sharper and driven purely by the hunger. In the end you'll be out of control, unrecognisable. And that's when I'll put you down." He links his fingers around his knee and leans in close to me. His hot breath scorches over my skin. "It's something I'd rather not do, Alex, so it'll be easier all round if you just listen to what I'm telling you and drink this." He reaches down, retrieves a flask from the floor beside him, and holds it out for me to take.

Ignoring him, I close my eyes and start to massage my temples in a rhythmic motion.

I don't want to do this. I feel trapped. I hate feeling trapped. I'm in this whole other world now, a world I have no comprehension of, a world I don't want to have comprehension of. But what other choice do I have?

I open my eyes. Nathan still has the flask in his hand but now it's resting against his knee.

I reach out and take it from him. "What's in here?" I ask, nerves apparent.

He sighs impatiently. "Blood."

I look at him sharply, tired of the sarcasm that comes naturally with him. "I know it's blood, I'm not a complete idiot," I snap. "I meant *whose* blood?"

He raises an eyebrow.

"Yours?" I cringe.

He throws his head back and laughs, a slow, dry laugh. "No. I should have said it's animal. Even though human blood is your natural craving, you can survive on animal's blood, it's just not as good for your needs. You'll require to feed more often than you would with human blood."

My body goes rigid with anger. "Should have mentioned!" I shriek. "Are you having a fucking laugh?! I think it's a pretty important thing to tell me!"

He leans back on the bed, levelling our eyes. "You swear too much." A pirate smile lurks around the corners of his mouth.

I hunt for a smart reply but take too long and lose my chance. I'm caught somewhere between hot and cold, with no comeback. I can feel the anger reddening my face.

Biting on the inside of my cheek, I look down at the flask in my hand. Knowing there's animal blood inside has calmed me a bit. Don't get me wrong, the thought of drinking animal blood is disgusting, but not as disgusting as the thought of drinking blood that has come from another human being.

"So ... this is animal blood?" I lift the flask up.

"Pigs."

I cringe. The poor pig.

"You're lucky we live on a farm," he adds. Getting up, he goes over and switches the light on, flooding the room with brightness. "You'll have an endless supply of it for the duration of your stay."

"I'm on a farm?" I ask, my eyes following him as he sits down in the only chair in the room.

Oddly, I hadn't even thought about exactly where I am, but then. I have had other things on my mind.

Nathan's eyes roam my face curiously. "You couldn't tell from the smell?"

I shake my head.

He scratches his temple. "Have you noticed any differences in yourself at all?"

I know it's a loaded question but still I have to ask, "Differences?"

"Increased sense of smell, better hearing, sharper eyesight, an increase in your strength," he ticks off.

I shake my head again and bring my knees up to my chest, hugging them.

"Try now," he says, leaning forward in his seat.

"Try what?"

"Your sense of smell. Inhale and tell me what you get."

I give him a look.

"Just humour me," he pushes.

So I do. I close my eyes and take a deep breath in through my nose.

I can smell his aftershave again. I focus harder, trying to smell more, then suddenly it hits me and I can smell everything on him just as clearly as if he were sat here on the bed pressed up against me. I can smell the natural earthy smell of him, his aftershave – cedar wood and ginger, the water on his skin from his recent shower, the subtle scent of the soap he washed with. I can even smell the remnant trace of the foam he used to shave with. He shaved. I hadn't noticed.

I open my eyes to find his already on me. I let my eyes drift down to his smooth chin. "Stubble suits you better," I say without thinking.

His eyes flicker surprise. He rubs his hand across his chin.

"I could smell the shaving foam on you," I add, a flush rising up my neck.

"What else?" His eyes hold mine with a surprising amount of depth.

"Cedar wood and ginger from your aftershave, water and soap."

"Try again," he urges. "Reach your senses out further."

I do as I'm told.

Inhaling past his scent, I let my senses roam further. Then I catch the distinct smell of manure, fresh cut grass, and rapeseed. Rapeseed. The smell reminds me of home and I start to ache inside for all things familiar.

"What else you getting?" he asks. His deep voice soothes over my skin almost intimately, taking the aches away.

"Cut grass," I utter. "Manure and the scent of rapeseed as clear as if I'm standing in the field with it." I'm desperately trying not to think how off the charts this actually is.

Slowly I open my eyes back up. I find Nathan's eyes still fixed on me. I swallow down, nervously.

"It'll probably all be a bit overwhelming for you at first," he says, "but you'll soon get used to it."

That's it? Gee, thanks for the lesson, Nathan.

Suddenly feeling the need for fresh air, I rest the flask down on the bed, clamber off and, go over to the window and open it up wide. It lets in a welcoming blast of cool night air. But the second it's open, all I can hear is the sound's of owls hooting, crickets chirping, mice squeaking, even insects scuttering around the ground. I guess my hearing's kicked in too. Wonderful. The sound's are like ticks in my ears. I slam the window back shut, frustrated, and rest my forehead up it.

"Am I still in Hackness?" I ask, my tone grumpy, my breath fogging up the glass.

"No. You're in Wykeham. It's only about ten miles away from … "

"I know where Wykeham is," I cut him off shortly.

An unexpected thought pops into my mind. I turn around and lean up against the window ledge. "What were you doing out in the woods the night you saved me?"

"I was out running," he responds without hesitation, his expression instantly blank.

His answer's too quick. He's hiding something.

"Pretty late to be out running," I observe.

"I like the night."

"Why Hackness woods?"

"Why not?"

"Surely there are places around here to go running?"

"There is," he answers unblinking, "but I like Hackness, its quiet."

That's bullshit if ever I've heard it; everywhere in this region is quiet.

I keep my steady eyes on him as I curl my fingers around the edge of the window ledge. "How do you know all this stuff about Vârcolacs again?" I hedge my bets.

"I never told you the first time." His smile is all fox. "Drink the blood and I'll tell you everything you want to know." He nods in the direction of the flask on the bed.

I give him a long look and walk over and pick the flask up off the bed. I take it back over to the window with me and rest up against the ledge again. My fingertips edge around the cool metal. I look down at it. There's blood inside here. Pig's blood. And I'm going to attempt to drink it. Yes, I know just how insane this is.

With a resigned sigh, I pull the outside cap off the flask and place it down on the window ledge. Then I take a deep breath and very slowly unscrew the lid. At the exact moment of release, the smell floods my nostrils. Sweet and sickly, like honey, it swims into my mind and body, coating my insides.

A sudden, new and unexplainable hunger consumes me. Saliva floods my mouth. I feel an ache there too and another ache deep within me, a need – no, a want - from a part of me I didn't even know existed. My heart's beating faster, my pulse is quickening. My veins feel like they're pressing up against the thin veil of my skin. Every orifice of me is crying out for this and then suddenly nothing else matters. I'm consumed. I'm moving the flask toward my mouth. The cool silver touches my lips. My tongue tingles in anticipation. I tilt the flask upwards but it clangs awkwardly against my teeth. Confused, I put a finger up to my mouth. My finger catches on my tooth, my incisor. It's longer. It feels sharp. I touch the other one. It's the same. Oh God, are they ... fangs?

Panicked, I look over at Nathan. "Have I got fangs?" I can't say the words without feeling sick. Oh God, they're catching on my lip as I speak. I cover my mouth up with my hand.

He nods. "It's a natural reaction for you when you're around blood," he says mildly.

I feel anything but mild.

"I can't do this," I blurt out, panicked. I hold the flask out away from me like it's a bomb that's about to go off any second.

Nathan comes over to me. "Yes, you can." He holds my eyes as he pushes the flask back toward me. "You have to."

I look from his face to the flask, and back up at him again.

"The fangs will retract once you've fed." He gives me a firm look of encouragement.

I take a deep breath and close my eyes.

Okay. Count of three. One ... two ... three. I pinch my nose and throw back the contents.

It tastes exactly as it smells, sweet. And I feel good. Eased. Better than I've felt in a long time. It's kind of like foregoing the sex and just heading straight for the orgasm.

But now it's done and the lust has gone, and I'm just left feeling dirty.

Then realisation hits. I start gagging. I thrust the flask into Nathan's hand. Pushing past him, I head straight for the bin. Leaning over it, gripping the edge of the desk for support, I start retching. I retch until my throat starts to burn but nothing comes up. It's almost as if my body doesn't want to part with the blood. And that thought only manages to make me feel worse.

"You okay?" Nathan places a glass of water on the desk beside me. I didn't even realise he'd left the room.

I nod and wipe my hand over my mouth. Nathan's right, the fangs have retracted. I didn't even feel them go. Too busy trying to throw up, I guess.

I pick the glass of water up, rest wearily against the desk and drink it down in one go.

"Why don't you get a shower, clean yourself up," Nathan suggests, gesturing to the chest of drawers over to the right of him.

I see sitting on top of the drawers a towel, wash bag and some clothes, which oddly I'm only just noticing for the first time. I wonder when he put those there.

I nod my agreement. "Where's the bathroom?" I ask.

"Door straight across the hall." He jerks his head in the appropriate direction. "Come downstairs when you're done."

Nathan turns to leave and lifts his arm, rubbing the back of his neck, and that's when I see the lump in the back waist band of his jeans. My eyes close in on it, and don't ask how I know, but I just instantly know what it is.

Fear clouds my judgement and I can't hold my tongue even if I wanted too. "That meant for me?" There's a clear edge to my voice.

Nathan pauses and turns half back, glancing across at me. He reaches behind him and pulls the gun out of his jeans, holding it up in front of him.

My body goes rigid with nerves.

"I didn't know how you were gonna be when you woke up," he says in an even tone. "I didn't know how you would react to the blood when I gave it to you. So, yeah, it was meant for you." He lowers the black shiny gun. "But only if you made it the case."

The temperature in the room suddenly chills and the hairs on the nape of my neck stand on end. He fixes his eyes to mine, pinning me to the spot. There's a darkness there that sends a shiver hurtling down my spine. "And I'll use it in the future without a second thought if you ever force me to." He tucks the gun back in the waistband of his jeans and, without another word, disappears out the room.

I exhale, realising I've been holding my breath the entire time. My whole body starts to tremble.

Collecting myself, I slowly walk over to the chest of drawers on unsteady legs. I see there is a pair of dark blue skinny jeans and a T-shirt. The T-shirt is white with a picture of a black bow on the front. There's also a pair of Converse trainers. I never wear trainers. And there's also a matching white bra and knicker set. All of this stuff is new. It still has the tags on. Nathan has bought me underwear. I don't know how I feel about that. I check the size on the bra – 32D. My size. How did he know exactly what size bra to get me? Then I know exactly how I feel about it as a deep eerie shudder runs through me.

I gather all the clothes up, leaving the trainers behind, grab the wash bag and head straight for the bathroom.

It's not until I'm safely locked in the bathroom when I realise Nathan never answered my question about how he knows about Vârcolacs. I feel a flash of annoyance.

Come on Alex, it's not like you're going to go downstairs chasing after him demanding answers, is it, especially not when he's carrying around a gun with your name on it. Fine, I'll just wait until I've had my shower, and then I'll ask him, if I dare.

To be honest, I really could do with a shower. It's apparently been days since I last had one and I'm starting to smell like a builder's armpit. And I need to brush my teeth, and my tongue. Well basically scrub clean the whole inside of my mouth.

I locate the light switch and turn it on. Seeing the window is open, I cross the bathroom, the tiles cold and unwelcoming beneath my bare feet, and close it.

Dropping my stuff onto the floor, I look around the bathroom. It's generic: a white toilet, sink and bath, with a shower over it. The tiles on the floor are black. The walls are painted a light green. There's a white shower curtain hanging over the railing and a green bath mat hung over the side of the bath. There are a couple of different bottles of men's shower gels and shampoos sitting on the corner of the bath alongside a blue sponge.

In the toothbrush holder there are three toothbrushes, which I take to mean Nathan doesn't live here alone. Everything in here looks like men's stuff, not a womanly product in site, which also means if there are other people living here, they aren't female. Not that it would matter either way.

Maybe Nathan lives with his dad and brother. He did say they were with him looking after me after the attack, and that they were the ones who got rid of the Vârcolac that attacked me and Ca ...

A sharp pain stabs me in my chest taking my breath with it. I lean up against the wall. A clotted sigh escapes me as a tear rolls down my cheek, followed in quick succession by another and another. I roughly wipe my face. The silence echoes all around me. It's haunting.

I walk over to the sink and run the cold water tap. Cupping the water into my hands, I press it to my face, washing my tears away. I grab my towel from off the floor and wipe my face dry.

Everything's gone. In the blink of an eye I've lost everything I cared about. And I've only got myself to blame.

I just drank blood. I have fangs. I've been turned into a freak, a complete and utter freak. I feel all wrong; dirty and violated.

I don't want to be like this. I want to be normal again. I gulp back my tears.

Moving away from the mirror I go and turn the shower on, turning it up hot. Steam quickly rises, cocooning me. I pull the T-shirt off, ignoring the scar that brands me, climb under the water, and attempt to scrub the 'hideous' from off me.

Chapter 7

Shifters

I've scrubbed myself clean. It hasn't helped. I don't feel any better. But then, I didn't really expect I would.

I've dressed in the clothes Nathan gave me. The size ten T-shirt fits fine but the jeans are a bit too big for me. They're hanging off my hips, but I suppose it's better they're too big than too tight.

I wring the water out of my hair and rub the towel roughly over it, trying to rid it of the excess water. My hair holds water like a sponge.

I look around the bathroom for a hairdryer. There isn't one. I hang my wet towel over the side of the bath and go back through to the bedroom to see if there's one in there.

After a good search through the desk drawers, chest of drawers and wardrobe - which is empty of clothes I notice - I come to the easy conclusion that there isn't one in here. My damp hair has soaked a wet patch into the back of my T-shirt. I really don't want to go and ask Nathan for a hairdryer. I go back to the desk and get an elastic band I spotted in there, and tie my hair back into a ponytail.

I sit down on the edge of the bed.

I probably should go downstairs now. I stand up and get the trainers. Size five. I guess Nathan must have checked my Jimmy Choos before he burnt them.

Burnt. Carrie. I'm going to be sick.

I just make it to the bathroom in time.

When my stomach's empty, I rinse my mouth out with cold water from the tap, and swill it clean with mouthwash. Then I go back into the bedroom, put the trainers on, tie the laces up and go downstairs.

I find myself in a longish hallway.

I look right. I can hear voices and the sound of a television coming from behind the closed door.

I look left. It leads to the front door.

If I turn left I can leave this house and get away from all of this. If I turn right it takes me to Nathan and to my new and very much unwanted life.

There's another door directly in front of me that is wide open. A quick glance tells me it's the living room.

I look at my surroundings. It seems to be a big house, well bigger than the two bed Eddie and I had, and every part of it I've seen so far is decorated in neutral colours, like the carpet under my feet. It's dark brown and the walls are painted beige. There's no colour, no knickknacks, no mementos – no woman's touch. If there was once a woman here, she's been erased.

I look left again. My eyes rest on the front door.

All I have to do is walk to it, open it up and leave. It's that easy. I don't have to stay here. I don't have to listen to anything else Nathan has to say.

I turn my body in the direction of the front door and take a step toward it.

But if I leave where will I go? I can't go home. I've got nowhere to go and no one that can help me, except for Nathan, that is.

I pause and look right.

With a resigned sigh, I walk down the hall toward Nathan, each step I take getting heavier the closer I get to him.

When I reach the door, I take a deep breath and slowly push it open.

I find myself in a brightly lit, large, open plan kitchen-diner. Nathan looks up at me as I enter. He's leaning up against the kitchen counter to my far left with a glass in his hand.

I smile. He doesn't return it and I wonder if I've done something wrong.

A flush rises in my cheeks. I look away, glancing around quickly, taking in my surroundings. Directly in front of me is the dining area. The TV I could hear is fixed up on the wall to my right and it's currently hosting the rugby. Adjacent to the TV is a large, dark brown, wooden dining table with six white leather chairs pushed underneath, and two of those chairs are occupied by, I'm assuming, Nathan's dad and brother.

"Hiya love, you alright?" Nathan's dad says.

I notice he looks good for his age. He has warm dark eyes and hair to match, with just a showing of grey. Nathan looks nothing like his dad.

"I'm Jack, Nathan's dad," he adds, patting a hand to his chest. "And this is Sol, my youngest." He thumbs in Sol's direction.

Sol smiles a very confident smile at me.

I can tell he's Nathan's brother. He's just a younger, slighter version of him. The only difference I can see between them is Nathan has a more indie style hair cut, whereas Sol's hair is cut short and styled to precision, just like his clothes. Sol seems to care about his appearance in stark contrast to Nathan's 'I've just fallen out of bed and put on yesterday's clothes' look. Nathan may have had a shower before he woke me up earlier but, if so, he's still put back on the same rumpled clothes he was wearing this morning.

"Hi," I utter nervously.

"It's really nice to meet you properly," Sol says with a noticeable swagger to his surprisingly deep voice. "And when my dad says I'm young, he just means I'm younger than these two oldies." He nods his head in the direction of his dad and brother. "I'm nineteen and very experienced for my age," he adds in a lower tone, bordering suggestive.

Nathan snorts out a laugh. My face instantly goes red.

"Sol, for God's sake, stop flirting!" Jack chides. "Sorry about him, love," he says to me, rolling his eyes heavenwards. "His hormones never calmed down once they set in when he was a teenager."

"Yeah, we've considered getting him neutered," Nathan adds, a goading tone to his voice.

I see Nathan and Sol share a look, then Sol says, "Sorry, when did you last get laid, Nate? Oh yeah, about a year ago." He smiles smugly. "Me, you ask? Oh well, I got some yesterday."

I flick a glance in Nathan's direction. His green eyes briefly meet mine. I feel a jolt inside. It surprises me.

"Ignore those two idiots," Jack says to me, sliding a disapproving look at them both. "They're always like this. You get used to 'em after a while - well eventually." He smiles. "Do you want a drink?" But before I get a chance to answer, Jack turns to Nathan and says, "Make yourself useful and get Alex a drink, will you?"

"Do you want a drink?" Nathan asks me.

I glance at him wearily, unsure of what drink is actually on offer. I don't think I could stomach any more blood right now. Or ever again.

"A normal drink," Nathan adds, seeing my hesitation.

I spy a bottle of Jack Daniels on the counter. That must be what he's drinking.

"Jack Daniels?" I ask.

"Jack Daniels it is."

He puts his own drink down on the counter, reaches up and gets a glass out of the cupboard, pours a small measure of whiskey into it and holds it out for me to take.

I walk toward him and take the glass. "Thanks." I stare down at the brown liquid. I'm not a big whiskey drinker, more of a vodka girl, but right now I'd drink glass cleaner if it had alcohol in it.

I down it in one. It goes down like water. In the past when I've drunk whiskey, I've breathed fire after a one sip.

"Refill?" Nathan asks, raising an eyebrow.

I press the back of my hand to my damp lips, drying them. "Yes, please." I hold my glass out as he pours again. A larger measure this time, I notice.

Nathan gets another clean glass from the cupboard, tucks the bottle of Jack Daniels under his arm, picks his own drink up and heads for the table.

Cradling my glass to my chest, I follow behind him.

He puts his own drink down, places the clean glass on the table in front of his dad, pours some Jack Daniels into it, and sits down.

"Thanks, son." Jack looks over at him appreciatively.

I sit in the chair beside Nathan and put my glass down.

"Don't I get any?" Sol asks.

"Since when do you drink whiskey?" Nathan questions.

Sol's eyes briefly flicker in my direction, then straight back to Nathan. "Since forever."

"Sorry, I thought strawberry milk was more your drink of choice." With a sigh Nathan gets up from his seat and goes to get Sol a glass.

He comes back, sets the glass down on the table in front of Sol with a slight bang, and sits down again.

Sol takes hold of the bottle of Jack Daniels and pours himself a large measure. He picks up the glass and, with a defiant look in his eyes meant for Nathan, takes a really big gulp of whiskey. The moment it's down he starts spluttering and coughing, his face turning bright red.

Nathan lets out a laugh. I stay quiet in my seat. Under normal circumstances I'd find this funny but this isn't exactly normal circumstances.

Jack leans over and pats Sol hard on the back. "Cough it up, lad," he says, letting out a low rumbling laugh himself.

"Good stuff, isn't it?" Nathan smirks at Sol and downs his own remaining whiskey.

"Fuck off," Sol snaps, wiping his mouth on the back of his hand.

Nathan eyes him over his glass, grinning.

A smile breaks Sol's stony face. "You're a real arse at times, you know," he says, a small laugh escaping him.

"So I've been told." Nathan slides an innocuous look my way. My face flushes. I look away.

"Do you want something to eat?" Jack asks me, thankfully changing the subject.

I shake my head.

"You sure?" he questions.

"I'm sure. But, thanks."

I take a sip of my drink and put it back down on the wooden table, keeping my fingertips resting up against the glass.

Jack picks the remote control up off the table and points it in the direction of the TV, turning it off. The kitchen is suddenly eerily silent.

"So ... Alex," Jack says putting the remote control back down, "Nathan says you have some questions."

That's the understatement of the century if there ever was one.

I slide a sideways glance at Nathan and look back to Jack. I nod my head lightly.

Jack pulls a pack of cigars out of his shirt pocket. "You mind if I smoke?" he asks.

I shake my head. Even if I did, it's his house and not my place to object, but I like the fact that he cared to ask.

He puts a cigar between his lips and lights it up with an old Zippo lighter. My dad used to have one of those lighters and he, like Jack, used to smoke cigars, only one a day, right after we'd eaten dinner. He'd go sit out on the back porch as my mum wouldn't let him smoke in the house and I'd go and keep him company.

It was nice. I really miss it.

I inhale the scent of the cigar smoke and watch as it curls around the air. A pang of nostalgia and longing overtakes me.

"You want one?" Jacks offers and I realise I've been staring.

"No, thank you," I utter, embarrassed.

Jack reaches over and pulls the glass ashtray, which was sitting in the middle of the table, toward him. He taps the end of his cigar on it, dropping ash in. "So you want to know how we know all about your kind – Vârcolacs, I mean," Jack says getting straight onto the point.

Leaning forward, I rest my forearms on the table and wrap my hands around my glass. "Pretty much."

He takes a noticeable breath. "We know about Vârcolacs and all the other supernatural beings out there because we're a part of it. We're shape-shifters." He takes another puff of his cigar but keeps his eyes fixed firmly on me.

I'm pretty sure a tumbleweed blows through the room.

I look at Nathan agog, but he doesn't meet my stare. I flick my widened eyes to Sol. He meets them and smiles in that awkward way people do when they really don't know what else to do.

Okay, so I don't really know what I was expecting, but it wasn't that.

"Shape … shifters, as in … shape-shifters," I finally say.

"Is there any other type?" Nathan bites.

I turn, surprised, and see Jack give him a look. Nathan gets out of his seat, taking his glass with him and puts it with a clatter into the sink.

"So, erm … what do you … shift into?" I ask Sol in a quiet voice.

"We can change into anything we want," Sol answers, "but only animals. We can't change into other human beings."

"Oh," I say.

Silence reigns for a moment. Nathan sits back down at the table beside me. He doesn't look happy.

I decide to turn the subject away from them and onto myself, even though I am curious. I shift in my seat, turning to look at Nathan. "Nathan, you said earlier that when I was been bitten by the Vârcolac it should have killed me, not changed me. So how did I survive?"

I'm met with shrug. Nathan turns his head to look in my direction. His hair falls in front of his eyes. He brushes it away. "Maybe there's something different about you. Maybe you're special," he says. He doesn't sound like he thinks I'm special. "Or maybe over the years, as women have evolved and your bodies have somehow become stronger, you've become able to cope with the change. They've probably just never discovered this fact because Vârcolacs are so accustomed to you dying, they stopped trying to turn you. To them you were just dinner and obviously no one's been stupid enough to try and save a woman from them, well apart from me, that is, and when I did, well then obviously I changed everything." I see the regret in his eyes.

I'm fast coming to the conclusion that Nathan doesn't really like me and that saving me is probably what he would class as one of his bigger mistakes in life.

It's fine. Really.

I rub my hand over my face. "From what you said earlier, I'm to take it that it's not a good thing I survived and became one of them?"

Nathan taps his long fingers against the table top. "No. If the Originals find out you exist—"

"Originals?"

"The first Vârcolacs," Jacks inputs. "There's two of them, Matthias and Isaiah. They're twins."

"So where did they come from?" I'm starting to get so anxious that I'm fidgeting with thin air. "What I mean is, if they're the first, then how did they become that way?"

Jack stubs his half-smoked cigar out and lays the remainder on the edge of the ashtray. He leans forward, resting his elbows on the table. "There's a lot of myth surrounding them but the legend as we know is that in the early part of the 1600s there was a cross-breed between Demetrius, the son from the original head vampire family, and a werewolf, Grace. She was the daughter of an important pack leader. That's how Matthias and Isaiah were created. Demetrius and Grace were in love and she got pregnant. It was a pretty damn stupid and dangerous thing for them to do. Vampires and werewolves don't mix at all. They don't get along."

"That's putting it mildly," Sol chuckles. "They hate one another," he adds, looking at me.

"Cross-breeding for them is deemed sacrilegious," Jack says.

"But I thought vampires are supposed to be dead? How could she get pregnant if he was ... dead?" My voice suddenly sounds really small and tinny.

"The first family can procreate," Nathan tells me, "but not 'made' vampires. They are 'dead'. What happened with Demetrius and Grace should never have happened, but it did. They hid their relationship and her pregnancy from their families. Only Grace's sister, Genevieve, knew. Grace had the twins in secret. They were planning to leave the country together, taking the twins with them, but somehow Demetrius' family found out about their relationship, but not the twins. His father, Elijah, was furious. He put the order out for their capture. Grace and Demetrius tried to run but they were found and killed for their crime."

"He murdered his own son?" I say aghast.

"They're vampires, Alex." Nathan says this with an almost mocking tone to his voice. "They're not known for their kindness."

"But still, his own son." I give him a look of contempt.

He shrugs. "Elijah's not known for his weakness. He had to make an example of Demetrius and Grace. Obviously killing her didn't help relations between vampires and the werewolves, not that Elijah would care either way."

"And the twins?" I ask tentatively, even though I know they survived. I wouldn't be in this position right now if they hadn't.

"Fortunately for them, the twins were with Genevieve when Demetrius and Grace were captured. After Grace had been murdered, Genevieve revealed the twins' existence to her parents. Matthias and Isaiah were all they had left of their daughter, so they raised them, keeping their existence a secret from the vampires who they knew would hunt them down and kill them if they ever discovered them. Matthias and Isaiah grew up and turned into what they still are today, the self-proclaimed Vârcolacs, half-breed, immortal blood drinkers like their father, with the ability to turn into a wolf just like their mother. But Isaiah was cocky and tired of living in the shadows. He had big plans to create an army so they'd be well protected and could kill the vampires that had murdered their parents, so he talked Matthias into coming out. Matthias, though reluctant, agreed and Isaiah outed their existence to the vampires in the midst of trying to build his army which obviously didn't go exactly as he'd planned. You see, they can't create any immortals like themselves, like vampires can. Isaiah hadn't done his homework first. Any male who is changed will only live a human life with a slight extension, just like werewolves do. They're not as strong as the Originals either who have a strength equal to vampires. So they'd exposed themselves to their enemy and were still as vulnerable as before." Nathan leans back in his chair, stretching his long legs out under the table. "The vampires have been hunting them ever since. The Originals live in hiding but they still have a strong allegiance to their werewolf 'family' who help keep them hidden. The Originals believe the only viable way to ensure their long-term survival is to have more like them, more immortals, and then they can finally have what they've always dreamed of. They can eradicate all vampires and put themselves right at the top of the food chain."

"So how can having me as a Vârcolac help them get what they want?" My voice comes out scratchy and hoarse.

There's an uncomfortable ripple of silence across the table. It sets my nerves on edge. I take a sip of whiskey.

"Well, like Nathan said, the Originals want full-bloods, just like them," Jack pauses, "and they believe the only way to do this is to breed them, and to be able to do this they need a … "

"Female Vârcolac?" I finish.

Jack looks at me with sorrowful eyes.

"If they find out about you," Nathan says in a tapered voice, "then you'll become their baby breeding machine for the rest of your life." He turns his head and looks me in the eye for a long moment and I can see it all there in his eyes reflecting back at me, like a flash-forward of my possible future.

Something crawls over my skin – fear, I think.

"Don't you worry though, Alex," Jack says in a confident voice, giving the table a bang with his hand so hard it makes me jump, "you'll be safe here with us."

But I don't feel confident or safe at all. I'm here with three men, one of whom is barely that, who happen to be able to change into animals when they feel like it.

"We'll make sure the Originals never know you exist," Jack adds. "Think of this as your home, now and for the foreseeable future." He waves his hand around, smiling through tight lips. "We'll take real good care of you."

I see the quick look that Nathan gives Jack, the one Jack chooses to ignore, and I know unequivocally that Nathan doesn't fully agree with Jack's statement. Nathan wants me here until he can find a suitable place to put me. He doesn't want me here for good, confirming what I already knew.

I'm all alone.

I squeeze my eyes shut, wanting to block it all out, block all of them out.

"You will be okay." Nathan's voice comes close to my ear.

You. Not we - you.

He touches my arm. I open my eyes, surprised. I yank my arm away from him. It's his turn to look surprised. I don't know why he's pretending to be nice to me when he clearly doesn't want me here.

And I'm about to say so when Nathan sighs loudly and leans back in his chair, raking a hand through his mussed up hair. "Great, just what we didn't need," he grumbles.

I stare at him, confused.

"You ready." Sol grins clearly amused. Nathan laughs. Jack mutters something unintelligible under his breath.

Okay, so I'm clearly left out of the party here.

Then I hear a car screech to a halt outside. A knot tightens in my stomach.

"Five, four ... " Nathan starts to count down on his fingers. Sol joins in. Jack picks up his cigar from the ashtray and lights it back up.

"Who's that?" I ask none of them in particular, gesturing to the outside with my shaky hand.

"Three ... "

"Cal," Jacks answers, his cigar perched precariously between his lips. A big puff of smoke emanates from out of his mouth.

"Two ... " Nathan leans over, picks Sol's glass up off the table and throws back the contents. "One." He bangs the empty glass back down.

I'm just about to ask who Cal is, but before I get a chance, the back door flies open and standing there is a huge bloke.

And he doesn't look happy or friendly in any way.

Chapter 8

Brothers

"So you are all okay, then?" Cal marches into the house, leaving the back door wide open, letting the cold air in. "Because Dad tells me you're all sick, dying from the bloody flu, and I'm not to come into work because you don't want me to pass it onto Erin. But you've all been acting so shady when I've rung to check on you, and Sol is the worst liar in the world, so I know something's going on, and then I walk in here and find you all fit as fiddles drinking bloody whiskey, and ... " He suddenly stops mid rant and appears to sniff the air. Then his eyes locate and lock onto me.

I shiver and it's not from the cold. My brain instantly goes on high alert. I shift in my seat. Nathan reaches his hand back and puts it on my arm, firmly holding me in place like he thinks I am going to bolt.

Well, actually, he isn't far wrong. Something about Cal has set me on nerves' edge and wanting out of here, now.

"Vârcolac?" Cal's eyes widen in disbelief. "But ... she's a woman? How? What the fuck is going on here?" He's aggressive demeanour is suddenly gone and he just looks kind of dumbstruck. He shakes his head roughly as though trying to clear his thoughts.

Seeing Cal's reaction to me is a bit of a wake-up call. He's looking at me with a mixture of horror, anger and mild panic. And even though Nathan, Jack and Sol have told me what the calamity of being me is, it is a little different when you see it actually being played out in front of you.

"Does someone want to explain to me just how the hell she happens to be a Vârcolac?" Cal drags his hand down his face, removing with it his perplexed expression. He turns around, slamming the door firmly, like he's worried someone might be out there and see me. Then he spins back on his heel and points at no one in particular. "And while we're at it, can you explain why the bloody hell she's here with you three?"

Nathan removes his hand from my arm and turns to Cal. "Just take it easy," he says calmly.

Cal laughs, a sharp laugh. "I'll take it easy when you tell me just exactly what the fuck's been going on here."

My hands start to shake. I can't seem to control the tremor. I grip hold of my glass for something to do with them. It shatters in my hands.

I stare down at in shock as a sharp pain sears through my right hand. Blood trickles out down onto the table. I turn my hand over. There's a deep cut in my palm. Blood continues to seep out, carelessly dripping on the table as the whiskey from my glass drips onto my jeans. But I don't move because I can't. I'm frozen to the spot and all I can do is stare down at the broken glass in front of me.

I just broke it with my bare hands. My eyes are brimming with tears. The room is eerily silent.

"I'm so sorry," I stammer, finding my voice.

"It's okay, love," Jack says kindly.

Nathan takes hold of my arm by the wrist. "Let's get you cleaned up." He guides me to my feet and leads me over to the sink. I hold my other hand beneath my bleeding one so I don't drip any blood onto the floor.

Jack follows behind us and gets some kitchen roll and disinfectant spray out of the cupboard next to where I'm standing, presumably to clean up the mess I've just made.

"Don't worry about it, love," Jack says quietly to me. "I've done much worse after a few glasses of whiskey." He winks conspiratorially at me.

I try to smile but my lips are quivering and it just feels awkward.

Nathan runs the cold water tap and puts my hand under it. I wince at the sting. I can see my blood washing down the sink. I look away. Sol and Jack are already cleaning up the table. Cal is leaning up against the back door moodily, his arms folded across his chest.

Leaving my hand under the increasingly cold water, Nathan gets a first aid kit out from the cupboard under the sink. He turns the tap off and carefully dries my hand with a towel, wrapping it around and pressing firmly down onto my palm to dry the cut out.

"How bad is it?" I ask warily as he examines the cut.

"Not bad. It'll be healed in a few minutes."

"What?" I look up at him alarmed.

"I already told you, you heal quickly." His tone is suddenly off.

I know he's already told me but it's just not something I can get easily used to hearing. And when he gets all antsy like this, it just makes me want to question him further.

"How did I break that glass with my hands?" I ask in a lowered tone. This wasn't a cheap, crappy glass. This was a thick whiskey glass, not that I can normally break any type of glass with my hands but, well, you know what I mean.

"Because you're bloody superwoman," Cal says from across the room, sarcasm practically dripping from his voice.

Nathan turns to say something to him but Sol beats him to it. "Give it a rest, Cal."

Cal opens his mouth to retaliate, then seemingly changes his mind. Sighing loudly, he pulls a chair out and sits down at the now clean table.

Nathan takes the towel off my hand. I see the bleeding has calmed. He rips open a large plaster. "You know how you did it," he finally answers, staring straight into my eyes. His eyes are so green, so piercing, they're intrusive, almost like he's, for some reason, trying to extract information straight from out of my brain. Either that or he's trying to leave some there.

He looks down at my hand and sticks the plaster over my cut. "Leave this on 'til it heals." But he doesn't let go of my hand.

"So I'm taking it this is what you've all been busy with?" Cal says, obvious impatience in his voice. Nathan lets go of my hand. "A female Vârcolac ... " Cal shakes his head, " ... so are you gonna explain what the hell happened, who the bloody hell she is, and why the hell you're involved, or do I have to wait till Christmas?"

"Alex, sorry, you haven't been introduced properly. This is Cal, my obnoxious older brother," Nathan says, gesturing towards him. "Cal, this is Alex, the only female Vârcolac in the world." He thumbs in my direction.

Sol snorts out a laugh. Even I have to hold off a smile.

So Cal is Nathan's older brother. He looks nothing like Nathan. He looks like Jack, except his features are sharp and uncharacteristic. The only similarity between him and Nathan is his size and, of course, his direct manner.

"Funny," Cal retorts, "are you gonna answer my fucking question or not?" His face is flushed with rage.

Nathan leans up against the sink and sighs loudly, folding his arms across his chest. "Why do you automatically assume this is my doing?"

"Because this has got you written all over it. You were always the one bringing the stray animals home when we were kids." Cal's eyes flit in my direction but don't actually settle on me. "And if you're mixed up in something dangerous, I need to know about it."

"Why?" Nathan's tone is brusque.

"Why?" Cal looks incredulous. "Because, brother, whatever you do will automatically have repercussions on me."

"Ahh, what a surprise!" Nathan lets out a slow, satirical laugh, shaking his head. "So now we're getting to it. This isn't about me, dad and Sol and how it affects us, this about you. What a fucking surprise that is!"

Cal looks so angry I'm pretty sure he's considering coming over here and taking a swipe at Nathan.

"Why don't you both just calm down," Jack says, finally intervening. "Cal, have a drink."

Cal eyes the bottle of whiskey Jack is holding up like a golden carrot and I take this as my chance to escape the furore.

"I'm gonna go outside and get some fresh air," I say in a quiet voice to Nathan. "I'll leave you all to talk."

I've already started to move away from him but he reaches out and grabs hold of my arm, stopping me. "I'll come with you."

I can tell from his tone he's not coming with me out of the goodness of his heart. He's probably worried I'm going to try and do a runner.

"Stay here," I say in a soft, placating voice. "I won't go far, just outside into the garden. You all obviously need some time to talk." I nod towards

Cal who is slumped in his chair and is currently laying into the bottle of Jack Daniels like his life depends on it.

Nathan hesitates, twisting his lips in contemplation. "Okay," he finally concedes, "just don't go far." I can tell he's not a comfortable with me going outside on my own, but right now I couldn't care less, I just want out of here.

"I won't go far," I reiterate.

I'm at the back door when Nathan's voice comes from close behind me, "Put this on, it's cold outside." He rests a black leather jacket over my shoulders.

I turn, giving him an appreciative look. "Thanks." I slide my arms into the sleeves and, without another word to anyone else, I slip out the back door.

The cold instantly sweeps over my face, wrapping itself around me. The evening air is surprisingly chilly for July, but I don't care, I'm just relieved to be outside and away from them.

I zip the jacket up. It's way too big for me. The sleeves are hanging down past my hands. I'm guessing its Nathan's jacket as it smells of him. Oddly, it gives me a sense of comfort.

Hugging the coat to me, I look around. The garden is closed in by a low fence. To my right is a path leading up to a gate. Parked up by the gate is a silver truck, I'm guessing Cal's. In front of me is another path which runs right through the garden and also has a gate at the end of it.

The voices inside suddenly become raised.

I quickly make my way down the path leading into the garden, leaving the hassle behind.

It's so quiet out here. There are no sounds of traffic or people. I'm literally in the middle of nowhere with nothing but nature to keep me company, and it's tranquil.

The garden has solar-powered lights dotted all around the edge of the garden. It's not a big garden for the size of the house, but it's well tended; someone obviously takes pride in it. I'd take a guess and say Jack.

I continue walking down the path, heading toward the gate.

When I reach it, I lean forward, resting my stomach against it, and have a nosey at what's out there. The gate opens up straight onto the farmland and it is a vast expanse. It seems to go on for miles. I can see a forest further out on the perimeter, spreading right across the back of their land, and the track that runs down the side of the house, splitting the land, appears to lead straight into the forest. I spy a barn over to my right the other side of the track. It's all lit up and looks welcoming.

I open the gate, let myself out into the field and head straight for the barn.

Chapter 9

Headlines

The main door to the barn is wide open. I wander inside. The barn's not as big inside as it looks from the outside, but it does look exactly as a barn should look. There's a tractor looming over to my left and a work bench fixed up against the wall behind the tractor which is littered with all kinds of different tools. To my right, on its own, is a magnificent looking, shiny red motorbike. It's a Ducati. I know nothing about motorbikes but it looks impressive, and expensive. I wonder if it's Nathan's.

At the back of the barn, taking up a large chunk of space, is a big stack of hay bales. I wander over to them and climb up onto the first lot, that are stacked three high, and rest my back up against the higher stack behind.

I close my eyes. I don't want to think anymore, I just want to clear my mind of everything and sit in peace.

It's easier said than done and I'm not left alone for long. It's maybe been five minutes max when I hear Nathan approaching. I know it's him because I can smell him.

This super smelling thing of mine is going to take some serious getting used to but I guess it comes in handy at times.

I open my eyes and, as expected, Nathan comes into view a few seconds later, walking with purpose toward me.

I repress a sigh.

"Hey," he says climbing up onto the hay bales and sitting beside me.

"Hey," I say.

Silence.

If he's got nothing to say, why is he here? Checking up on me, most likely. I close my eyes again and rest my head back against the hay.

"So you can change into an animal." The words are out of my mouth before I even realise. But still, I open my eyes and turn my head to catch his reaction.

His eyes are already on me and they look cautious. "Yes," he finally answers.

"You always been able to do that?"

"Since I was thirteen. The ability comes in at puberty."

"Ahh." Pause. "So, do you have a favourite animal you like to change into or ... "

"Wolf."

"Any reason?"

"Nope." Or none that he's willing to share with me.

I look out at the blackness that is casting its shadows in through the open barn door, threatening to infringe on the light.

"You can shift as well, you know," Nathan says out of the blue.

"What?" My head swivels round on my neck.

"You're part werewolf remember." His tone screams 'stupid'. It irks me, to say the least. "The only difference you have from them is you're not ruled by the moon," he adds a little less caustically. "You're like shifters in that respect. You only change if and when you want to."

Great. So not only have I changed into a monster that drinks blood but I can also turn into a dog. This just gets bloody better and better.

I lean forward, resting my elbows on my thighs, my chin cupped in my hands, my lips turned downwards, and stare dismally at my feet. "Does it hurt when you change?" I utter into my hands.

"No. For me it's as natural as breathing."

I shift my chin onto one hand and look round at him. "Will it hurt me?" I run my hand over the scar on my stomach.

"No. It'll just feel ... uncomfortable, odd, the first time you shift. But the more you do it, the more it'll become a natural thing for you to do."

My mind starts to whirl. There's so much I don't know about myself. I start to run a list of all the things I know about vampires and werewolves, well all the things I've seen in the movies.

"Not everything you think you know about vampires and werewolves applies to you," Nathan says as if reading my mind.

I can't hide the surprise from my face. "You read minds as well?" I ask half-serious.

A smile turns up the corners of his mouth. "No. Just faces."

I shuffle around so I'm facing his side and pull my legs up, crossing them in front of me. "So is any of the stuff in the movies true?"

"Some."

I pause before asking the question which has been on the edge of my mind since I discovered what I am. I mean, I might feel alive but that doesn't necessarily mean I am. I am part vampire after all.

"Nathan, am I ... dead, like vampires are?" I hold my breath in anticipation of his answer.

"Is your heart beating?"

I rest my hand lightly against my chest. "Yes."

"Then you're not dead."

And now I just feel stupid for asking. Nathan has the amazing ability to make me feel idiotic, seemingly at any given opportunity, and I just keep leaving the door wide open for him.

Looking at anything but him, I start to chew on my fingernail.

Nathan moves around to face me. "Vârcolacs are still living creatures, Alex. You're still very much alive, you're just different now, and you need different things to keep you alive."

I stop chewing and bring my eyes to his. "Blood."

"Yes." He nods.

"Can I still go out in daylight?"

"Yes."

"Garlic?"

"No effect."

What else? What effects werewolves? "What about silver?" I ask.

He nods again. "Silver bullets straight in the heart work best." He taps his chest in the place where his own beating heart sits. "Once they're in there, there's no getting them out."

I feel a shudder deep inside. "No wooden stakes then?" I let out a shaky laugh and run my finger over the damp patch on the thigh of my jeans that is still wet from the spilt whiskey before.

"Well, yeah, I'm guessing it'd eventually kill you if someone stabbed you in the heart with a wooden stake. You're not immortal, Alex." He smirks and yet again I feel like an idiot. "You're strong, you heal quickly, so you'll bounce back from most things, but silver in your system is the real killer. It's like a disease once it's in your blood, hence why, if I wanted to kill a Vârcolac, I'd go for the heart, silver straight into there and it'll flood their system, killing them in a matter of minutes."

"Is that how you killed the one that attacked me and Carr … " My voice wilts as the pain ruptures deep inside of me.

"I caught him off-guard when he was … busy." His tone quietens. He stares straight ahead past me. Nausea washes through me and my head starts to throb. "I broke his neck," he continues, his voice still lowered. "It left him incapacitated. I carried you back to my car, got my silver blade out of the glove box, went back and stuck it straight into his heart."

I inhale deeply, pulling tears back with it.

It should make me feel better hearing how he died. But it doesn't. My brain is so messy, I'm struggling to make sense of anything anymore.

"Are you okay?" Nathan asks. I feel like it's all he asks me.

"I'm fine." I shake the thoughts out of my mind and yank the elastic band out of my hair as it suddenly feels tight. I put the band around my wrist and rub my scalp, brushing my hair out with my fingers and fanning it out around my shoulders. I catch my hair on the plaster on my hand. I'd forgotten about that. Pulling it free, I look at it. There's a tiny blood stain where my blood has seeped through. A strand of my blonde hair is still stuck under the plaster. I pull it free.

Then, without a word, Nathan reaches over and takes hold of my hand. I raise a confused eyebrow at him but he's not looking at me. His eyes are on my hand. His large hand is warm and dwarfs mine, making mine look almost child-sized. He picks at the corner of the plaster and peels it back, pulling it right off.

I can't help the gasp that escapes me. The air just rushes straight out of my lungs.

The cut has gone. It's healed completely. Just like he said it would.

"It's gone," I say, voice quivering.

He gives me a knowing look and lets go of my hand, leaving it feeling cold.

I bring my hand closer to my face to examine it, and run my fingertip over the place where the cut should still be. "Do you heal this quickly?" I ask, trying to keep my voice steady.

"Not as quickly as you do," he answers. "But, yeah, a lot quicker than a normal person would."

"Do you have the good hearing and other stuff as well?"

I want to talk to him about it. I want to know what I'm working with here. However, he apparently doesn't because he moves away from me, sitting himself on the edge of the bales, letting his long legs dangle down. For a moment I wonder if he's just going to jump down and leave without another word, then he finally answers a quiet, "Yes."

I get the distinct impression Nathan doesn't like to talk about his abilities. Dejected, I stare at my newly healed hand.

"I'm sorry about Cal's behaviour before," Nathan says, breaking the silence and surprising me. "He can be a bit of an arse at times. That's why we hadn't told him about you yet."

"Run in the family?" The words are out before I can stop them.

He looks sideways at me, his eyebrow raised. "What, being an arse?"

I feel my cheeks turn pink. "Hmm." I nod, lightly.

He rests his chin on his shoulder, his even eyes fixed on me. "No, that quality's just reserved for me and Cal."

"Sorry, that sounded ... what I meant was ... I didn't mean your dad and Sol ... I meant ... I mean ... " I'm flustered. I take a quick breath, " ... I like them, and you of course."

A smile flickers over his face. "Of course."

My cheeks turn from pink to red. I sweep my hair around my neck and start twisting strands around my finger. "What about your mum?" I ask.

"What about her?" His sudden cool tone sucks the air right out of here.

"Well, I just wondered where she is?" My words are careful, measured.

"I don't know." He shrugs averting his eyes. "She left, seventeen years ago. I was twelve, Cal was fourteen, Sol was two. He doesn't remember her." His voice has gone as flat and cold as I've felt since I woke up this morning.

"I'm sorry ... "

"Don't be," he cuts me off. "I'm not." He glances back at me but his face is unreadable, impassive.

"I lost my parents," I blurt out. "They died."

Where the hell did that come from? That's the first time I've spoken about them in years. I always think of them. Always. I just never talk about them. If I do, it makes the fact they're not here all the more real.

"I know," Nathan says, blindsiding me. "It said in the papers about your parents, about how they died in a car accident when you were sixteen."

I stare at him, confused. "Why would it be in the papers about my parents? They died ten years ago."

"You're a missing person. It's a big story in the news at the moment and ... well, in these sorts of cases they tend to give a back story about the ... victims." He hesitates, then asks, "Do you want to see the newspaper?"

It's my turn to hesitate.

Do I want to see the newspaper? No. Yes. No.

"Yes," I hear myself saying, despite all my reservations.

Nathan jumps down from the bales, lithely landing on his feet, and goes over to the tractor. He opens the door, climbs halfway in and emerges back out a second later with a folded newspaper in his hand.

Blood starts to beat in my ears as he walks back toward me. He climbs up the bales and sits down again beside me, closer this time I notice, and hands me the paper.

It's my local newspaper, the Scarborough Evening News. I notice the date at the top of the page. "Is this today's?" I ask.

"Yep."

I unfold the paper, revealing the front page.

There's a sizeable picture of me and Carrie on the front. I recognise it instantly. It was taken last Christmas Eve. Angie and Tom had a party at their house. Eddie came with me. We were just getting back on track after I had found out about his first indiscretion.

Carrie looks beautiful. Her arm is around my shoulders, eyes sparkling, smiling widely, with her red hair ablaze around her face. I look drunk. Actually, I was drunk. It really is a great photo of Carrie, though. It captures the essence of her. I know that Angie and Tom have it in a frame on the mantelpiece in their living room. Angie loves this picture, she was the one who took it.

My face starts to tingle with the memory.

"Your story's made the nationals as well," Nathan informs me. He doesn't sound happy about it.

The national newspapers? Hackness is a really small place and I used to live in Scarborough. Both Carrie and I went to school there, so I can see why our disappearance would have a big impact on the local community. But to make the national newspapers, well you're either a celebrity, a criminal or ... you've been murdered.

My throat starts to feel tight. It's getting hard to breathe again. A fat teardrop leaks from my eye and lands on the paper, directly onto the picture of me and Carrie. Dismayed, I quickly try to dab it dry with the sleeve of Nathan's leather jacket. Instead I smudge it.

The picture's getting ruined. Panic grips me tight. It's the only picture I have left of Carrie. It's all I have left of Carrie.

Nathan, seeing my upset, pulls the sleeve of his top down and dabs the paper dry. He does a much better job than me. Now there's only a slight smudge on the part of the picture with me in. Carrie looks fine.

I exhale with relief. "Thank you," I utter gratefully.

"I wasn't thinking when I brought you this." He indicates the newspaper with his finger. "I should have realised it would upset you. Do you want me to get rid of it?"

"No." I wipe my wet eyes dry with my hand and rub my hands against my jeans before touching the paper again. I can't risk any more smudges.

I stare down at Carrie.

She's gone. She's never going to get married or have kids, or go travelling like she always talked about doing. I've stolen her life from her.

I try to breath but stale air ghosts its way through me.

"She was really pretty," Nathan says in a measured voice. I glance at him. "You guys look like you were having a good time in this picture," he adds.

"We were. Carrie was the life and soul of the party."

"You were close?" he inquires.

"Like sisters." I stare down at the picture. "She was my family. Her, Angie and Tom, they were all I had left in the world."

"You got no other family? Grandparents, aunties, uncles?"

"No." I shake my head. ""My mum and dad were both only children and my grandparents on both sides died a long time ago." I let out a sad breath, tracing my fingertip over the picture. "I'm an orphan."

The silence that follows carries a heavy weight.

I let my eyes drift over the paper. I read about mine and Carrie's disappearance and the odd circumstance surrounding it. There's the mention of my parents' death that Nathan has just mentioned. It goes on to say that Angie and Tom have put up a reward for anyone who has information about my and Carrie's whereabouts, leading to our discovery. A hundred thousand pounds.

Angie and Tom are wealthy, but still, a hundred grand is a lot of money even for them.

There's a quote from Angie in the text saying, 'We're not missing one daughter, we're missing two.'

I feel sick and it aches all the way through my chest, straight into my hollow heart. It's all I can do not to throw the paper down and run straight to them. If only there was some way I could go to them and tell them what has happened. It won't bring Carrie back but it will allow them some peace.

I look to Nathan, pleadingly. "Isn't there any way I can tell Angie and

Tom what has happened, end their suffering?"

He stares back at me with sympathetic eyes and I already know his answer before he speaks. "We've already talked about this, Alex. You know it isn't a possibility. If you go to them, you'll only end up putting them in danger too."

Frustration practically burns up my insides. I know he's right but I don't want him to be. I owe everything to Angie and Tom. They deserve more than this from me.

I stare back down at Angie's words, letting them burn into my retinas, and something catches my eye. Eddie's name. Eddie's in here, of course he is. He was my boyfriend after all. I scan the text. The story on him only just starts when it ends, saying, 'Turn to page 5 to continue ... '

I turn the pages quickly. There's more about me in here but I'm not interested in me, I'm only interested in Eddie.

I see a small picture of him halfway down the page. He looks distraught. It makes my heart hurt. And, as I stare harder at the picture, things start to stand out, like the police station behind him. This picture is of Eddie leaving the police station. I swallow down hard. As I read the text directly below the picture, it says Eddie's a suspect in our disappearance.

Oh God. He might have cheated on me but I don't want Eddie to go to prison for something he didn't do. My heart starts to beat erratically.

I let my eyes scan over the words, picking out the important parts.

'Alexandra Jones and Eddie Thomson had been in a relationship for three years ... Eddie Thomson works for Tom Ross, Carrie's father ... Jones and Thomson had argued the day before her disappearance ... Jones discovered he'd been cheating on her ... They argued and had split up the day prior to Alexandra and Carrie's disappearance ... Jones had moved out of their two bed house on Princess Street ... the last call received to Jones' mobile was from Thomson ... Thomson was taken in for questioning but was released without charge when his alibi was corroborated ... the night of their disappearance Thomson was with a woman, Serena Travers. She confirmed to police officers yesterday that he had spent the night with her at her house on Scalby Road, Scarborough.'

My heart sinks down to the stony floor.

He called me begging me to go back to him and all the while he was at her house. Carrie was murdered, I was left fighting for my life, and Eddie was getting his jollies on with his tart.

I fucking hate him, the bastard. And I truly hope he feels so guilty that it swallows him whole and he chokes the fuck to death on it.

My whole body is shaking with rage. I'm so angry I don't know what to do with it.

I jump down from the bales and begin pacing the floor, the paper still tightly clutched in my hand.

"You okay?" Nathan asks me, concerned.

"No!" I yell, throwing the paper to the floor. "I'm not bloody okay. I'm having a really shit time of it, if you hadn't noticed!"

"I noticed."

I stop pacing at his firm tone and stand there facing him.

His serious eyes meet mine for a long moment. "You can be as hurt and pissed off as you want, Alex, but it's not going to change anything. This is how it is for you now and you're just gonna have to find some way to accept it." He sighs. I feel like an irritation. "I don't know what other way I can say this to you to make you understand."

Does this guy have no heart at all?

I feel all consumed by my grief again. I'm so close to the edge. I could scream.

So I do.

I scream until my head throbs and my throat feels sore. And when I'm done, I open my eyes and see Nathan just looking blankly across at me.

And now I feel even worse, not better.

"What if I don't want to accept my situation?" I cry at him. "Then what?" My head is buzzing around like there's a swarm of bees inside.

He shuts his eyes briefly in silent apology and I can't bear to look at him for a second longer.

I grab the page of the newspaper featuring the picture of Carrie up from the floor and, clasping it to my chest, I turn and stalk out the barn.

"Where are you going?" Nathan's deep voice is at my side within a matter of seconds.

I stop and spin around to face him. My heart is pummelling my rib cage.

I push my hair angrily off my face and scowl up at him. "I'm going back to your house, Nathan. You don't have to worry, I'm not going to try and leave. I mean, it's not like I have anywhere to go." I can feel my bottom lip starting to quiver. "I know I'm stuck here and I know you hate that thought as much I do ... " My voice breaks, betraying me. I bite down hard on my bottom lip.

Nathan frowns down at me. His light eyes look almost black in the darkness. "Alex, you're not a prisoner here, but it's also not possible for you to leave at the moment. You already know this." He exhales, raking his fingers through his hair. "And it's not that I don't want you here, it's just ..."

"I don't want to hear it!" I cut him off with a wave of my hand, blinking back my pathetic tears. "Really, I've heard and seen enough crap today to last me a lifetime. No more! I don't want any more." My loud voice echoes around nature's silence.

"What do you want?" His question catches me off-guard. He takes a step toward me, towering over me, the toes of his boots nearly flush with my trainers, leaving a veil of air between us.

I feel off-balance. I dig my feet into the ground to steady myself and look up at him. "What?" My voice comes out sounding weaker than I intended.

"Just what is it that will make all of this better for you?" His voice sounds dry and intense, and he's wearing an unfathomable expression on his face.

My heart has set a battering ram against my chest. I'm sure it's about to crack through a rib any second now.

I take a shaky step backwards. "Nothing," I say affected. "Nothing will ever make any of this better. Just leave me alone!" I shove him away from me, hard in the chest, and then I'm turning on my heel and running toward the house, leaving Nathan behind.

And this time he doesn't follow me.

Chapter 10

Hope

I've lost everything. Everything. My humanity. My life. My best friend.

Every day is like a hangover, worse than the one before. I've been in this house for a week and that week has felt like a year. I sleep sporadically and the little sleep I do have is plagued by nightmares because all I think about, every single second, of every single day is of what I've lost ... what I've become ... that night ... Carrie.

Her death is like a noose around my neck, tightening with each passing moment, sometimes spurred on by a memory, sometimes by a flashback.

I don't know how to get out of this perpetual state of melancholy or if I even want to. Maybe my guilt and grief will eventually just come and consume me whole. Or maybe it won't. Maybe this is just how it's meant to be for me from now on. A lifetime of punishment for what I've done.

For every breath that Carrie has lost, I'm to feel each agonising minute of this misery as if it's brand new.

I can't bring myself to eat and I only drink blood because Nathan forces me to.

I hate it. And I hate him for making me do it.

If I at all cared about sustaining myself in any way, that would be the last on my list of ways of doing so. Well, actually, it wouldn't be on my list at all.

'But it's the way it is, so you just have to get on with it,' as the habitually cold and hard Nathan puts it.

He hates me. I know he does. He doesn't say it but he doesn't have to. I can feel his resentment for me emanating out of him like a bad odour. He barely looks at me and he always keeps his distance. I don't blame him. I'm me and I hate me. I deserve to be hated.

Any form of communication Nathan and I did have disintegrated after our confrontation that first night in the barn.

The only time I see him is when he comes to bring me blood and there's no interaction, no conversation. I think I'd die of shock if he came in and said, 'Hi Alex, how are you doing?' Actually, me dying of shock wouldn't be such a bad thing. Maybe I should ask him to try it.

Our conversations, if you can call them that, are limited to single syllables.

Nathan: 'Blood.'

Me: 'No.'

Nathan: 'Yes.'

...and rinse and repeat.

Mainly, I spend my time alone trapped here with my painful memories and dwelling thoughts, wondering just why it is the people I love most die.

I'm so lonely.

But then this room could be filled with a hundred people and I'd still be lonely because the people I want to cure this loneliness I will never see again.

Jack and Sol are nice people. They're kind. They try hard with me, try to help me, try to be my friends. And in another life I would have loved to have called them friends. But not now.

Now I don't want friends.

Sol on a few occasions over the first couple of days tried to coax me out of my room, which was fruitless. The only time I ever leave my room is to use the bathroom. He soon gave up and now just comes in here and sits with me after he finishes work on the farm. He chats animatedly, telling me about his day and any other topic he can think of. I don't have anything to add to the conversations, so I just sit on my bed and listen politely, waiting for the moment when he leaves so I can fold in on myself.

I just want to go home. I want back that safe feeling that only home can give you. I want everything I had back, except for Eddie. Actually, I'd endure a lifetime of Eddie if it meant I could have everything back as it was.

I wish there were a time machine I could climb into that would take me out of this room and back to that moment before we stepped into the forest. I'd do it all so differently. I'd leave my phone where it lay in the forest. We'd never go in for it. And everything would be okay. Carrie would still be alive.

I stare blankly into my regret from my seat by the window. It's pitch black outside. There isn't a star in the sky. The moon isn't visible for me to see. It's almost if as the sky knows my misery and is in mourning with me.

The house is empty. Jack and Sol are on an overnight trip away. They left this afternoon, farm business I assume. I didn't ask, they didn't tell. So, for tonight it's just me and Nathan. Whoopee.

Nathan's not in the house at the moment. I heard him go out a few hours ago. He won't be far away, though. Nathan may keep his distance but he always has a watchful eye on me.

A sigh escapes, drifting off into the darkness, followed by an unexpected tear. It trickles out from the corner of my eye, slides down my cheekbone and soaks into my hair. I bring my knees up to my chest, resting my bare feet on the edge of the wooden chair, and wrap my arms around my legs and hug them tightly to me.

Movement in the garden catches my eye and I hear the back door open and bang shut. Nathan's home.

The next thing I know my bedroom door is opening and Nathan's standing in the doorway, a huge shadow in the darkness. "I need your help." He sounds stressed.

I put my feet down to the floor. "What's wrong?"

"My horse, she's in labour, she's having problems delivering. I need your help."

Horse? I didn't know he had a horse.

"Sure, just let me put my shoes on." I lift my weary body out of the chair. I go to the wardrobe, retrieve my trainers and slip my bare feet into them.

Nathan's shifting from foot to foot in an agitated manner. Feeling pressured, I don't bother to fasten the laces and instead just tuck them down the sides. "Okay," I say, walking toward him. "Let's go."

I follow him out of my room, across the hall and down the stairs. He's moving quickly. I pick up pace to keep up.

I really don't know how I'm going to be able to help him and his pregnant horse, or why he even thinks I can. I'm generally useless at everything, and that's when I care. Right now I don't care about anything.

"Have you rung a vet?" I ask as we're hurrying through the garden, me following in his wake.

He gives me a look over his shoulder, harsh enough to make me shrink back. "Yes." His answer is brisk.

I let it slide. I really don't have any fight left in me anymore.

"Two hours they said ... two fucking hours. They'll both be dead by then," he mutters to himself.

As we cross the field, I pick up on the sound of a distressed horse crying out in obvious pain. Nathan starts to move quickly, hearing it too. I keep up with him easily, surprising myself. I've never been much of a runner - a few feet and I'm usually doubled over with a stitch. Must be another side effect of my new super-self.

I follow Nathan across the field toward the barn, past it and down the side. As I turn the corner, I find myself looking upon a small paddock and stables. I didn't know these were here but then I didn't even know Nathan had a horse. It shows how very little I do actually know about Nathan and the place I currently have to call home.

Nathan heads straight for the stables. He slides the bolt open on the stable door and opens it up just enough for him to fit through.

"Hey beautiful," he coos. "You hanging in there, okay?"

I'm guessing he's not talking to me.

It's strange to hear him sound so caring. On the rare occasion he has been 'nice' to me, he's still only ever spoken with a severity to his voice.

"You coming in?" he says tersely, holding the door a pinch open for me.

And there he is, the Nathan I've come to know.

I slide in through the small gap he's left for me without a word. I don't know how small he actually thinks I am. I have to suck in a couple of inches just to fit through.

He closes and bolts the stable door behind me. And then I come face to face with the most beautiful horse I've ever seen.

Not that I've seen many horses up close, but she is stunning. And I get his adoration for her. She's huge. Her coat is dark brown and shiny, and she has this little white patch just nestled between her eyes. It looks like a star.

She also looks like she's in pain. She's pacing around the far end of the large stable, kicking hay around in her endeavour, her long tail swishing about.

Nathan goes straight over to her, talking to her soothingly, and she immediately responds to him, nuzzling him as he takes hold of her head collar and strokes her gently on her neck.

I find myself watching him curiously. I really can't figure him out, at all. He seems so cold and distant, yet here he is showing love to another creature. Maybe because of what he is – a shifter – he has a natural affinity with animals.

"There's going to be a lot of blood when she gives birth." He turns, giving me a hard stare. "Do you think you'll be able to control yourself?"

He might as well have just slapped me. I feel my face start to tingle and my throat thicken.

How is he able to upset me so easily? Considering I don't care about him in the slightest, you think I'd be able to just brush him off.

Swallowing past the thickness, I say in the most even voice I can manage, "If you don't trust me, then why ask for my help?"

He pushes his dirty blonde hair off his forehead, keeping his hard gaze fixed on me. "Because currently you are all I've got. You're the only person around for a good mile and I can't do this alone. I need someone to help keep her calm while I deliver this foal."

He just called me a person. I haven't felt much like a person for a really long time, and to hear him say it means more than I realised it would. It's like salve on an open wound I didn't even know existed, which probably sounds crazy, considering he's just asked if I'll be able to refrain from killing his horse.

I take a cleansing breath in. "I'm not a monster, Nathan. I didn't ask to be made into one of these things." I sweep a hand down myself. "And, yeah, we both know I need blood to survive but I'm still the same Alex inside. I'm still the same girl I was before this happened, and I know you didn't know me back then, obviously, but I was a good person. I would never hurt anyone. I love animals. I couldn't even kill a fly and I hate flies. But if that's how you see me, if you think I'm capable of murdering something in cold blood, I should leave now." I gesture to the stable door behind me.

He's looking at me with in that way he often does. It's like a mixture of confusion and complete and utter dislike.

I'm feeling a bit confused myself, to be honest. I actually sounded articulate then and that happens rarely, if ever.

I hold eye contact with him but he's staying silent and I'm starting to falter. Taking his silence as he thinks I should leave, I turn away and reach over to unbolt the door.

"Okay … " He heaves out a sigh.

I look back at him but keep my hand on the bolt. I'm not sure if I read his tone right, you can't really tell with Nathan, so I ask, "Okay, you want me to leave or okay, you want me to stay and help?"

"Stay." A frown creases his brow. It looks like it physically hurt him to say that.

I can't help but feel a little sense of triumph.

"You can trust me," I reinforce, moving back into the stable.

He stares at me for a moment longer than necessary. I start to feel nervy. I wrap my arms around myself.

The horse stamps her back leg, demanding Nathan's attention. He strokes her face. "Come here." He gestures to me.

Swallowing my nerves down, I loosen my arms and walk toward him. "Have you done this before?" I ask.

He glances down at me and I notice for the first time how dark the skin around his eyes is. He looks really tired. "Once," he utters, "on a cow."

"Oh." I tuck my hair behind my ear. "So what do you need me to do?"

A yawn escapes him and he rubs his eyes. An image of me touching my hand to his face, pushing my fingers into his hair, suddenly flickers through my mind. I blink hard.

"Well, right now I need you to stay with her and keep her company," he says, moving past me, heading out the door. "I'm just gonna go and get a few things I need to deliver the foal."

Okay, so what the hell was that? Now I'm imagining touching Nathan. I can't think of anything I would rather do less. I'm obviously losing the plot.

Clearing my mind, I turn to the horse and slowly reach my hand out to her. She eyes me suspiciously for a moment, then carefully moves her head toward my hand and starts to sniff it, inhaling my scent.

"This baby of yours causing you problems, huh?" I murmur, rubbing the side of her face.

She nudges my arm with her head, almost as if responding.

"Probably a boy, then," I reply. "Men are always trouble."

Nathan returns a few minutes later carrying a bucket filled with soapy water, a pile of towels and a blanket.

"What's her name?" I ask, gesturing to the horse, realising I'd not already asked and he hadn't told me.

"Honor," Nathan answers while rolling the sleeves up on his blue sweatshirt. He starts to wash his hands and arms in the bucket of soapy water.

"Honor." I stare into her huge black eyes. "A beautiful name, for a beautiful girl. How old is she?" I ask, casting another glance Nathan's way.

"Five."

"Have you had her from a foal?"

"No, I got her three years ago. She was a rescue horse."

"Rescue horse?" I am surprised. I wouldn't have pegged him for the type to voluntarily take on a rescue animal. I'm a rescue and he doesn't much like me, but then I guess that says it all. He just doesn't like me.

"Was she badly treat?" I ask concerned. I can't bear the thought of people being cruel to animals.

"Hmm." He lifts his dripping hands out of the water and grabs a towel.

I feel a flash of anger. How anyone could have hurt her, how anyone could hurt any other living creature, is completely beyond me. What gives someone the right to do whatever they want to others? I start to feel a tightness in my chest, bad memories threatening to invade. I take a deep breath in. "How did you come to get her?" I ask him.

"An old friend works for the RSPCA. She told me about Honor. I adopted her."

An old friend, a girlfriend maybe. I feel a twinge inside my stomach.

It takes me a moment to find my voice. "Well, I'm glad your friend got her away from those horrible people and that you adopted her," I say, ignoring whatever it is that's going on with me tonight.

Nathan comes over to Honor and starts checking her swollen stomach with his hands. He looks up at me, his eyes wide and serious. "Time to get this foal out."

Then everything moves really quickly.

I talk to Honor, trying to keep her calm, while Nathan attempts to deliver her baby. It's hard and stressful, mainly for Nathan. I can tell he is really worried, even beneath his hard, calm exterior.

"Okay," Nathan puffs breathlessly from the other end of Honor, "I've got my hands on it. Keep her as still as possible while I pull it out."

I take a firm hold of Honor's head collar with both my hands. Steadying myself, I press my feet into the floor. I look straight into her black glossy eyes. She looks terrified. "Don't worry," I whisper to her, "your baby will be fine. Nathan won't let anything happen to it."

Nathan starts to pull, Honor shunts me forward, and I nearly lose my footing. "Keep her still," he yells at me.

I steady myself again and hold her face close to me. She's breathing heavily into my arm, her hot breath scorching my skin. "Just stay still. A few more seconds girl, that's all," I whisper gently in her ear.

"Got it." Nathan lets out a sound of relief.

I glance past Honor to see Nathan down on his knees. A foal is his arms. Ignoring the fact it's covered in blood, and other questionable things, I watch, holding my breath, while Nathan rubs the foal over vigorously with a towel.

"Can I do anything?" I ask, worried.

He shakes his head, looking up at me through the mess of hair that's fallen over his eyes. "No need. The foal's fine." A smile edges his face.

It's my turn to let out a sound of relief. "See, I told you your baby would be fine," I utter to Honor. Letting go of her, she turns and goes straight over to where Nathan sits with her new baby.

Nathan puts the foal down and gets to his feet, leaving them to it. "Well done, girl," he says, patting Honor on her back as he walks past her.

I watch with fascination as the foal tries to get to grips with its gangly legs. That's all it is, long legs and this cute, skinny little body.

It's crazy to think there's new life in this room and I have had a little helping hand in making it happen. For a moment I actually feel of use, like I have a purpose again.

I don't know what to do with the feeling. Shoving it away, I go over to Nathan who's crouched down, washing his gunged-up hands and arms in the bucket. His clothes are covered in blood and gore. Then I realise I never felt the urge to feed at all, I never even gave it a second thought. Maybe it was the stress and intensity of the moment keeping my mind occupied and away from the blood. Well, whatever it was, I'm thankful for it and I feel a momentary sense of victory over the monster inside me.

"So what we got, a boy or a girl?" I tip my head in the foal's direction.

"A girl." He picks up a towel and dries his hands on it. "You wanna name her?"

I look at him wide-eyed. His eyes hold mine with a surprising amount of depth to them. "You want me to name her?" I edge out just to make sure I haven't heard him wrong.

"Wouldn't say so if I didn't mean it," he drawls, getting to his feet. He picks up the dirty towels and bucket of water, and walks out the stable without another word.

Was Nathan actually just being nice to me then? I lean up against the wall and look over at Honor, getting distracted by the foal as it tries to get to grips with feeding. It's endearing to watch.

The foal is really cute. I know all foals are cute but this one has to the cutest one ever. It's got chestnut fuzzy hair and a white mane. She's the complete contrast to Honor's dark colour, all bright and colourful.

"How they doing?" Nathan asks, coming back in the stable.

"Fine. The foal's having her first meal."

Nathan leans up against the wall next to me and folds his arms across his chest. He lets out a long, noticeable breath.

I turn my head to look at him. "You look tired," I observe.

"Mmm," he murmurs, letting his eyes close for a long blink.

"Why don't you go to bed? I can stay here with them both," I offer.

"Nah, no need."

He still doesn't trust me to leave me alone with them. I thought I'd already proved I have no intention of hurting them. I feel my hackles rise. "I'm not going to hurt them if you leave me alone with them," I bite, a clear edge to my voice.

He glances sideways at me, giving me a hard stare. "I know you won't."

His tone is equally as acerbic as mine. "They'll be fine on their own. The foal is feeding so I'm happy. We can both go get some sleep."

"Oh," I say, the wind blown out of my angry sails.

Nathan pushes off the wall and goes over to Honor. "Proud of you, girl." He takes her face in his hands, patting her affectionately, then he walks past me and opens the stable door, waiting for me to go through first.

"Bye, Honor. Bye, Honor's baby," I murmur before leaving.

Nathan bolts the door, locking them safely in for the night. The air has got significantly chillier while we've been in the stable. I rub my bare arms with my hands, trying to generate warmth.

"You cold?" Nathan asks.

"A bit."

"I'd offer you my top, but ... " he gestures down at his blood stained sweatshirt.

"One for the bin?"

He nods, laughing lightly. We continue to walk side by side in silence.

"So, have you picked a name for the foal yet?" Nathan inquires, breaking the silence.

I have actually.

"Hope," I say, giving him a quick glance.

"Hope." He nods. "Yeah, I like it." I feel secretly pleased that I've actually got something right. "Oh, and thanks, Alex," he adds in a casual tone, "for your help. I know how hard it must have been for you but you did real good, and I couldn't have done it without you." He looks at me and smiles. A genuine smile. It lights up his whole face, even in this darkness.

And without realising, I smile back. It blindsides me. I'm so shocked at the sensation that I touch a finger to my lips to see if it's real. And for these few seconds all my pain and self-hatred just drift away.

But I quickly remind myself, reprimand myself. Happiness is not something I deserve.

"No problem," I mutter dismissively, letting the self-hatred flood back in.

Wrapping my arms around myself, I look up at the sky. There's a star out which has managed to break through the darkness, lighting up its small part of the sky. One single solitary star. And for a moment, I wonder if the world is actually trying to tell me something.

Chapter 11

Knee Deep

"He wants us to what?"

"Muck out the stable." Sol's face breaks into a grin.

I like it when Sol smiles. It lights up everything around him and it's almost, in a way, as if he's smiling for me too.

I glance from his grinning face over the stable door and down at the waiting mess. There's horse manure and dirty straw everywhere.

"Does Nathan always give you the shit jobs, pardon the pun, or is it just because I'm helping you out?"

Sol laughs heartily. He has one of those contagious sounding laughs. It almost makes me laugh too. Almost.

"Nah, Nate does his fair share," he says. "Well more than that really. It's just my turn, nothing whatsoever to do with you. You just lucked out is all when you offered your kind services."

I made the fatal error of offering my help today when I heard over breakfast that Cal wasn't coming in to work today because he's sick. It was a half-hearted offer on my part I didn't think Sol would take me up on. How wrong was I? And looking at all of this, I wish I'd kept my mouth shut.

Honor, seeing me, wanders over and pokes her head over the top of the stable door. "Morning, beautiful." I stroke her face. She nudges my shoulder gently with her nose. She's expecting food. I always bring something with me when I come to visit.

I'm just about to get her apple out my jacket pocket, when Sol asks,

"Would you mind putting the girls out into the paddock while I get the wheelbarrow and pitchforks. Oh, and I'll get you a pair of wellies," he adds, looking down at my trainer clad feet.

"Sure," I say.

"Cheers," he replies, walking away.

I turn back to Honor, giving her my full attention. "Don't worry, I didn't forget." I get the apple out of my pocket and hold it out in my palm for her to take. She gently takes it and begins happily munching away on it. I wipe the saliva gift she's left on my hand onto the back of my jeans.

Hope, seeing her mother eating, trots over to me, worried she's missing out. "Don't worry, baby, I brought you one too." I offer Hope her apple and she swipes it greedily from my hand. I smile.

I do smile now, occasionally, but not intentionally. I try and stop them if I know they're coming, because for every smile that lasts a few seconds, I feel an hour's worth of guilt. I don't mean to feel happiness, just sometimes it creeps up on me without my realising.

I reach over to get Honor's head collar off the hook beside the stable door and see Sol is still here. He's standing at the end of the stable, casually leaning against it, watching me.

"Hi," I say, uncomfortable. He doesn't look embarrassed I've caught him staring, as I would.

"She really likes you, you know." He nods his head forward.

"Honor?" I say, casting a glance in her direction.

"Mmm." He nods again. "She's funny about who she trusts, you know, with her having been badly treated 'n' all, but you she definitely likes."

It's nice to hear that Honor likes me, that she trusts me enough to like me. I'm just about to thank him for saying so, when he adds, "She's a bit like Nathan in that respect."

"What?" I ask confused, ignoring the fact he hasn't once looked away from my face.

He pushes off the stable and stands up straight. "Picky about who they like."

"Oh." I scuff my trainer against the concrete path, looking down. He doesn't need to remind me Nathan doesn't like me. It's a fact I'm already well aware of. Not that it matters either way.

"Nathan does like you," he says as if reading my thoughts.

"Now I know you're lying." I give a little awkward laugh for effect.

"Don't be so sure."

I look up in time to catch sight of him disappearing down the side of the stable.

I stare after him for a moment, confused, feeling out of tune, like I'm missing out on something important.

Honor gives a sharp neigh, demanding my attention, bringing me back round. "Okay, girl, I'm all yours." I slip her head collar on and fasten it up.

She's eager to be out of the stable, so I keep hold of her by the collar and open the stable door. She's out in a flash, pulling me along with her. I clip the lead to her head collar and start to jog with her out into the sunshine. Hope comes trotting out behind her mother, her tail high, looking proud and incredibly cute. I jog at Honor's side to keep up with her and keep a watchful eye on Hope to make sure she doesn't go wandering off.

I slow Honor down to a walk as we approach the paddock gate. I lift the latch, push the gate wide open and walk them both in. Closing the gate behind me, I put the latch back on, then slip Honor's head collar off.

"Go have some fun." I pat her affectionately on her back. She trots off, quickly picking up pace with Hope hot on her trail.

I come back out of the paddock, latch the gate behind me, and rest my arms upon it, watching Honor and Hope cantering around.

It's been three weeks since Hope was born. After I got back to the house the night she was born, I went straight up to my room, climbed into bed and slept for seven hours straight, completely dream, well nightmare, free. That hadn't happened since I'd arrived. When I woke, I felt slightly more normal than I had in a long time, so I got out of bed, showered, got dressed, and before I knew it my feet were taking me out of the house and I was heading straight for the stables.

The further away I walked from the house, and the closer to Honor and Hope I got, I started to feel a sense of calm washing over me. I liked the feeling.

I knew Nathan wasn't in the house when I'd left. I also knew with certainty he would be at the stable when I arrived there. But I didn't mind that I would see him. We'd got on okay the night before - well, really well for me and Nathan - and I thought things were actually going to start to get better between us.

I was wrong.

From the moment I got there he was just as frosty and cold toward me as ever, if not frostier. It was almost like the night before hadn't happened. If it weren't for Hope, I'd actually think I'd imagined us getting along.

And this is how things have continued ever since. I'm fine with it. I just accept it for what it is. Nathan will never like me, he'll always resent my being here and the fact he felt he had to save my life that night, because of what it now means for him, and I get it, I really do.

So on Hope's first day in the world, I hung out at the stables with them both, except for when the vet came to check Honor and Hope over. I went back to the house before he arrived, waited until he'd gone, then I went back to the stables. Mainly I was alone with the horses, as Nathan was out on the farm, working. I was happy with this arrangement. I was glad to be in company where I didn't have to make pointless small talk with someone who hates me.

Then, when I went to bed that night, I found the same happened again. I slept right through. Not as long as the first night, but still I'd slept more in two days than I had over the last seven prior to meeting Honor and Hope. So, once again I got up, got dressed and headed out to see the horses. But this time I stopped by the kitchen to get some carrots to take with me.

Jack was in there making himself breakfast; him and Sol had returned home from their trip late the night before. I smelt the toast he was making and found I actually felt hungry. I managed a slice of toast and a cup of coffee. We sat together eating breakfast, making small talk and, before I knew it, I was talking to him about that night, the night that irrevocably changed my life. I didn't plan on talking to Jack, or anyone, about it ever but once I started I couldn't seem to stop. It was gushing out of me. I don't know if Jack has magical powers of some sort because I couldn't stop the words from flowing. And if I'm being honest, it was actually a relief to talk to someone.

I sat at the table with Jack for a long time, swinging through a range of emotions. He listened patiently. Then, when I'd said all I could and cried all the tears I had, he simply asked me, 'What would I want Carrie to do if she were me?'

I paused for a long moment. I knew just exactly where he was heading with this. Still, I answered truthfully.

I said, 'I'd want her to live her life. I'd want her to move on. I'd want her to be happy.'

Jack smiled lightly, squeezed my hand, gave me a knowing look and got up from the table taking our breakfast plates with him, leaving me to contemplate my own words.

So that's what I'm trying to do. I'm trying to move forward. I'm trying to make the best with what I have left.

It's not easy.

I have good days, I have bad days, and I have really, really bad days, but now I have someone to talk to on those bad days. It helps some.

I'll never get over Carrie's death. I'll always know I'm to blame, irrespective of how many times Jack tells me I'm not, but I will at some point learn to live with it.

Leaving Honor and Hope to enjoy their time in the paddock, I make my way back to the stable. I meet Sol on his way back pushing along the wheelbarrow that is carrying a couple of pitchforks and spades. He sets the wheelbarrow down outside the stable door.

"Smallest size I could find was a nine," he says, pulling a pair of dark green wellies out of the wheelbarrow and holding them up, one in each hand. "It's been a long time since we've had to cater for a woman. What size are you?"

"A five."

"Oh."

"Don't worry they'll be fine," I say kindly. I take them from him, sit down on the path and pull my trainers off. I put my feet in the wellies. They're massive. I could probably fit two feet in one.

Awkwardly, I get up to my feet. I try taking a step forward in them. It's like walking in flippers. This is going to be interesting.

"I look like an idiot," I grimace.

"Yeah, you do a bit." Sol meets my eyes and laughs. I allow myself a smile. Sol's green eyes sparkle as the sunlight catches them. His eyes are not as striking as Nathan's, but they are nice nonetheless. And when Sol looks at me, I know he's looking at me, not through me as Nathan does. It matters. To be seen means a lot now I'm invisible to the rest of the world.

Sol winks cheekily at me, picks the wheelbarrow back up and pushes it inside the stable. He sets it down just to the side of the door and unloads the pitchforks and shovels, leaning them up against the wall.

He hands me a pair of gloves and a pitch fork.

"Thanks." I give him a begrudging look.

"Aw, stop moaning and get on with it, woman!" he chuckles good-naturedly, nudging me with his elbow. I nudge him back. His face breaks into a grin. I laugh. Guilt stabs me hard in the chest. I stop laughing.

"Guess we better get on with this," I say my mood instantly dropping.

If he notices my abrupt change, he doesn't say anything and I appreciate it. He just gives me a nod of agreement, puts his gloves on, picks his pitchfork up and starts working.

Sol is a good friend to me, one I don't deserve or should be allowed to even have, but I'm really not sure how to stop him from being my friend or if I even really want to.

Holding the pitchfork under my arm, I put my gloves on, and joining Sol, I dig into the soiled straw and start moving it into the wheelbarrow.

It's unreal how much mess one horse and a foal can make in a day. We fill the wheelbarrow in no time and it still looks like we haven't even made a dent. Sol takes the wheelbarrow away to empty it onto the manure pile around the back of the stable that Jack uses for his gardening, then comes back and we start filling it up again.

Sol starts to talk as we continue working, easing off the silence. Normally he talks and I listen but, this time, I find myself joining in, asking him questions mainly about Nathan, curiosity finally getting the better of me because I know nothing about him - he never gives anything away about himself. Sol and Jack, on the other hand, are open books. I already know tons of stuff about them.

He tells me Nathan was in the army. That doesn't surprise me. It definitely goes some way to explaining why he's so regimented and good at being a hardass.

Sol also tells me Nathan left the army three years ago and that he served in Iraq. He says he's a hero. Apparently Nathan saved some people's lives while on duty in a northern Iraqi town called Shirqat after a suicide bomber detonated his explosive vest at a busy local market.

It seems Nathan makes a habit of going around saving people's lives.

It's obvious from the way Sol talks, how proud he is of Nathan and how much he looks up to him. It sets off a longing in my chest for Carrie which I quickly seal off.

Sol stabs his pitch fork into the straw, taking a break. He lifts his arms above his head, stretching his long, lean body upwards. His T-shirt rides up, revealing an incredibly toned stomach. I look up at his face. Sol is a really good looking guy and he has a charming manner about him. I bet he does well with the ladies.

"Do you have a girlfriend?" I ask him.

I catch the look of surprise in his eyes before it quickly clears and I realise how much of an intrusive question that may have been, especially just asking out of the blue like that.

"Sorry," I say, abashed, pressing my lips into an awkward line.

He drops his arm back down to his sides. "Don't be." He smiles. "And no, I don't have a girlfriend."

"Oh," I say, not expecting that to be the case.

"You seem surprised." He laughs but I can tell it's forced.

"No, I'm not surprised. I mean, well, I just got the impression you would have ... not that it's a bad thing to be single, because it's not, obviously." Sol's looking at me, eyebrows raised, eyes assessing me intently. I feel all hot and flustered. "But anyway, I'm sure you'll have a girlfriend soon," I add pointlessly at the end.

"I'm fine with it." He shrugs his shoulders. "Just keeping my options open."

"Best thing to do," I say awkwardly. "You don't want to get tied down too young." I rub my nose. "What about Nathan? Does he have a girlfriend?" I regret the words the instant they leave my mouth. All I wanted to do was change the subject and that was the best I could come up with?

Sol picks his pitchfork up. Looking away from me, he answers, "Not that I know of," his tone suddenly flat.

"And Cal?" I ask, just so he doesn't think I'm only interested in his and Nathan's private life, which of course I'm not. Why would I be?

"Married to Erin. She's pregnant. I'm gonna be an uncle soon." He turns looking at me, a smile lifting his lips. He drops the contents of his pitchfork into the wheelbarrow.

Now my curiosity's piqued. "Is Erin one of your kind?" I ask him.

He stands his pitch fork upright again and rests his arm on the handle. "Yeah. It's preferred that we marry our own kind. You know, to keep up the lineage. It's not forced or anything, but we do obviously keep our ... um ... abilities to ourselves. You know, humans wouldn't understand and it would be a bit hard to explain to a human girl if you had a baby with her that it's very likely that when the baby hits puberty it's gonna be able to shift into an animal of its choice at the drop of a hat." He screws his face up. "It's just easier to be with our own kind, you know."

I nod. Then it hits me out of the blue. I'm never going to be able to have a normal relationship with anyone ever again. I'm never going to have children. Who would want me like this?

A hollow feeling sets up residence in my stomach. I had always taken for granted that at some point, when I met the right guy, I would settle down, get married and have kids. It was just a given. And now it's not. That choice has been forever taken away.

I feel a sudden overwhelming sense of loss for the children I'm never going to have, a loss for the future I could have had.

"You want a brew?" Sol asks, interrupting my thoughts.

I can feel tears glimmering in my eyes. I don't want him to see them, so I look down and start working again. "A brew would be great." I somehow manage to keep my voice steady even though the tears have turned hot and are burning their way down the back of my throat.

Sol leans his pitchfork up against the wall with a clang. "We've got a kettle and that in the barn, but we've only got coffee there. Will that do you?"

I swallow down. "Coffee's fine."

He pulls his gloves off. "Milk and sugar?"

"Milk."

"Powdered okay?"

"That'll be fine," I say quickly, wishing he'd just go and leave me alone.

He shoves his gloves into the back pocket of his jeans. "Won't be long, and no slacking while I'm gone." He leaves me with one of his trademark cheeky smiles before exiting the door. But even that doesn't help.

The second he's gone, tears spill from my eyes. I wipe them away but more quickly follow.

I'm being stupid. I know I'm being stupid. I need to pull myself together.

I press the palms of my hands to my eyes and force myself to take a few deep breaths. When the tears are finally dried and gone, I force my body back to work.

Then as quick as that my area is all done. I look around and see there's still some mess that needs clearing up over in the far corner that Sol hadn't got to yet.

I look down at my huge wellies, then at the wheelbarrow to my right, then back to the mess.

It'll all probably fall off the pitchfork if I walk the distance in these wellies. I'll use a shovel.

I swap my pitchfork for a shovel and flipper my way over to the mess. After a bit of faffing, I manage to get some of the manure onto the shovel. Then, very carefully so not to drop it, I slowly walk back, heading straight for the wheelbarrow.

And don't ask how I mange it because I have no clue, but somehow I step on the toe of my right welly with my left, lose my balance and trip forward. As I fall, I instinctively put my hands out to stop myself, dropping the shovel. It clatters to the floor and horse shit flicks up everywhere, well mainly onto me, and I land hard on my hands and knees on the concrete floor.

"Oww!" I cry from the instant pain. I might be stronger nowadays but this still hurts like hell.

Cursing out loud, I sit back on my haunches, rubbing my bruised knees.

Great. Just bloody fucking great. I'm bruised and covered in horse shit. It's everywhere: it's in my hair and all over my clothes. Why does this stuff always happen to me?

I yank my gloves off and, using my sore hands, rub my face clean, getting the manure off my skin, then shake my head roughly, running a hand over my ponytail, trying to get the manure out.

"Sitting down on the job?" I hear Nathan's deep voice come from the doorway.

Fuckety fuck.

I haven't heard him coming. Wouldn't you just know when I think it can't get any worse, Nathan arrives to ensure it does.

I look up at him. He's got a look of amusement spread across his face which instantly grates on me. I've never met anyone who can get under my skin as quickly as he can.

"Piss off," I snap.

His look of amusement instantly disintegrates and I regret my harshness. But I'm not apologising, no siree.

He glares at me with hard eyes and, not taking them off mine, pulls a New York Yankees baseball cap from out of the back pocket of his jeans, pushes his hair from off his forehead and puts it on, pulling the peak low, shading his eyes.

I notice he hasn't shaved and has the beginnings of stubble. It suits him much better than being clean shaven. It fits in with his hobo look.

"Well ... " he says with a deep exhalation of breathe, "I had come to ask if you wanted to sack this off and come out with me, but I'm guessing by your mood probably not."

Out? He wants to take me out? On what planet is this?

"You want to take me out, with you?" I ask, a slight stammer creeping into my voice.

"Yep," he answers and pushes his hands into the back pockets of his ripped jeans.

Okay, so this is an unexpected turn of events. I'm not really sure what to do, I mean I don't deserve to be able to go out but ... I haven't been off this farm since I arrived here a month ago, and I am supposed to be trying to move forward, and it would be nice to see some different surroundings for a change.

"That would be great, but ... I thought I wasn't allowed to go out in public in case anyone recognises me?"

He pulls his hands free from his pockets and readjusts his cap, lifting the peak so I can see his face better.

Nathan really is good looking. His eyes look almost luminous in this light. It's such a shame he's an arsehole.

"Don't worry," he says mildly. "Where we're going there won't be anyone around."

Sounds ominous. Nerves flutter through my stomach. I really don't know how I feel about being alone with Nathan for an extended period of time but I hear myself saying, "Okay, that'd be great." My voice apparently has more confidence about this than my brain does.

"You're probably going to want to get cleaned up." A smile plays on his lips as he gestures to my crap-covered clothes.

I glance down at myself, realising I'm still sitting on the floor with the horse manure. I quickly get to my feet, feeling self-conscious and I wipe my hands over my clothes, trying to dust them clean, only to realise all I've managed to achieve is to wipe crap all over my hands again. I hold them out awkwardly by my sides. "Yeah, I need to get a shower." I nod, embarrassed.

"I'll meet you back at the house in an hour." Then he's gone, almost like he was never here.

I'm going out. With Nathan. Now there's a sentence I never thought I'd hear myself say.

I wipe my hands on the only clean part of me, the back of my T-shirt, and head for the door. I consider going to see Honor and Hope before I go but I see they're right over the other side of the paddock, grazing on the grass, and decide against it.

I stop by the barn to let Sol know where I'm going but he's nowhere to be found. Maybe he's popped back to the house.

When I get back, I look around for him. I check the kitchen, living room, I even knock on his bedroom door, but there's no answer. Maybe Nathan saw him and told him he was taking me out and he might have gone back to the stables already to finish off. We've probably just missed one another. Without giving it another thought, I go straight to the bathroom, peel my stinky clothes off and jump in the shower.

As the hot water hits my head, I realise I'm actually looking forward to going out with Nathan. And I really don't know what to do with the thought. It feels alien and I can't seem to find a suitable place for it in my mind.

Chapter 12

Stripped Bare

I've left my hair down. Nathan bought me a hair dryer last week. It makes a change to wear it down. I'd forgotten how much I like the feel of it over my shoulders and running down my back. I always used to wear my hair down in my old life, set poker straight by hair straighteners, but for the last month it's just been tied back into a ponytail. I haven't really cared to bother with it.

I haven't got any make-up on because I don't currently own any. I've always felt naked without mascara. I've got really huge blue eyes. I know that may sound like a nice combination but trust me it's not. I've always thought my eyes were too big for my face. They stand out, and not in a good way. Mascara helps to make me feel a little better about them.

I'm wearing my dark blue skinny jeans and ribbed black vest top. I don't have many clothes. When you've got a man buying clothes for you, things are going to be pretty basic. So, I've made the best of what I have with what I've got.

I assess myself in the mirror. I still look like crap.

I pick up the tub of Vaseline I've found in the bathroom cabinet and slick a bit of that over my eyelashes to give them a sheen, and then I rub some on my lips. Okay, that'll do.

I instantly hate myself for actually caring about my appearance. Carrie can't care about her appearance anymore, so why should I be able to?

Stop it, Alex. You're trying, remember.

Still, I don't even know why I'm bothering to try and look nice. I'm only going out with Nathan, and considering there isn't going to be any other people around, it's not exactly going to be anywhere special. It's a pointless exercise really.

With a sigh, I head downstairs to find him. I can't hear him in the house anywhere, but just because I can't hear him, doesn't mean he's not here. He can be pretty stealthy when he wants to be.

I poke my head into the living room but it's empty. I go in the kitchen. Jack's sitting at the table reading the newspaper, a steaming cup of coffee in front of him, a lit cigar resting in the ashtray. I like the sight. Jack always seems to give off a warm, homely kind of vibe. He glances up at my entrance and smiles warmly. "Hiya, love."

My eyes instinctively flicker to the newspaper. I resist the urge to ask if I'm in it. The media interest in my and Carrie's disappearance has reduced in the absence of leads as to our whereabouts, obviously.

"Hi," I reply distractedly, my eyes flitting about. "Do you know where Nathan is?"

"He's waiting out front for you, love."

"Oh, okay, thanks." I turn, going back through the door I just came in.

I feel a bit awkward that Jack knows I'm going out with Nathan. I don't know why. It's not like we're going on a date or anything.

"You look pretty," Jack says from behind me.

I can't stop my face from going red. "Thanks," I mutter and hasten to make my way down the hall and out the front door.

Great, I do look like I've made an effort. If Jack noticed then Nathan most certainly will. He's as sharp as a tack and I don't want him thinking I made the effort for him because I most certainly did not.

I open the door to see Nathan leaning up against the driver's side of a black Range Rover. I notice he's changed his clothes from the ones he had on earlier. He's wearing black motorbike boots, faded blue jeans and a fitted black T-shirt with a picture of Jim Morrison on the front. He's actually looks a bit tidier than normal – well, for him, anyway. Even his hair looks like it's seen a comb.

His lips almost curve into a smile as I approach and if he notices I've made an effort, he doesn't comment on it.

He climbs into the driver's seat and I walk around to the passenger side, get in and put my seatbelt on.

Nathan roars the engine to life and the CD player comes on in the middle of The Killers' 'Read My Mind'.

Well at least he's got good taste in music.

He swings the car around, and instead of turning right and heading down the long drive to the main road, he turns left and drives down the dirt track heading straight for the forest.

We don't speak for the first minute of the journey and it's a very long minute.

Obviously I'm the first to break the silence. "Is this your family's?" I ask.

"What, the car?"

"No, the forest." I point a finger at the bracken we're entering. "Do you own this as well as the farm?" The daylight collides with the trees, bringing in a darker edge to the day. I feel a sudden chill on my bare arms. I rub my hands over them.

"Yep," he answers.

"Wow, you guys have a lot of land."

"Mmm."

Silence.

"Sol said you were in the army," I mention, trying to reignite the conversation.

He gives me a sideways glance. It's almost a look of suspicion. "Yeah, I was," he replies slowly.

"Did you like it?"

"What?"

"Being in the army."

He shrugs. "It was okay."

"How long were you in for?"

"Seven years."

Jesus, this is like pulling teeth. "What made you enlist?"

He takes a deep breath. It's one of those, 'I really don't want to talk to you about this but you won't let up' kind of breaths. "I wanted to do something useful," he replies, impassive, not taking his eyes off the track ahead.

"And farming isn't?"

"Yeah, it is, but I just wanted to branch out on my own for a bit, try something else, see what that was like."

Well at least his sentences are getting a bit longer.

"How'd that work out for you?" I inquire.

"I'm back here, aren't I?"

"Hmm." I nod. "Sol said you saved some peoples' lives while you were serving in Iraq."

His face freezes, hardens, and I instantly know I've said the wrong thing. As I'm quickly discovering, it's like treading land mines talking to Nathan.

For a long moment he says nothing and I think that's it, end of discussion, but then he says in a flat voice, "Yeah, and I also saw a lot of people die too."

So he obviously doesn't hold himself in the same hero status as Sol does.

"But you saved people's lives," I say, turning to him. "That has to count for something, surely?"

"Ask the ones I didn't save."

And all that does is remind me of Carrie. She was someone he didn't save. If only that Vârcolac had fed on me first, killed me first, then it would be Carrie sitting here having this conversation with Nathan, not me. And I wish more than anything it were that way. Not that I would ever want to condemn her to a life of this - but rather that than gone.

"Why did you save me that night?" The words are out before I can even consider them.

Nathan slams on the breaks, skidding us to a sudden halt. "Why all the questions?" He turns his hard eyes onto me.

Without warning, my hackles rise. I don't know why but I have this sudden urge to pick a fight with him. I've gone from cold to hot in the space of five seconds and I have absolutely no idea where it's coming from.

I try to rein myself in. "I don't know." I shake my head. "I guess I just wanted to get to know you." And I leave out the part about saving my life.

His eyes narrow on me. "Why?"

"Does there have to be a reason?"

He looks at me with a 'yes' face.

Losing all my resolve, I throw my hands up in the air. "I guess I just thought it was the polite thing to do considering I currently live in your house. God, I was just trying to make conversation!"

"Try the weather next time." He gives me one last piercing stare, looks straight ahead out through the windscreen, and puts his hands back around the steering wheel.

I'm so angry I can barely breathe. My chest is pumping up and down and my heart is just about ready to explode. "Why did you save me?" I ask him bluntly.

I see the whites of his knuckles as his hands tighten around the steering wheel. "I didn't expect you to live."

And that just pisses me off even more than I already was. It's not like I haven't heard that from him before. "Yeah, but that's not really answering my question is it? If anything it just highlights my point!" I spin around in my seat to face him. "You thought I'd die anyway so why put your life at risk to save someone who in your mind was as good as dead? I just don't get it!"

"Do you have to?"

"Yes!" I cry.

"Why?" He looks at me angrily. "Just why is it so fucking important you know?"

"Because I need to understand why I'm still here and Carrie's not!" The sound of my screaming voice quickly fades away and all that's left is a tense silence that even the music can't fill.

After a moment, he shakes his head and says in a quiet voice, "I don't know." He genuinely looks and sounds like he doesn't, like it's still a mystery even to him, but I don't believe it. "I guess it's just not in me to walk away. It's not who I am. And when I heard your screams, I became a part of it whether I liked it or not. I guess I just lucked out that night."

And there it is. He just can't help himself.

Tears sting my eyes at his careless remark over the event that changed my life forever. "Do you enjoy being a bastard?" I ask in a flat voice.

"It can have its upsides." He shrugs, casting an unemotional glance my way.

Then the tears spill. I've heard enough. *Fuck him.*

I get out and slam the door so hard it shakes the whole car. I start to walk quickly back up the track in the direction of the house.

"Where are you going?" Nathan calls out. He's out of the car now, I hear his door open.

"As far away from you as possible!" I yell back at him. I wipe the tears from my eyes. I hate that he can upset me like this.

He jogs up alongside me, passing me by and stops in front of me, forcing me to an abrupt halt.

"Alex?"

I refuse to look at him and just stare down at the muddy ground beneath my feet.

I hear him sigh. "Look, I'm sorry. I was out of line."

But I don't believe his apology for one second. "You really lack sincerity," I say coldly.

I move to go around him but he steps in front of me again, stopping me. He takes hold of me by my arms. "I am sorry, really."

But I can't hear him anymore because the feel of his hands on my skin is like I'm being blasted by ten thousand volts. It's the most intense sensation I've ever felt.

Blood is beating in my ears. I drag my eyes up to his. The normal hardened edges around them have softened. Something funny happens inside my stomach. I swallow down, trying to quash the sensation. "I get that you hate me, Nathan." My voice comes out breathy. "But I just wish..."

"I don't hate you," he cuts in, looking astonished. Releasing his hold on me he steps back and I'm grateful for the space.

"So why do you act like you do?"

"I don't, do I?" He changes tack when he sees my expression change to absolute surety.

"You act like I don't exist."

"No I don't."

"You ignore me."

"That's bullshit. I'm with you all the time." He highlights the 'all'. I don't miss that.

"No, you're not. The only time you see me is when you bring me blood, and that's brief to say the least, and what you say hardly qualifies as talking. There was the night when Hope was born, that was okay, you were sort of nice to me then, but the next day it was back to the same old you pretending like I don't exist."

He drums his fingers irritably against his forehead. "Just what exactly do you want from me, Alex?" His question throws me. I really hate it when he does that.

But really, what do I want from him? I hadn't even realised it bothered me that he didn't like me. In many ways him hating me made it easier for me to hate myself. But now, for some reason, I'm finding myself wanting him to like me, wanting him to be nice to me. And it's just another alien thought which won't fit anywhere in this screwed-up head of mine.

"I ... er ... " I fumble around for words I'm not entirely sure of. "Well, I guess I'd just like you to be a bit nicer to me."

"And what's this?" He gestures around with an open hand.

I give him a confused look.

"This, me taking you out away from the farm, getting you out of the house. Isn't that a nice thing to do?"

"Oh," I say. When he puts it that way, I guess he does have a point. "Well, yeah, I suppose, but you haven't really taken me anywhere, well not yet, but then I have no clue where we're actually going. But anyway ... " I pause, collecting my thoughts, bringing myself back on track, " ... the point is it'd just be nice if you'd talk to me a bit more, be a bit nicer to me." I fold my arms across my chest

He presses his lips together, inhales a deep breath in through his nose and breathes it out again. "Okay, I'll make sure I talk you more if that'll make you happy."

I don't actually know whether he's been sarky or serious, so I opt to choose the latter as I'm getting pretty tired of arguing with him now.

"Well, okay. Thanks." I unfurl my arms.

"Now will you get back in the car?"

I meet his brilliant eyes. "Sure," I say through my dry mouth.

Once we're both back in the car, Nathan shifts into first gear and sets off down the track again.

And now, after that battle, I really don't want to talk. It kind of defeats the point of the argument but at the moment I'm past caring, so I stay silent for the remainder of the journey. Well, all five minutes of it.

We're deep in the heart of the forest when Nathan slows the car to a stop at the point where the track narrows to a foot path.

"We're here," he says, turning the engine off and getting out of the car.

"Here where?" I ask opening my door and climbing out.

"The best part of the forest for hunting."

"What?" I shut the car door a bit too hard.

Nathan sighs. "The best part of the forest for hunting." He reiterates the words, single and distinct.

I ignore his sarcasm. "You brought me out here to go hunting?"

He nods.

"Hunting what?"

"Rabbits, deer, that kind of thing."

I wrinkle my nose up. "You want me to kill Bambi and Thumper?"

"Yeah, if that's how you want to put it," he says around a smile.

"Oh I don't know, Nathan, I don't think so. I don't want to hunt. I mean I wouldn't know how to and I've never even held a gun in my life, let alone shot one."

He lets out a sharp laugh. It instantly gets my back up. "Do you see any guns?" He gestures around with empty hands.

"Well how would I know if you've got one? You usually carry a concealed weapon somewhere on you, don't you?" My tone is acerbic.

He gives me a look. "Alex, I brought you out here because I thought it might be an idea to teach you how to hunt and feed yourself just in case you ever find yourself needing to."

What? It was bad enough when I thought he wanted me to kill them with guns, but this - no way.

"So let me get this straight." I rub my nose. "You've brought me out to hunt and kill animals with my bare hands?"

A smile ghosts his face. He scratches his cheek. "Well teeth, but basically, yes."

Oh God. This is his idea of going out? No wonder he hasn't got a girlfriend.

"This is your idea of going out?" My voice comes out shrill.

Here was me thinking I was going to do something nice. Of course I know I can't go out amongst people anymore, well for the time-being anyway, but I thought ... well I don't know what I thought but it certainly wasn't this.

"What did you think we were gonna be doing?" Nathan asks, his tone pedantic. "I brought you into the middle of the woods, for God's sake." He shakes his head in a patronising manner.

And I feel like a complete idiot.

"I don't know." I cast around for something to say. "I thought maybe we were going to have a picnic, or going hiking, or something ... " I trail off, my face flaming. "I want to go back to the house." I say shortly.

"For fucks sake," he grouches, "you complain I'm not nice to you. Well, this is me being nice." He shoves his hands in his rear jeans pockets.

"This is your idea of nice?" My voice shoots up another octave.

"Yep." He nods.

"Well, it's not mine." I fold my arms stubbornly across my chest.

"Well, it's all I've got to offer you at the moment," he sighs, resigned. "So take it or leave it but I'm going hunting. You can do as you please."

He pulls his T-shirt off over his head.

"What are you doing?" I splutter, gesturing to his bare chest.

My eyes involuntarily take a quick tour of said chest. He's all muscle. He's taut and toned, and his skin is incredibly smooth. I notice he's wearing army dog tags around his neck. My eyes are drawn to a tattoo on the left hand side of his ribcage. It looks like some kind of Arabic lettering. There's quite a bit of it and it stops just shy of his waist.

"What does it look like I'm doing?" he says smartly, snapping me back to the now.

"It looks like you're undressing in front of me." My voice breaks, making me sound like a teenage boy right before puberty.

I'm trying to keep my eyes level with his, desperately trying not to look at his chest. It's way harder than you'd think.

He runs his hand through his hair, down his neck and hangs his hand off his shoulder. "I'm going to shift."

"What? Shape shift?"

He gives me a stupid look.

My annoyance and embarrassment quickly evaporates and now all I feel is curious. "Are you going to change into a wolf?"

He raises an eyebrow. "Well I was going to turn into a pigeon but I'm not so sure I'd be able to scare the deer into submission." He smirks.

I get the sudden urge to wipe it off his face. "Hardy bloody ha," I retort. I hate being mocked. I think he forgets this is all new and very alien to me.

"Look," he says in a placating tone. "If I shift with my clothes on they'll shred and I need them to go home in as I haven't got any spares with me ... unless you want me to go back home naked." He raises his eyebrow again, this time in a suggestive manner and shrugs his shoulders, T-shirt still in his hand. "I'm easy either way."

"Well I'm not," I say hotly, my cheeks flaming. "Do what you have to." I waft my hand. "I just don't care to see any of your ... goods."

Goods? Did I really just say that? Oh God.

He makes a sound almost approaching a laugh and throws his T-shirt onto the bonnet of the car. He reaches down and yanks his boots off revealing bare feet. *Doesn't he ever wear socks?* He tosses his boots near the car and starts to unbutton his jeans.

I avert my eyes, shifting uncomfortably. "What should I do while you're gone?" My voice has gone hoarse. I clear my clogged throat.

Nathan takes the car keys out of his pocket and throws them to me. I catch them easily. "Take the car back home. I'll head that way on my hunt. Just do me a favour and leave my clothes and boots at the top of the track, will you?"

I'm finding it hard to focus. His jeans are undone and hanging off his slim hips. I can see his boxer shorts. Surprisingly for him, they're Dolce and Gabbana. I imagined Nathan would be a Next kind of guy when it came to buying boxer shorts, not that I think about Nathan and his choice of underwear in any way at all but, anyway, whatever, they're black and quite nice.

I'm starting to feel really warm.

I set my eyes on his face, avoiding any more of his nakedness. "I can't drive," I finally say.

"Seriously?"

"Why would I make it up?"

"I'll teach you sometime if you want."

"Sure." I shrug.

He drops his jeans to the floor. My pulse races up. He steps out of them, bends down, picks them up and throws them on top of the car bonnet next to his T-shirt.

He's standing here before me in just his tight black, designer boxer shorts and nothing more.

I can honestly say I've never been as uncomfortable in a man's presence as I am in his right now. I'm not a prude, far from it, but this guy has no modesty whatsoever. And I'm pretty sure he's aware of just how uncomfortable he's making me feel. I'm just wondering why he's enjoying torturing me like this.

My skin is prickling and a flush of heat is rising up my neck, threatening to heat my face again.

Pull yourself together, Alex, he's only a man - a good-looking, sort of sexy man, if you like the unwashed, scruffy, muscular type - but he is a man nonetheless. And not a very nice man at that.

"Are you gonna take those off as well?" I point towards his boxer shorts.

"Yeah, I was gonna. Why?" A tiny smile creeps onto his face. He pulls his dog tags off over his head and tosses them onto his pile of clothes.

"Because, well, I need to know so I can turn around, or close my eyes or something, to give you some privacy." Actually I could have turned away for the whole time he was undressing. I hope he doesn't note that.

"Thanks for the courtesy." His eyes smile almost sexily at me and that sets off a whole different kind of thought reaming through my mind.

Stop it, Alex. Stop it now.

I turn around and start to chew on my thumbnail and I hear the gentle thud of his boxer shorts as they land on top of his clothes.

Nathan is naked. Right now. Behind me, completely naked.

Oh God.

"You sure you don't want to come with me?" he asks.

"No."

"You're gonna have to learn to feed yourself one day."

"Yeah, well today's not that day," I say defiantly, folding my arms across my chest.

"I'll be about an hour." I can almost hear the shrug in his voice, followed by a movement behind me and the rustling of leaves.

Curiosity gets the better of me and I turn around, moving forward quickly, trying to catch a glimpse of him changing form, but all I see is what I think is a glimpse of brown fur moving at high speed.

With a sigh, I turn back, pick Nathan's boots up off the floor and gather his clothes off the bonnet. I throw them all onto the driver's seat, climb onto the passenger seat and lock myself in the car.

I might be stronger than I used to be but I'm still a girl and I need to feel safe, and currently I'm sitting in the middle of the woods all alone with Nathan off God knows where. I lean over, put the keys in the ignition, and turn the music on. The Killers CD has come to an end and the changer moves onto the Kings of Leon. I recline my seat back, rest my feet up on the dashboard and let the dulcet tones of Caleb Followill wash over me.

I must have fallen asleep because the next thing I know I can hear a tapping on my window. I open my eyes to see Nathan's bright green ones staring down at me. Sleep driven, I fumble to sit up and wind the window down.

"Can you pass me my clothes?" he asks impatiently.

I lean over, grab his clothes and hand them over, desperately trying to ignore the fact he's still completely naked out there, not that I can see anything waist down anyway.

That actually sounded like disappointment in my head. Just when exactly did I turn into a sex fiend?

Nathan quickly pulls his clothes on and makes his way around to the driver's side. He picks his boots up off the seat, jumps into the car and slips his feet into them.

He looks fresher. His cheeks are flushed and he seems, I don't know, I guess I'd say lighter, not as tense as he normally does.

"Was your hunt okay? I ask as I put my seat back up to vertical.

"Yeah, it was good." He turns the engine, shifts the car into reverse, and starts to manoeuvre it around. It takes him a good few attempts as the track is quite narrow.

"And you ... fed?" I ask tentatively.

He casts a glance my way. "Mmm."

"But you don't need to feed like I do."

"No."

"So why?"

"Natural thing for me to do. Are you warm?" he asks, changing the subject.

"I'm okay."

"I'm hot. You mind if I put the air con on?"

"No." I shake my head.

As he leans over to turn it on, his bare arm brushes against mine and I get that electric shock sensation again. This time I do jump away from him. I feel like I've just been scalded. My arm is sizzling where he touched it and my heart is thumping in my chest.

He gives me an inquisitive look. My face flushes. I turn away and stare out of the window, confusion plaguing me. Why do I get that sensation when he touches me? Maybe it's something to do with me being a Vârcolac. Yeah, that's probably it.

Nathan turns on the air con and I now welcome it. I feel him press down on the accelerator, picking up speed and I watch as the trees and bushes whizz by. When I start to feel calmer and cooler, thanks to the air con, I say to him, "Your tattoo's nice."

He glances at me intermittently. "You noticed that, huh?"

"Hard not to," I reply, raising an eyebrow. He laughs. I smile back. "What does the lettering mean?" I ask.

He takes a deep breath, pressing his lips together into a tight line, and I wonder if I'm asking too many questions again. "It's the names of the people I saved in Iraq," he says in a low voice.

"It's in Arabic?" I inquire.

He gives me a long curious look. "Yeah, you speak Arabic?"

"No." I shake my head. "I just recognised it. My ex, he had some tattoos. He liked script. Guess I don't need to ask why you went for Arabic?" I add, looking to move the subject away from Eddie.

He chuckles to himself. "Actually that had nothing to do with it." He slides me a look. "I got it 'cause it looked the nicest." His face breaks out into a grin and I find myself laughing.

"Wasn't one of them your friend?"

"Yeah, Craig. His name's first on the list. He's the reason I have the tattoo. He got me drunk, talked me into it. It sounded like a good idea at the time." He grins again.

"Well I bet you're his best friend nowadays. I know if someone saved my life I'd ... " I stop abruptly, never finishing the sentence which has just sucked all the air right of the car.

I stare back out of the window and Nathan says nothing.

Then it hits me. I've laughed and smiled with Nathan and I haven't felt guilty once. For some reason, being with him keeps it at bay.

I sly a glance at him. He's staring straight ahead. His jaw is set, his whole body tense. He's feeling uncomfortable because of what I've just said. Emotion ripples through me for him.

And right now I can't decide if that's a good thing or not.

Chapter 13

Over and Over

You know the old saying 'You get what wish for', well I'm getting it, and more.

I asked Nathan to talk to me more. I asked him to be nicer to me, to act like I exist and, true to his word, he's followed through. But somehow in all of this, we've also ended up spending more time together, quite a lot in fact. I think I've seen more of Nathan in this last week than I did in the first four weeks of my being here.

Sounds great, doesn't it? Well it's not because I've discovered I do actually like being around him. He makes me laugh without the guilt. He makes me forget all the bad stuff. When I'm with him, I forget what I now am. Oh God, I'm starting to sound like a slushy Mills and Boon. Okay, basically the problem is ... I like him. More than I should.

I didn't even realise it was happening until it was too late and now I can't seem to switch it off. I've tried, believe me, and the worst thing about it is that this is my own doing. I've got no one to blame but myself.

All I want right now is for him to turn back into the bastard he was before so I can stop feeling this way.

My emotions are all over the place. My head is a complete and utter mess, worse than it was before.

All Nathan has to do is look at me and my insides fall to pieces. So much so that I have to remind myself just to breathe most days.

I wish there was some way I could turn these feelings off, turn the part of me off that's turned onto him.

I realised four days ago.

I was in the kitchen with Nathan. I was sitting at the table reading a magazine, just like I'm doing now, but instead of watching Jack cook, I was watching Nathan. He was frying bacon. The kitchen stank but in a really good, unhealthy greasy way that only bacon can do. He was talking about the new Arctic Monkeys' album. I was half-listening while reading the magazine. It was one of those Sunday newspaper supplement magazines and there was a piece on relationships, you know the 'How to Keep Your Man Happy in Ten Easy Steps', and my mind flickered. I started to think about how I'm never going to have that problem, how I'm never going to be in a relationship again. I felt sad. Then I thought about Eddie. And as those thoughts filtered through my mind, Nathan turned toward me. He knew I hadn't been listening to him, I could tell from the look on his face. He smiled and his green eyes sparkled under the lighting. He was still speaking but I couldn't hear him anymore. My world tilted on its side, then realigned, but everything was different. It was a like a light switch went on inside of me, and I had no way of turning it off.

And now I have no idea how to act around him. I feel like I'm back at school, and he's the cool mysterious popular guy and I'm the awkward gawky teenager with a red hot crush. I constantly feel uncomfortable around him, which is hard going considering I'm pretty much always with him. I'm trying my best to pretend that nothing has changed, trying to pretend I don't feel this way. It takes every ounce of strength I have just to get me through the day.

I don't think Nathan's noticed the difference in me. Well I hope he hasn't. God, could you imagine how he would react if he ever discovered I was feeling this way about him? He'd probably laugh, say something hurtful, or run screaming in the opposite direction. Or all three combined.

So, basically, he can never know.

I just need to get these feelings under control and work on getting rid of them, fast.

I've thought a lot about why I'm feeling this way about Nathan and I'm putting it down to the fact it's because he's being nice to me now. Add in the fact he did after all save my life, and you've got yourself a good set of ingredients for one hell of a serious crush.

And I guess in a way I feel connected to him. He's the only other living person who was there when my old life was ripped away from me.

I have, however, come to the definite conclusion that my crush on Nathan has nothing to do with the fact that I've seen him pretty much naked, that he has a great body, that he can in fact be quite sweet when he lets his guard down, that he is all mysterious and deep, and that he runs around saving people's lives like some kind of bloody superhero.

Well, okay, maybe they do add to it just a little bit, the illusion of him.

But any psychologist would tell you that grief can make people do and think things they normally wouldn't. Not that I know any psychologists, but I'm sure I'm right. I think I read it in Cosmo or somewhere that grief can make people act out of character, do things they wouldn't normally do, like have feelings for someone they wouldn't normally have.

Don't get me wrong, I do think Nathan is good looking, and yes, if I saw him in a bar I'd look twice, well maybe three times, but he's not someone I'd ever consider to be boyfriend material. He can be arrogant and callous, he has messy hair, and his clothes look like they've never seen a washing machine, let alone an iron. He visits a razor once every blue moon - okay, I'll admit I do like the stubble, but he just looks unkempt all the time - and he has this no care, no-nonsense attitude about everything, whereas I care about everything, right down to the minute detail.

But now it seems all the things I saw to be a problem in Nathan are the things pulling me in. I've gone from intensely disliking the guy, to wanting to rip off his clothes in a matter of days.

And yes, I know just how very screwed up that is.

I know nothing will ever come of this crush. I don't want anything to come of it, so it's pointless to think about the necessaries. But really someone needs to tell this to my raging hormones. Seriously. Or at the very least sedate me until it passes.

I know exactly how Nathan views me. He sees me as your average, run of the mill, freak of nature. And yes, he's being nice to me but that's only to keep the peace, nothing more. He will never see me otherwise because it's the truth, I am a freak, and like Sol said, they stick with their own kind anyway...

"You want another coffee?"

"Hmm?"

"I asked if you wanted another coffee, love."

I look up from the magazine I've been pretending to read for the last five minutes, and over at my current half-full cold cup of coffee. "Oh, erm, yes please, Jack."

Jack comes over and I hand him my cup. He glances down at the contents and smiles. Taking it over to the sink, he rinses it out.

Jack's cooking dinner. I offered him my help but he wouldn't hear of it, so I decided to keep him company instead. Great company I turned out to be. All I've done is analyse my feelings for Nathan and sit here on nerves' edge wondering when he'll be home. He's been out all day at some animal auction. I really want to see him, and I really don't. It's insane. Four days ago I wouldn't have cared less where Nathan was - to be honest, the further away from me he was the better - but now I literally have to mentally prepare myself to see him.

This is an absurd situation that I've created in my own mind and it's the only place it currently resides. I intend to keep it that way.

Yes, I know I'm ridiculous and seriously messed up.

"You okay?" Jack enquires, mild concern lacquering his voice as he pours us both a coffee. "You seem miles away."

"Oh, yeah, I'm fine," I say with way too much enthusiasm as he walks over and puts my cup down in front of me. He takes a seat opposite.

I can feel my face starting to heat. I'm so crap at this covering up business. How Nathan doesn't know I fancy him is beyond me. I may as well walk around with a sandwich board, saying 'I heart Nathan', ringing a bell.

"Anywhere good?" Jack asks. He takes a sip of his coffee. I can see he's eyeing me closely. Jack should be a detective. Really. The man can sense bullshit at fifty paces.

"What?" I evade.

"Where you were?"

Oh well, I was just off daydreaming about your middle son, you know, the moody, sexy blonde one, goes by the name of Nathan ...

"No not really." I shake my head, pressing my lips together, desperately trying to conceal the truth.

Jack puts his coffee down and leans back in his chair. He pulls his cigars out of his shirt pocket and lights one up. I feel like I'm under a spotlight. I'm starting to sweat. My palms have gone clammy. I rub them surreptitiously on my jeans.

"I'm looking forward to dinner," I say, grasping for normality.

Jack smiles. "Yeah, me too."

Actually that was a lie. I'm not looking forward to it at all.

Cal and Erin are coming. It's the first time I'm going to meet Cal's wife and the mother of his unborn child, and I can't say I'm overjoyed at the prospect. I have her painted in my mind as being as scary as he is. Well, she'd have to be to put up with someone like Cal; either that or she's a saint of some kind.

I know Cal was reluctant to bring Erin with him tonight and that's because I'm here. I could tell from the way the conversation went that he had with Jack. I wasn't meaning to listen in, honestly, but with this hearing of mine, it's sometimes hard to tune out.

Cal doesn't like me, and I mean he really doesn't like me. He avoids me like the plague when he's here during the day working, and makes no secret of his feelings about me. Mostly I just keep out of his way. I may not like him but they are his family and this is the place where he grew up, his home, and he should feel comfortable here. I'm only a visitor, not a permanent fixture, and I really need to remind myself of that, and regularly. I can't get comfortable here.

From what I can tell – well, after asking Sol - Cal and Erin used to come around for dinner really regularly, before I arrived and disrupted everything, and I think this is Jack's way of trying to inject some form of normality back into their lives.

I pick my coffee up, blow on it and take a sip. Jack's being uncharacteristically quiet and it's unnerving me.

"Are you sure I can't do anything to help." I nod in the direction of the kitchen.

"No, it's all done, thanks love. Just the lamb to go in in a few minutes."

I take another sip of my coffee and rest the rim of the cup against my lower lip.

"Has Nathan ever told you he was in the army?" Jack says out of the blue.

He's sussed me. My stomach ties into a thousand knots. I move the cup away from my mouth. "He did, well Sol did, and I asked Nathan about it."

"Yeah, Nate's never been one to blow his own trumpet." He smiles fondly to himself and takes a puff on his cigar. The smoke billows up into the air. "Did he tell you about all those people he saved?" he asks, holding his cigar between his teeth.

The knots tighten further. I put my cup down. "Briefly."

"He's a hero, my boy. Eight people he saved. They were on duty, him and his best mate Craig. They were walking down the street through the market. Nate stopped to talk to some local kids, Craig kept on walking. There was a suicide bomber right there in the middle of the market, real close to Craig. Craig spotted him, knew something was wrong, but he was too late. The guy blew himself up for whatever godforsaken cause he thought he believed in. Craig was technically dead for a short while but Nate got him breathing again. Then he spent the next hour until help arrived searching through the rubble pulling people out. He saved eight people that day. One was a kid of about ten. His mother was dead, though. Nate tried to revive her, but it was too late."

There's a lump in my throat that won't go down.

Jack flicks the ash from his cigar into the ashtray. "Forty-one people died in that blast. It would have been forty-nine if it wasn't for Nate. But even though he saved those eight people, he still blames himself for the ones he couldn't save, especially the boy's mother. It's one of his bigger regrets," … pause … "but not as big as the night he saved you."

The skin on my face prickles. "Wh … what do you mean?" The words wobble out of my mouth.

He rubs his face. "He hates that he didn't get there in time to save Carrie." He pauses again, almost like he's collecting his thoughts so as to say this just right. He looks directly into my eyes with his steely blue ones. "But mainly, he hates that he didn't get there in time to save you."

I touch my hand to my face and realise there's a tear running down my face. I discreetly brush it away. "He did save me." My voice sounds inept.

Jack shakes his head, gently. "No love, not in the way he wishes."

I feel sick. Another tear rolls down my cheek. I don't bother to wipe it away. "Why are you telling me this, Jack?"

"Because I care about you. You're lovely girl, you're like one of my own now, and you've had to endure way more than anyone ever should in their lifetime, and I don't want to see you get hurt again. I know Nathan. He's a good boy but he can be hard. He doesn't really get … close to people. He can hurt them, a lot, without meaning to. It's just his ... way."

I stare at Jack, at a loss for words.

He stands up and stubs his half-smoked cigar out in the ashtray. "Best get the lamb in the oven or we'll all be going hungry tonight." He tries to give me a lasting smile, but it doesn't work.

Jack knows I have feelings for Nathan and he's telling me to quit now because Nathan would never be interested in me, because of what I am. He's trying to save me the hurt and embarrassment. The mortification drenches me. Even though I already knew all of this, it still doesn't make it hurt any less. I feel so stupid and pathetic, and weak.

I want to get up and leave but I can't; I'm frozen to this chair. Pride has me stuck. Jack may be right about my feelings for Nathan but if I get up and leave, I'm just confirming to him that's he is right, and I can't do that. All I have left is plausible deniability.

So, instead, I sit here, torturing myself, desperately trying to hold onto my dignity, as I once again attempt to read my magazine.

But for a long time all I can manage to do is read the same sentence over and over.

Chapter 14

Instinct

"Aww, Alex, you should have seen Sol when he dressed up as Kylie at our Halloween party last year. He wore the gold hot pants and everything. It was hilarious. And he could have easily passed for a woman." Erin laughs heartily from her seat beside me, and reaches over and pinches Sol's cheek as he sits adjacent to her at the end of the table. "He looked so gorgeous. I'm gonna bring the photos with me next time I come."

"Don't you dare!" Sol warns, laughing.

"*You* dressed as Kylie?" I lean forward to look down the table at Sol, raising a playful eyebrow.

He screws his face up. "I left it 'til the last minute to get my costume and it was all the shop had left … and anyway … " he looks back to Erin, "it's not my fault I've been blessed with great features." He casts his hand over his face, and looks at me again and winks.

I laugh. He's so cheeky.

"Womanly features aren't something you should brag about," Nathan quips.

Sol pulls a face at him. Nathan grins smugly back. They're like a pair of kids at times.

I rest back in my chair and look over at Nathan who's sitting opposite me. "So what did you go as?"

He looks at me for a long second before answering, "A Viking."

I smile, impressed with his choice. You can't beat a burly Viking. But now all I have in my mind is a picture of Nathan dressed as a Viking. I mentally shake myself out of it.

"Jack dressed as Frank Sinatra," Erin says, pulling my attention to her. "Cal was Jack Sparrow and I was Catwoman, not that I could fit into that costume nowadays." She juts out her lower lip, patting her heavily pregnant stomach.

"Well, I still think you look lovely," Cal says smiling at her.

"Brown nose," Sol jokes.

Erin playfully smacks Sol on the arm.

I can see the obvious connection between Erin and Cal, and for a fleeting moment I really envy what they have.

Erin has been a complete surprise, and for that matter, so has Cal. He's actually being nice. Well, not yet to me directly, but he has made eye contact a few times and he did sort of smile in my general direction when he arrived, but I was standing next to Sol at the time, so he could have been smiling at him.

I'm guessing it's Erin's influence on him. She's nice and very warm and friendly. I instantly liked her. She's the type of person I would have been friends with in my old life. She's been incredibly friendly toward me from the offset, which must have been difficult for her knowing how Cal feels about me, which is a view I'm a hundred percent sure he will have aired to her. He's not exactly one to keep his feelings secret.

I was expecting Erin to come in with an already inbuilt air of hostility toward me, wearing the same look of distaste as Cal does whenever he's forced to be around me. I had painted her in my mind to be as abrasive as he is, but she is nothing like that at all.

The moment she walked through the door, she honed in on me straightaway, wearing a huge toothy smile, all dark brown eyes and long black hair swishing about. She practically oozed kindness and not the fake kind either. You know how some people just have a natural, genuine charm about them, well Erin has that. She reminds me of Carrie in that respect.

Carrie.

And as quickly as her name filters through my mind, so appears the familiar squeeze on my heart, the chill blanketing my skin, the sting of tears at the back of my eyes.

Carrie would have loved being here at this dinner, she would have loved all of them, and they would all have loved her.

I take a silent, deep breath and count to ten, forcing myself back to normal. Well, as normal as I can get.

I glance at Erin, then over at Cal. Visually, they look well suited, but their personalities are worlds apart. She's warm and friendly. He's cold and not so friendly.

All I can think is that Erin sees something in Cal that no one else sees, or he allows them to see, which has to be something good, right?

And because of how lovely and genuine a person Erin is, I have to consider the fact maybe Cal isn't as bad a person as I thought, that my initial instinct could have been wrong. It's not the first time I've been wrong about someone, take Eddie for instance.

It's obviously just around me, or should I say with me, that Cal has issues, which is understandable.

I tune back into the conversation. Jack's talking. He's telling us about

Dave, an old farming mate of his, who he ran into at Tesco's this morning. I stop listening again the moment I hear the word 'fertiliser'.

I steal a quick glance at Nathan. His eyes are on Jack and he's absentmindedly picking at the food left on his plate with his fork. He looks relaxed, happy, and incredibly handsome in only the way he can. Seriously, if anyone else dressed like Nathan does, people would be handing them money in the street. Still, my heart does a little flip-flop.

How is it that all the things that irritated me about him a week ago now have my body fizzing on sight? Sets my heart beating just that bit faster? Makes my head go light every moment he happens to cast a glance my way? Makes me want to blurt out every thought and feeling I've ever had for him as I throw myself begging into his arms?

Stop Alex. You have to stop these thoughts. Remember what Jack said to you a few hours ago. Just keep reminding yourself of that.

I did worry that Jack might tell Nathan I have feelings for him but so far he hasn't, and I don't think he will. I don't think it's his style.

I know Jack is only looking out for me, and I appreciate it, I really do, but it's all so easier said than done. The second Nathan walked through the door a few hours ago, I was lost to him again, all my resolve gone, just like that. My brain seized up and left me to the mercy of my hormones. And all I want is to be around him despite the all-engulfing, infuriating, tangled way he always leaves me feeling.

Nathan looks at me unexpectedly, catching me staring. I quickly look away, focussing my attention onto Jack.

I know he's still looking at me. I can feel his quizzical stare. I ignore the temptation to look back at him, pick up my glass and take a sip of my wine for something to do.

I put my glass back down on the table. Nathan shifts his position in his seat. His foot brushes against the bare skin on my leg under the table. Heat sears, almost painfully, up my leg. I wish I'd worn my jeans now, not my shorts. Did he do that on purpose? No, why would he? To get my attention for some reason, maybe?

I look at him.

He smiles and mouths, 'Sorry.'

I smile back. It feels awkward and clumsy.

With shaky fingers, I pick my wine up again and take a big gulp, then another. It coats my insides like warm honey. But still, my leg is burning from his touch, it's kindling, like wood crackling white.

Every single time Nathan touches me, I get that feeling of electricity sparking, and now I know I don't feel like that because I'm a Vârcolac, I feel it because of him. It's like all my feelings are imploding at once. Nathan's touch can set off lightning bolts to strike under my skin. It's exhausting, he's burning me out. I've never in all my life had a reaction to anyone like I do him.

I know it's just chemical. The intensity and level of my feelings probably do have something to do with the changes I've been through. My body is so screwed up it doesn't know its left from its right anymore, which is why I know these feelings for Nathan will go as soon as I sort myself out.

Erin reaches over and picks up my plate, which is still bearing half the meal Jack made, and sits it atop her own empty plate.

"I'll take them," I say, taking both our plates from her hands. "You stay there and take it easy."

She smiles gratefully at me and says, "Thanks."

I go around the table collecting all the plates. As I approach Nathan, my heart starts to up its tempo. Heat is practically radiating off me. He looks up at me as he hands me his plate. "Thanks," he says, low.

I mutter something incoherent and quickly move away, carrying the plates over to sink.

I will get past this. I will stop feeling like this.

"Who's up for some dessert?" Jack asks, an enticing tone to his voice, as I take my seat back at the table. "It's Lemon Torte with Jersey Cream."

There's collective and very enthusiastic yeses from Erin and Sol.

"None for me, thanks," I say quietly.

"I've got to put the horses in for the night, dad," Nathan says, getting to his feet. "Save me some for later."

"Yeah, me too," Cal adds. "I'll go give Nate a hand." Cal gets up and kisses Erin on the top of her head. "Won't be long, babe."

I end up with some dessert. Jack was insistent; said I need to put some meat on my skinny bones. I've never thought of myself as skinny before, but he is right, I do look a tad on the thin side. I've lost a fair bit of weight since I've been here and I don't look good for it. Still, I can't seem to eat the dessert. I just pick at it, forking tiny amounts into my mouth at a time.

I think it was a race between Sol and Erin as to who could finish first as their plates are cleared in no time. That's typical of Sol, though, and Erin is eating for two after all.

I glance at Erin's pregnant stomach. There's a tiny baby in there. I feel a sharp stab of envy. Erin is doing the one thing I'm never going to be able to do. Well, not unless I want to create an abomination, that is.

"When's your baby due?" I ask Erin.

"Thirtieth of September," she answers. She wipes up a bit of left-over cream from her plate with her finger and licks it off. "I've got just over five weeks left."

"Not long then." I smile.

"Nope."

"Do you know what you're having?"

She shakes her head, smiling. "We wanted a surprise." A big yawn escapes her. "Sorry," she says, covering her mouth with her hand.

"You tired, love?" Jack asks.

She pushes her chair back, allowing her to stretch her legs out. "Yeah, it just came over me all of a sudden. I'll go get Cal, tell him I'm ready to go home. I hope you don't mind me leaving straight after dinner."

"Don't be daft," Jack chides good-naturedly. "You've got to take good care of yourself and my grandchild." He smiles warmly

"I'll go get Cal for you," I say getting up. "Save your legs." Really, I could do with the walk and fresh air after all that food.

"You sure you don't mind?" she asks.

"Course not." I pull my cardigan on.

I head straight for the stables, thinking they should have Honor and Hope out of the paddock by now. I'm just near the front of the barn, probably only about fifty feet away from the stables, when I hear them talking. And I don't what it is that stops me from moving or why I expanded my hearing in the first place, but what I'm hearing isn't exactly filling me with confidence ...

"Nate, you need to think about what you're going to do about Alex. Just be serious and think about it for a minute. You can't keep her hidden away here forever."

"Why not? She's safe here."

"I disagree. I think it's only a matter of time before she's discovered by them, and you know what'll happen to you, to all of us, when they find her here. Alex being here puts us all in danger, and I've got Erin and the baby to think about."

"They won't find Alex because they're not looking for her. They don't even know she exists."

"It's just a matter of time, Nate, just a matter of time." Sigh. "You really don't have many options."

"So what do you propose I do, Cal? Throw her out into the streets, let her fend for herself. That'd be plain fucking stupid and you know it. I might as well just deliver her to their doorstep."

Silence.

"Please tell me you're not serious." Nathan sounds angry.

"Just hear me out," Cal's tone is mild but forced.

The hairs on the back of my neck prickle, sending a shiver running down my spine.

"No," Nathan says.

"Just listen for a minute before you start kicking off. If you give Alex to the Originals, if you give them the one thing they've wanted for the last four hundred years, you'll be a fucking hero in their eyes. There'd be no comeback for you killing the arsehole who changed her in the first place, and we'd all be safe. There'd probably even be a reward in it for you."

"Money? Jesus Christ, Cal, do you actually have any comprehension of what you're actually suggesting I do?" Nathan's voice is full of incredulity. Well, at least that's what I think it sounds like and what I'm really hoping it is. "You want me to actually sell Alex to them?!"

"No." Cal's voice breaks ever so slightly. I hear him swallow down and the increase in his heartbeat tells me he's lying. "That's not what I'm suggesting at all."

"Yes, it is."

"No, it's not. This is about all of us - dad, Sol, Erin, the baby - about our lives. You know what the Vârcolacs are capable of and what you've got us into by saving her. Don't get me wrong, I like Alex, I do, but ... "

"No, you don't. You don't have any fucking regard for her whatsoever."

Sigh. "Fine, I don't like Alex, but that's not the point ... "

"It's completely the point."

"Fucking hell, Nate!" Cal sounds exasperated. "What is it with her? If I didn't know better I'd think you'd ... " Silence. "Have you?"

"No."

"But you want to."

"We're done talking."

I hear Nathan's footsteps move across the floor and the stable door bangs shut. It opens quickly again as Cal follows him. I slide inside the darkened barn, pressing my back up against the brick wall and hold my breath.

"Nathan, wait."

"I don't wanna hear it, Cal, seriously."

"Just stop a minute, will you?"

Nathan stops walking. "What?" There is nothing in his tone that's interested.

"If you've got feelings for Alex, then this all makes a little bit more sense, and I get it, I do. She's a stunner but you know nothing can ever come of it."

"I don't have feelings for Alex. I feel responsible for her, that's all." Silence. "You know, Cal, when you come out with ridiculous shit like this is the time when I wonder just how the fuck we're related at all."

My heart drops down to the cold, hard ground. Bitter tears bite at my throat.

"Nice, bro, thanks." Silence. "Nate, you know I'm just worried about us all, worried what could happen if they find out about her."

"They won't, so nothing will happen."

"Fine." Sigh. "Just say you'll consider what I'm saying."

"Consider it, considered it, and Alex stays put." Nathan starts walking again.

"Okay, fine," Cal says, following him. "Whatever you think is best."

I keep hold of my breath and still my beating heart as they pass by the barn. Then I let the tears flood into my eyes as my weary body slides down the wall to the floor. I pull my knees to my chest and wrap my cardigan around them.

Well, at least now I know I should always trust my instincts when it comes to people. Looks like I was right about Cal after all.

Chapter 15

In His Hands

I don't know what I feel most. Disappointment, I think.

I'm disappointed with myself. And that's not because I thought for a brief, stupid moment that Cal might actually be a good guy, but because, even as much as I hate to think it, Cal is partly right in what he said last night.

I am putting them all in danger by being here.

Nathan keeps me here out of some misplaced sense of responsibility, apparently. And I've allowed him to do so because I'm afraid to be alone. I've got no one and nowhere else to go.

I should leave. I know I should. But the problem is I can't seem to bring myself to. I spent all of last night trying to do just that. The furthest I got was the end of the drive. And yes, I know just how weak and selfish that makes me.

There are two reasons I can't leave.

One, I'm afraid.

Honestly, I don't think I'd survive out there alone. I've never truly been alone before. I've never had to fend for myself. After my parents died, Carrie, Tom and Angie took care of me. They did everything for me because I had no care to carry on. Then from their home I moved straight in with Eddie and he just took over where they left off. And now I've let Nathan, Jack and Sol do exactly the same.

It really would be easier if Nathan would just show me the door and push me out of it, because then I'd have no choice but to leave and finally try and fend for myself.

But if he did do that, it would crush me. You see, Nathan is reason number two as to why I can't leave. If I'm being completely honest, he's the only reason.

The thought of leaving and never seeing Nathan again is so painful that I can't even express it into words. I think I'm way past the element of a crush now. My feelings for him have gotten so out of control that I can't even distinguish just exactly what they are.

Am I in love with him? Quite possibly.

And even if I was the strong person I'd liked to be, the bottom line is I don't want to leave him. Not now, not ever.

I wish I were a better person but obviously I'm not. And no matter how hard I might try to convince myself to leave, it's clearly not going to happen anytime soon.

I roll onto my back and let my eyes drift over the clear sky above. There's not a cloud to be seen today and the sun is beating down hot. You don't see many days like this in my little part of the world, so you have to make the most of them while they're here. The freshly cut grass is cool beneath my back but the sun's hot rays are set to warm the rest of my body.

I love the smell of freshly cut grass. It reminds me of normality, something I miss with an almost physical ache. I run my fingers through it, disturbing it, redistributing the smell into the air. I close my eyes and inhale deeply. Then I hear Nathan's approach.

My heart starts to beat just that little bit faster and nerves ripple over my skin. I fight to ignore the feeling.

"Hey," he says. His voice sounds huskier than normal, I notice, and I can feel the cool of his shadow on my body as he stands beside me.

I inhale another deep breath, readying myself to see him for the first time since last night, then I open my eyes.

He's wearing aviator shades. They really suit him. My heart skips a couple of beats. I force a calm and say, "Hi," in the most even voice I can manage.

He smiles down at me. He looks exactly like my version of perfection. He makes my head hurt. "Weather's really great, isn't it?" he says, completely unaware of the internal battle that's raging inside me.

I rest up on my elbows. "Yeah," I answer, "it's lovely."

I notice he's carrying a shiny blue motorbike helmet in one hand and a black leather jacket in the other, and that he himself is dressed in black leather pants and a plain white T-shirt, and is wearing his trade mark motorbike boots. My first thought is he must be really hot in those leather pants. I'm warm and I'm only wearing a vest and my denim shorts. My second thought: he looks really hot in those leather pants.

"You're gonna need these." He tosses the helmet and jacket to me. I catch the helmet but the jacket lands in a heap on my stomach. "And you might want to put some jeans on too," he adds, nodding down at my bare legs. I don't miss how his eyes skim up them.

I sit upright, glancing down puzzled at the helmet and jacket. "Why? What for?"

"We're going out for a ride."

"Ride? On what?"

"My bike." He thumbs over his shoulder.

I look past him and see waiting on the other side of the garden fence the red Ducati that lives in the barn.

So, it is his bike. That makes him even sexier, if possible. *Crap.*

"I didn't know you rode a motorbike?" I say, putting the helmet down on the grass and sitting the jacket next to it.

He crouches down beside me, so close I can feel his heat. He pulls off his sunglasses, hangs them off his T-shirt and looks me straight in the eye. "There's a lot you don't know about me." His tone is low, intimate.

I feel a white, hot thrill shoot through my blood, throwing me off-balance. I put my hands down to the ground to steady myself.

"Go put some jeans on," he tilts his head in the direction of the house, "and we can get going."

Pulling myself together, I shake my head and say, "Thanks for the offer, but no thanks."

"What?"

"No way am I getting on that thing." I gesture at the beautiful, but monstrous, motorbike.

"Why not?" he asks, laughing.

"Well I could fall off it for starters ... "

"You're not gonna fall off it." He chuckles. "But if you did, you'd heal quickly anyway." His smile is all fox.

I pull a face at him. "Yeah, well that's not a theory I fancy putting to the test, thanks all the same."

I start to get to my feet but he takes hold of my arm, keeping me there. I glance at his hand, then up at his face. "Come out with me," he says, his tone is inviting and daring, and it's making me feel like we are the only two people in the world right now.

Trembles erupt deep within me. "I can't." My voice is barely working. "I can't risk being seen by people in case they recognise me, remember?"

"You won't be seen," he assures me, not moving his eyes from mine. "I'll keep you safe."

I can't think straight. His touch is distracting.

Then he lets go of my arm and the spell is broken. "I'm just gonna take us up to Dalby Forest, that's all." He lifts his voice but his tone is still smooth. "Come on, it'll be fun."

Fun? I really don't think I should be considering the word fun and Nathan in the same sentence in my current state.

I tuck my hair behind my ear. "You're not trying to take me hunting again, are you?" I let my obvious distaste at that thought spread plain across my face.

He laughs. It's a slow, dry laugh, and sexy as hell. "No, Alex. I'm not going to try and take you hunting again." I love it when he says my name.

He gets to his feet. "Don't make me beg." A grin plays like a tune on his face.

"Fine," I huff. "I'll come."

He smiles a winning smile.

I pick the jacket and helmet up, and get to my feet so that we're just stood here facing one another. I'm not sure what to do, or just exactly what it is he's waiting for. He still hasn't looked away from my face and my pulse has started to beat loudly in my ears.

"Jeans," he finally says, raising his eyebrows.

"Oh yeah, of course." I flush as the realisation thuds into me like a ton of bricks. "Hold these. I won't be a minute." Embarrassed, I shove the helmet and jacket into his arms and quickly make for the house.

Nathan's already sitting astride the bike when I get back, the helmet and jacket waiting for me on the seat behind him.

"You were quick," he comments.

"Would you rather I go back in and take a bit longer?" I flash my eyes at him.

He chuckles, shaking his head. "Just get your ass on the bike."

I slip the leather jacket on. It fits perfectly. I wonder where it came from. Maybe it belonged to an ex-girlfriend. Jealously spikes me. I hate that he can make me feel this way without even knowing. I try to zip it up, but the zipper's stiff and I can't do it.

"Come here." Nathan gestures to me.

I go and stand in front of him. He takes hold of the zipper, fits it in and pulls it up in one easy movement.

I slide my eyes up from the zipper, meeting his on the way up. "Thanks." My mouth is so sticky it is like talking through a mouthful of chewing gum.

His eyes smile at me. "No worries."

"Where you two off to?" I jolt away from Nathan at the sound of Cal's voice like I've just heard a gun go off.

Nathan pulls his own black helmet from off the handle bars. "I'm just taking Alex out for a ride to Dalby Forest," he answers in an even tone. He puts his helmet on. I can sense the tension between them. Even if I hadn't overheard their conversation last night, I'd know something was off.

I can't bring myself to turn around and acknowledge Cal, but I also can't let on that I overheard their conversation, so I force myself to relax and try to act no differently than I normally would around him.

"Well you've got a good day for it," Cal comments, pointing up at the sky. "I'll catch you later." And with a nod, he disappears into the house.

"You getting on or not?" Nathan says, his voice now monotone, and I can't tell if he's being arsey or joking.

"On," I say. I pick my helmet up, put it on and fasten the chin strap, then I gingerly climb onto the seat behind him.

He turns the key in the ignition. The explosion of the engine startles me as its power vibrates up through my body. My nerves instantly kick in.

I put my hands around his waist, holding on, but keep a safe distance between us.

He kicks the bike stand away and rolls it forward, quickly gaining speed.

Without meaning to, I squeal out when he takes the bend at the top of the driveway. I grip hold of him tighter, practically digging my fingers into his ribs. I feel his low laughter rumble through his body.

It's only a matter of seconds before we're at the end of the driveway. He stops the bike, resting his foot to the floor, and takes hold of both my hands and pulls me in closer to him. My heart stutters.

With a quick check, he pulls out onto the road and we roar off in a trail of dust, leaving my stomach still somewhere on his driveway and my heart completely in his hands.

Chapter 16

The Beginning

Nathan pulls up at the entrance to Dalby Forest to pay. He lifts his visor, gets some coins out of his pocket and hands them to the guy at the entrance.

He takes the ride slow down the main road, leading us right into the heart of the forest.

It's been years since I've been here. The last time I came was when I was a kid with my mum and dad. I'd forgotten what a beautiful place it really is. I always think of beautiful sights as being other places in the world, always forgetting about the ones in my own back yard. The trees are lush and green, the sun is beating down, and I can't think of anywhere I'd rather be right now than here with Nathan, my arms wrapped tightly around him.

After a few minutes, Nathan turns off onto a narrow track just wide enough for the bike to fit down. As we cut through the bushes it opens out onto a big lake completely surrounded by the forest. He pulls the bike around and parks it up by the bushes, and turns the ignition off. I climb off the bike. My legs are like jelly. It takes me a moment to get them working properly.

I lift my visor up a touch, allowing me to look around properly. This place is a hidden oasis. It's really secluded. The sun is glinting off the water, a rainbow of colours rippling down to the water's edge. "It's beautiful here," I murmur.

Nathan pulls off his helmet, hangs it on the handle bar and kicks the bike stand out. He turns his head to look at me, resting his chin on his shoulder. "I thought you might like it."

His tousled hair is stuck to his forehead from the helmet. The urge to want to reach out and brush it back off his face is overwhelming. I bind my hands together in front of me.

Nathan stands, leaving the bike between his legs and takes his jacket off. Then he swings his long leg over and gets off the bike. "You're okay to take this off." He reaches over and taps my helmet with his fingers. "There's no one around."

Hands shaking, I fumble with the chin strap. Finally I undo it. As I remove the helmet, my damp hair sticks to my head too - attractive. I run my fingers through my hair, trying to make it look nicer.

I turn and see that Nathan is watching me. He looks away and unhooks the rucksack that was fastened to the side of the bike. He sits the bag on the bike seat, opens it up and pulls out a folded-up picnic blanket and a small cooler bag.

I look at him with open surprise.

He shrugs. "You mentioned a picnic when I took you on the ill-fated hunting trip and I thought today was as good a day to have one."

A smile broadens my lips.

"Don't get excited," he's quick to add, moving away from me, "it's nothing fancy, just some sandwiches."

But I can't help it, I am excited. Nathan is doing something thoughtful for me. He has been thinking of me.

I take off my jacket and put it and the helmet down on the bike seat. I go over to where Nathan has set down the blanket on the grass a touch in from the shoreline.

I watch him as he sits down on the blanket, stretches his long legs out in front of him and looks up at the sky. Emotions squeeze tightly on my heart. I turn away, looking out over the lake.

Warm from the heat and wanting to feel the water on my skin, I pull off my trainers and roll up the bottoms of my jeans. Treading carefully over the pebbly edge, I step into the shallow water, letting the cool water tickle over my feet. I breathe in the clean air deeply, letting the tranquilly settle all over me like a shield. I feel a sudden sense of freedom here. I feel safe here, like nothing can touch me. I hadn't realised how much of a prisoner I had felt until just now, not that I've ever been a prisoner with Nathan, far from it. I've been a prisoner of my own being and Nathan bringing me here has done more than I thought it would. Maybe he knows more about me than I realise.

I turn around, the water splashing around my feet as I let a smile ghost my lips. "Thanks for bringing me here."

"No probs." He shrugs. A smile briefly flickers over his face. "So how was the ride?" He tips his head in the direction of his motorbike. "As bad as you thought it would be?"

"It was okay, I guess, well once I'd gotten used to the crazy speed you drive at."

He throws his head back and laughs. "I don't drive that fast."

I widen my eyes and put my hands on my hips. "Er, yeah you do."

He purses his lips. "You wait for the ride back, then. I'll show you what fast is." He flashes his eyes daringly at me.

I shake my head disapprovingly, then, suddenly feeling mischievous, I kick water at him.

"Oi!" he yells jumping to his feet.

"Afraid of a bit of water?" I taunt.

He pushes his tongue between his teeth, giving me a dangerous look. He shakes his head. My stomach tumults.

"Actually you look like you could do with a good wash ... " I tease, lifting my foot, readying to kick more water at him.

He moves so quickly I have no time to react and the next thing I know he's behind me, wrapping his arms around me, pinning mine by my side. His body pressed up against mine. I can feel his heat radiating through our clothes, and his heart beating against my back. It stutters mine into irregular beats, doing inexplicable things to me.

"Now what you gonna do?" he whispers jokingly into my ear. His hot breath blows down my neck, taking mine and I'm left breathless. My heart reaches out to him, stuttering, sending feelings so strong flowing through me I'm powerless to stop them.

Then I feel it. It's like a dirty bomb filled with pure emotion imploding between us, splintering off in all different directions. And I know he feels it too by the way his whole body stiffens against me.

"Alex," he practically breathes my name. He releases his hold on me but doesn't move away. I slowly turn to look at him, my whole body trembling. My shoulder brushes against his chest.

And when I meet his eyes, I just know.

The warm breeze passes by, moving the water around us, washing it up against our legs. "Your boots," I say, not moving my eyes from his, "they'll be getting soaked."

Without a word he slips his hand into mine and leads me over to our blanket. Nathan sits first, then me beside him, facing him. He doesn't let go of my hand and I don't want him to, ever again.

My mind won't take me anywhere close to the words I want to say, I have no idea where to go from here, and it seems neither does he. So, I opt for what I do best - small talk. "Do you ever come here to shift?" I gesture to the beautiful woods surrounding us, pushing my damp feet into the blanket.

"Sometimes." He runs his thumb over the back of my hand, his rough skin tickling mine, leaving a heavenly trail of warmth wherever he touches. "Not as often I'd like, though. It's a bit further out and I tend to stick to local places like ... " He pauses, not finishing his sentence. I see a flicker of regret in his eyes.

We both know what he was going to say. He was going to say the woods near my home, the woods where he saved me.

I know his eyes are on me so I avoid them and cast mine out over the scenery behind him. "It really is pretty here," I say, filling the awkward silence.

"Are you okay?" he asks ignoring my attempt. He slides his fingers in-between mine gripping hold of my hand.

"I'm fine," I answer instinctively. *Well, except for the fact I have no clue what's going on here between me and you*, I fail to add.

"Fine," he echoes, his tone disbelieving. It makes the hairs on my arms prickle. "You don't seem fine. I'd say the dead giveaway is that you can't even make eye contact with me when the subject of your attack comes up."

My insides freeze solid. I pull my hard eyes back to his. "And how would you expect me to be?" There's zero tone to my voice.

"I'd expect you wouldn't be fine. I'd expect you'd be hurting."

I shrug. Biting my lip, I look away.

"Talk to me, Alex."

My eyes snap up. "You want me to talk you?" I almost laugh. "Five weeks down the line and now you're asking how I'm feeling." I rub my face roughly with my hand. "And this coming from the man who told me I had to basically suck it up and get on with it on the first day."

"I was wrong and insensitive ... and I'm sorry." His tone is intense.

I flicker a surprised look his way and my gaze turns suspicious. "What's your end game, Nathan? Why do suddenly want to help me?"

"No end game." He grips my hand tighter. "I just want you to know that you can talk to me about anything."

I feel a wave of anger and grief coming from somewhere deep within. Tears are threatening my eyes. I look away, a sigh escaping me. "I miss Carrie so much it hurts like a physical pain inside that will never go away." I swallow back the tears. "I miss Angie and Tom. I miss my life, my job, my home, my friends, and I hate what I've become. I hate everything about me. I hate that I have to drink blood, but most of all," I pause, taking a breath, "I hate that I actually enjoy doing it." I look back at Nathan, my lips quiver and a tear leaks from my eye.

He reaches his hand up to my face and brushes my tear away, his touch gentle. "What about your boyfriend? Do you miss him?"

At the mention of Eddie, my free hand starts to fidget, picking at the fluff on the blanket. "Ex-boyfriend," I say, and even I can hear the bitter tone in my quiet voice. "We'd broken up before all of this happened. And no, Eddie is actually the one thing I don't miss."

"Would you have ever got back together if things had turned out differently?"

"No." I rub my eyes dry. "Being cheated on once was bad enough, but twice was a joke. I might have been an idiot to go back the first time but I'm not a complete idiot that I'd have done it again."

He runs his fingers up my arm. My skin hums and all I want him to do is kiss me now.

"What about you?" I ask, finding my weak voice as I fight the urge to lean into him.

"What about me?" he asks, his tone soft, his eyes taking hold of mine. Nathan has me, and whatever he chooses to do, I'll follow.

"Well, I'm assuming you don't have a girlfriend because I've never heard you talk about one." I'm nervous. I don't know if I want to know the answer.

"No. I don't have a girlfriend." His eyes flicker to my lips. I part them to let the breath I was holding out.

"Boyfriend?"

He throws his head back and roars out a laugh. "No!"

"Did you?"

"What, have a boyfriend?" His mouth is twitching with amusement.

"No, well, yeah." I'm flustered. "What I mean is did you have a previous, er, relationship?"

"Yes, Alex, I have had girlfriends. No boyfriends, though." He grins at me and winks.

Girlfriends - plural. Of course. You don't go through life looking like Nathan and only ever have one girlfriend.

"Anyone serious?"

"One."

Ahh. My heart gives an unpleasant twist.

"Was she like you - a shifter, I mean?"

"Yes."

"Why did you break up?"

"Because she didn't like what I became after I left the army."

"And what was that?"

He stares deep into my eyes. A sudden coolness overtakes the warmth. It sends an unexpected chill running through me. "Uncaring. Hard. Cold," he answers dryly.

I swallow down. "And what were you before?"

"Uncaring ... hard ... cold." He grins, his warmth instantly returning.

I hit him jokingly in the chest. He catches hold of my hand, keeping it there. I glance at it, then back to his face. His brilliant eyes are depthless and I'm falling further and further into them. I feel like I'm swimming in cool water on a hot summer's day, with no way of ever reaching the edge.

Nathan has both of my hands in his, my heart held in sync between them, and it can no longer keep up, left only with the option of tripping over itself, again and again, waiting for him to reset it.

I take a deep breath. "There must have been something good that she saw in you when you first got together," I say from out of my tacky mouth. I feel like someone's poured glue into it.

He shrugs, lightly. "You'd have to ask her that." He presses his lips together, letting his eyes drift into a long blink, and all I want is him, forever.

"Well, seeing as though I can't do that, you know, me being dead to the world an' all, I guess I'll have to go off my own impression of you."

He leans closer with interest. He's so close to me now that as he speaks his hot breath scorches over the skin on my face, blistering my lips. "Oh yeah and what's that?" He smiles. "Apart from what I already know - what was it you said? - that I'm an arsehole and a bastard."

I grin sheepishly, a blush rising in my cheeks. "I believe I actually called you an arse and that was when you were been an arse, but since you've been nicer to me, I know different."

He lifts an intrigued eyebrow.

"I know there's a lot more to you than you allow people to see. You're guarded but you care. You love your family a lot. I know you'd do anything for them, and the way you love your horses is amazing. And I also know that for some reason you think it's your job to save the world and everyone in it. I mean, look at what you did in Iraq, saving all those people."

"That was my job." He lets go of my hands and I instantly know I'm losing him. I can see him starting to close up.

"It wasn't your job," I say in a small voice, "and you saved me."

He hangs his hands on the back of his neck and closes his eyes. "You were different," he says, voice low.

My pulse races. "How so?"

He opens his eyes. The way they study me cuts straight to my heart. I swallow against the thickness in my throat. He opens his mouth to speak and closes it again. I see his face shut down completely and whatever he was going to say is lost. And after a long moment he simply says, "I don't know. You just were."

The frustration I feel is insurmountable. It practically blisters under my skin. "Can't you ever answer a question truthfully?" I challenge.

"Don't start." He casts a warning glance my way and all that he manages to do is to annoy me further.

Angry, I get to my feet. "Just when I think we're getting somewhere, Nathan, you shut down on me, again!"

"What the fuck are you talking about?"

"Nothing. I'm talking about nothing. Just forget it." I stomp off in the direction of the track.

"Why do you always have to walk away from me?" he calls angrily from behind.

He's right, this is twice now I've walked away from him when he's tried to do something nice for me, but I'm so sick of asking him this question and the instant I do he shuts down.

"Because you annoy the crap out of me!" I yell back.

He's behind me now. Hooking my arm, he swings me around to face him, pulling me close. "You know what?" His face is angry but his eyes hold a lot of depth. "You annoy the crap out of me too but it still doesn't stop me from wanting to do this."

Then he takes my face in his hands and kisses me.

Chapter 17

Surprise

I feel like the sky has fallen in on me. Of all the ways I ever imagined this would happen, this was not one of them. It didn't even radar on my list but it's gone right to the very top.

Nathan is nothing like I thought he would be. I imagined him to be rough and impatient. He's not, he's intense and passionate.

My legs are like jelly, nearly giving out, but Nathan's strong arms around me are keeping me upright. My body is shivering under his touch. Wherever his hands go, my skin instantly responds.

He inches his fingers down my back and grips a tight hold of my vest, pulling me closer to him. My arms snake around his neck, my fingers twist into his hair. He parts my lips with his. His tongue runs over mine, warm and inviting, and he tastes just like heaven.

I feel the desire pass through us. It's like lightning hitting a circuit breaker, blowing out all the fuses, and all my thoughts head south. Nathan lifts me at the hips. I wrap my legs around his waist. Then, without breaking from our kiss, he carries me back over to our picnic blanket.

He lays me down, resting himself on top of me, and our kiss deepens to something a little more than passionate.

My head is light with anticipation. He runs his hand under the hem of my vest, his fingers working their way up my side. My heart starts to beat out of my chest.

He sucks my bottom lip into his mouth. "Is this how all our fights will go from now on?" he murmurs, his voice breathy, as he trails his fingertip around the edge of my bra.

"Hopefully." I bite down on a smile.

He laughs, an intimate laugh, and starts to kiss me again, his hot breath mixing with mine as his hand runs down my arm, searching for my hand. Taking hold, he interlocks our fingers and moves my arm to rest up above my head. "Let's go home," he murmurs into my mouth.

My stomach tumults. "Will anyone be there?"

"No, they'll all be out working on the farm. The house will be empty." I can hear the smile in his voice.

I put my free hand under his T-shirt, feeling the ridges of his muscles on his back, and run my hand under it onto his hard chest. His muscles flex with my touch. A memory flashes through my mind of how Nathan looked that time I saw him naked when he stripped off in the woods, and it practically sets my pants on fire. I've never wanted someone as much as I want him and I really don't think I can wait the half hour journey back home.

I kiss him again, deeply, wrapping my legs around him, holding him to me. I never want to let him go. I feel him harden against me and any rational thought I might have had left flies out of my mind, and all I know is I want him, now.

"Is there anywhere else closer we could go?" I sound like I'm sixteen again and after a quickie with my boyfriend. My excuse: I'm not thinking rationally; I'm driven solely by lust and, really, who can blame me?

His mouth twists into a perceptive and sexy smile. "There's a hotel about five minutes from here." His pupils are wide and dilated, so much so the green of his iris is almost indistinguishable.

A flux of butterflies swoosh through my stomach. "Sounds perfect."

Nathan starts to lift himself up off me.

"Is this a private party or can we all join in?"

The deep voice jolts us the rest of the way apart. Nathan springs to his feet. I shoot up into a sitting position, all my breath leaving me in a whoosh.

We were so lost in each other, we didn't even sense them coming. And no, I don't need to look at them to know who or what they are. Vârcolacs.

And it's at this exact moment that I know it's all over for me. A tight feeling of impending doom slides through my stomach, not stopping until it reaches my toes.

When I do finally bring myself to look, I see the three of them standing just to the left of us about twenty feet away, blocking our only exit.

I clamber to my feet, and the second I'm standing Nathan takes hold of me and pushes me behind him.

I've so many thoughts flying through my mind, I don't know which one to address first, and now there's a chill in the air pushing the sun out and my clothes suddenly feel inadequate. I know with certainty they're not enough to protect me from whatever harm the three of them intend for me. And neither is Nathan. Nathan's undoubtedly strong and a trained fighter, and I might be freakishly strong nowadays but I'm no fighter, and that puts us at a considerable disadvantage to the three of them.

So basically, I'm fucked. There is no way out for me. Now all I can do is to try to ensure Nathan gets out of this unharmed.

One of the Vârcolacs takes a step forward, moving away from the other two. He's average height and build, has white blonde hair, really pale skin and bright blue eyes. He reminds me of an albino.

"Nathan," he says, addressing him like he knows him.

Does he know him? Oh God. Alarm shoots through me, my eyes darting up in panic to Nathan as my heart slams into my chest.

"Am I supposed to know you?" Nathan says flatly, but I hear a discreet undercurrent of menace there.

A strange sense of relief ripples in waves over my skin and I falter against Nathan, gripping a tight hold of his arm.

"No," The albino's mouth twists in the suggestion of a smile, "but I know you and I also know that you have something which belongs to me."

"And what would that be?" Nathan asks, almost conversationally if it wasn't for the set line of his jaw and the chill in his eyes.

Albino tilts his head in my direction. His eyes drift over me, a slow languid smile forming on his lips. My skin practically ups and crawls off my bones. "Wow, Alex, you really are a beauty. You were not done justice at all. The Originals are going to be very happy to meet you." He clicks his tongue in approval and I feel all kinds of violated, and completely and utterly terrified.

Nathan smiles but it isn't pleasant. "Well, it sure is a shame that they're not gonna get to meet her."

Albino's eyes shift back to Nathan, the muscles in his jaw tightening. Another one of them - black, slicked back hair - takes a step forward but Albino puts a hand out stopping him.

"So, Nathan, you're the one who killed Eric." Albino's tone is impassive.

"If you're referring to the lackey in Hackness woods." Nathan nods. "Well then, yeah, that would be me."

Albino laughs, and from his cool demeanour I can't decipher whether he's actually impressed or irritated. "You make that sound like you have more than one Vârcolac on your killed list?"

Nathan's mouth tips up but it's hardly a smile. "No, but I am working on it."

Albino gives another laugh, this one silent as he pushes his tongue between his teeth. "Okay, so here's how things are gonna go." He traces his fingertip with precision over his eyebrow. "You're gonna give the beautiful Alex to me, and then I might be kind enough to let you go with not so much as a hair harmed on your head."

Nathan laughs and scratches his chin. "Kind of you to offer but unfortunately we're gonna have to pass." His voice is even. Not a hint of fear. How is he keeping so calm? I listen to his heart. Yep, beating like a dream. I'm freaking out. My mouth is as dry as a waterless well and my heart has given out on me.

Albino laughs, a dry, papery laugh, then moves his lips back revealing his huge fangs.

A sensation – fear, I think - grabs hold of my heart, twisting and tugging at it, awakening it. And then I know what I have to do.

Swallowing against the thickness in my throat, I part my lips and say to the Albino, "I'll come with you. Just don't hurt Nathan, okay."

"No," Nathan says firm and low, tightening his hold on me. He looks down at me and I see it in his eyes, the fear. It ripples just beneath the surface. He's not afraid for himself, he's afraid for me, afraid of what he knows will happen to me when they do finally take me.

I give him a pleading look to let me do this, to let me save him, but he ignores me and moves his eyes from me back to Albino. "I'm taking it that it's money driving you here," Nathan says with a clear edge to his voice, his calm dissipating, "so we can work a deal. You walk away and forget you ever saw Alex and I'll pay you whatever it takes you to do that. You're not interested in Alex, it's only the Originals who'll want her. You're just interested in the money they'll give you when you hand her over, and I'll match it, whatever it is - and more if necessary."

Silence blisters the air, and for the first time ever in my life, I start to pray.

Albino takes another step closer to us, rubbing his forehead with his fingers. "You're right, Nathan, I'm not interested in Alex. I'm only interested in the money." He drops his hand down to his side. "But you're too late, the deal's been done. The Originals already know about her."

My body goes slack as the last shred of hope left is taken. I feel powerless and, completely and utterly vulnerable.

"I called them the minute I arrived here and got a whiff of her," Albino adds. "They're getting on a plane as we speak. Should be here in about … " He glances down at his watch, tapping the glass face with his fingernail., "… fourteen hours, and I'm under strict orders to keep her safe and sound. And honestly, you could have as much money as Richard fucking Branson and it wouldn't make me want to go up against them. I betray them and … " He slides the tip of his index finger across his throat in a cutting motion, "… and I kind of like my head. So thanks, but no thanks. But a question, though, farmer boy. If you have so much money, why didn't you just pay your brother's gambling debts off in the first place for him, and right now you'd be well on your way to riding Alex to the finish line, with us none the wiser."

I can't even be offended because my world has just come crashing down all around me. Blood starts to beat loudly in my ears.

"What?" Nathan says, his voice splintering.

"Your brother Cal. Seems he's got himself into a bit of debt, owes a lot of money to some very nasty people - not me, of course." Albino winks conspiratorially at me. My stomach curdles. "That's why he called. He wanted to sell the lovely Alex to me. Told me all about her existence, how you saved her like a knight in shining armour, and how she somehow survived the change to become our only one. Honestly, I could hardly believe my fucking ears. So, I told him I'd have to see her with my own eyes, and if she was the real deal, I'd give him the money he so desperately needs. He pays his gambling debts off and gets to keep his head in the process. I get Alex. I hand her over to the Originals and I'm rewarded handsomely. It's a win-win situation." He pushes his hand through his hair. "Well not for you, obviously," he adds, giving me an awkward smile.

It rolls right off me. The last thing I could ever imagine him to feel is awkward.

Nathan makes a guttural sound, bordering on a growl. "You're lying."

"Easy, boy," Albino mocks. "And believe what you want." He shrugs, uncaring. "But have a think about how I knew exactly where to find her."

Oh God, Cal sold me out. This was his intention all along. He was just testing the water with Nathan, trying to see if he could get him onside.

And when he couldn't, he went off and did it anyway.

I slide my hand down Nathan's arm, taking hold of his hand. His fingers close in around mine.

I look at the three Vârcolacs, the cocky Albino, the black haired one with the arrogant stance, and the silent Asian with the look of death in his eyes.

And I know I'm one of them. I'm their kind.

Something breaks inside me. Hot tears tumble down my cheek. "I'm so sorry," I choke, pressing my face into Nathan's back, my tears soaking into his T-shirt.

He sighs, a tired sound. "Okay, so we all know how this is gonna go. You want Alex, you gotta get past me first."

I lift my head, fear crackling my mind to alert. I want to cry 'no', to stop him from doing this, but I'm too late.

"You know, I was really kinda hoping you'd say that," Albino says with a smirk and then he's heading for us.

Nathan pushes me backwards, hard, away from him. "Run!" he yells, moving forward, heading for the three charging Vârcolacs, "and don't ever look back."

Love takes off masks that we fear we cannot live without and know we cannot live within.

James Arthur Baldwin

Chapter 18

Nathan

There's dirt in my mouth. I can taste blood. I lift my head up slightly and spit it out. My body feels like carnage. What the hell happened?

Fuuccck!!

I jump to my feet, stumbling forward as the memories flood my mind. My eyes struggle to focus as I scan the area searching for Alex. But she's long gone. She didn't make it. They took her.

How long have I been out? I check my watch - 17:20. Jesus, I've been out for hours. She could be anywhere by now.

Think practical, Nate. If you were them, where would you take her? She's worth a lot of money to them.

They'll have a safe house.

But where?

They're local but they won't keep her too close by. They'll know I'll look for her and they won't want me messing up their plans, but it will be somewhere close to an airport with the Originals travelling in by plane. Keep the bosses happy.

Surrounding airports - Leeds Bradford, Durham Tees and Humberside.

It depends where the Originals are flying in from? If I know where they're coming in from, I can get the airport and narrow down my search to that area.

Okay, so he said they'd be here in fourteen hours, so depending on the travelling to airport time from their end, I could be looking at China,

Singapore, Malaysia, Thailand, and just about any other country that sits in the southern fucking hemisphere!

Arrggh! This is fucking hopeless!

No, Nate, it's not. You can figure this out. Alex is relying on you to find her. You have to find her. You can't lose her, not now.

Okay, deep breath and calm down. Just think...

Cal.

I gonna fucking kill him.

Then I'm on my bike, yanking my helmet on, ignoring the pain that sears through my face from the pressure of it, and I'm tearing up the dirt and grass, down the track back onto the road out of here in seconds, heading for the only person who can tell me exactly where Alex is.

How could Cal do this? No, don't think, just drive. The sooner you see him, the sooner you'll get the answers you need, and the closer you'll be to getting Alex back, even if you have to beat it out of him.

I accelerate faster.

Cal should still be at the farm. He usually is at this time. I really don't want to have to do this in front of Erin, but I will if I have to, and then I guess she'll see what type of bastard she's married to, if she doesn't already know.

It feels like hours have passed before I finally hit my driveway. Swerving in, the back wheel spins out, nearly tipping me off, but I put my foot to the floor, gravel raking at my sole, and somehow I manage to keep on. Then I'm outside my house, skidding to a halt. I jump off my bike, letting it drop to the floor, not even bothering to turn the engine off.

Cal's still here. I could smell his betrayal from the top of the drive.

I throw the front door open and tear into the living room. I see him sitting as calm as fuck in the arm chair, drinking a can of lager, watching TV. He looks up at my entrance. I see a flicker in his eyes and I know.

I tear my helmet off and throw it as hard as I can at him, aiming straight for his head. He puts his arm up to protect himself. The helmet hits his arm and bounces to the floor, lager splattering all over him.

"What the fuck?!" he yells, wiping the lager from his face. But I'm already advancing, covering the room in a few strides. I grab hold of his shirt and drag him up to his feet.

"Where is she?" I say, my tone dark.

"Nate, what's wrong? What's happened to your face?" my dad asks, worried, getting up from the couch.

I don't answer him. I can't answer him. My only focus right now is Cal.

"Where is she?" I repeat, my voice harder.

"How the hell would I know where Alex is? I thought she was with you." I hear the small break in his voice. Most wouldn't, but I do. I know my brother and he's a shit liar, always has been. He attempts to push me away from him but I increase my hold. I have no intention of letting go, not until I have the answers I want.

"Don't mess with me, Cal. Just tell me where the fuck they've taken her?" I push him back into the chair, leaning over him, my face close to his as my hand goes up and around his throat.

Sol bursts in from the kitchen. "What the hell's going on?" His eyes are pinging between me and Cal, and dad. "Where's Alex?"

"Ask our so called fucking brother where Alex is," I hiss, not taking my eyes from Cal.

"What?" Sol sounds confused

I glance in Sol's direction. I feel an unexpected wave of guilt at what I'm about to tell him. I don't know why but I feel like I've not only let Alex down but I've somehow let Sol down too. "Cal sold Alex to the Vârcolacs."

"He sold Alex?" he says in a way that sounds like he sincerely hopes I'm joking. I wish I was.

I nod my head, briefly closing my eyes.

And I'll never forget the look of horror I see in his eyes.

"Tell me exactly how much you got when you sold her out?" I say, low, narrowing my gaze back onto Cal.

"I didn't ... "

"Don't fucking lie to me!" I roar. My tolerance has reached its limit. "They told me. The blonde one told me it was you right before him and his buddies kicked the shit out of me." I shove him harder into the chair. "How could you do this to Alex? I told you no last night." I move my face closer to his, my nose almost touching his. "Tell me just exactly how much is Alex's life worth to you?"

I see it flicker over his face and it just confirms everything I already know.

"Does it matter?" he finally says in a hard voice.

I feel sick to the pit of my stomach. I knew it was true, of course I did, but deep down some part of me was praying it wasn't.

I feel like I don't even know him anymore. He's a complete stranger to me now.

Rage burns through my veins, blurring my vision. "Of course it fucking matters!" I yell, pushing my hand hard into his throat as I propel myself away from him. He gags from the pressure. Coughing, he rubs at his throat. "I need to know exactly how much money it takes to buy you off so I can pay you and get my fucking answers." I try to grab hold of him again but he slides off the side of the chair, scooting around the back of it, out of my reach.

"You sold Alex?" Dad says in disbelief from behind me.

Cal exhales a defeated sigh. "I needed the money," he answers croakily, still rubbing his throat, looking past me at dad.

"But I thought you were clear." Dad's tone is imploring. "I paid off your debts. You promised you'd stopped gambling."

"Yeah, well obviously I didn't." Cal stares hard at dad.

My head is swivelling between them both. I feel like an extra in my own fucking show. My eyes settle on my dad. "You knew?" My lips have gone numb.

Dad sits back down with a slump and emits a tired sound. He suddenly seems years older, like they've finally caught up with him.

He looks at up me with sad eyes. "I only knew about the gambling, not about Alex." He shakes his head. "If I'd have known, well it would never have happened." He pulls his lighter out of his shirt pocket and starts turning it over in his hands. "Erin came to me a few months ago in tears. Cal had gambled away everything they had and remortgaged the house without her knowing. They were broke and with the baby coming, well she was desperate. I gave him the money to pay his debts off ... " He looks directly at Cal. "You promised me you'd paid them."

"I did." His shoulders hunch over as he looks down at the carpet and says in a quiet, almost desperate-sounding voice, "I just made new ones."

"Am I the only one who didn't know about his gambling problem?" I bellow, clutching the back of neck with my hand.

"No," Sol says in a disappointed voice from behind me. "I didn't know either."

"I thought I was doing the right thing by keeping you both out of it." My dad looks between Sol and me. "Never in a million years did I think he would do something like this. Jesus Christ, Cal!" My dad shakes his head disconsolately. "How could you do this to Alex?"

"She's a blood sucking Vârcolac for crying out loud!" Cal shouts, getting his gusto back. "Am I the only one that sees that? I really don't see the problem here. She's with her own kind."

I spin around on the spot. "You're a fucking idiot! Is that what you've made yourself believe, to make it acceptable for you to sell her to them?" I grip my head in frustration, pacing the floor. "She doesn't know the likes of them. She can't even hunt fucking animals, let alone … " I shake my head, disconsolately. "She has no concept of the arena you've just dropped her in. She won't survive."

"They won't kill her." He sounds so fucking cocky right now, it's taking everything in me to not pummel him to death.

"No, you're right they won't kill her." Sol's mouth crooks down at one side. "The Originals will just keep her prisoner and force her to have sex with them. They are going to rape her, repeatedly, over and over, so she can breed more of them, for the rest of her life. She'll give them a nice little start to their collection of pure breeds while they conduct tests on her to figure out what makes her so special that she survived the change, so they can replicate her, getting themselves some more Alexes and building themselves the grand fucking army they've longed for, for the last four hundred years."

And I see it. The flicker of emotion in Cal's face. He hadn't actually allowed himself to really consider what he was doing to Alex. He couldn't see past the money and that makes me hate him even more.

Sol has just said everything I already knew they would do to Alex, but hearing it out loud like that is making my gut twist into knots. I need to get her out of there but I don't know how. I've never felt so completely and utterly helpless as I do now, and I've faced some pretty fucked-up situations in my life.

I turn away from Cal. I can't bear to look at him anymore.

"I always knew you were selfish," I say in a low tone, staring out of the window as the remainder of the day sets to fade. "But this ... " I shake my head. "You've really outdone yourself this time, Cal."

I turn back just in time to see the mask sweep down over his face and I know whatever remorse he was feeling is gone, and he's back full of his usual shit and swagger. "I know what this is about," he gives an ironic snort. "The fact you've been desperate to tap up Alex since the moment you laid your eyes on her, and you're just jealous the Originals are gonna get to do what you've never had the balls to do."

I'm moving before I even realise. J jump over the armchair and I'm on him. Whatever self-control I had left is gone. I know it's my hand travelling toward his face. I know it's my knuckles cracking as they crash into his cheekbone. I know I'm punching him repeatedly over and over, but I feel detached from my body, like it's someone else hitting him and I'm just an observer sitting on the periphery, watching.

It's dad that pulls me off him.

And as I'm been dragged backwards, I look down at Cal, seeing my handy work. His face is a mess. He's covered in his own blood. It doesn't make me feel any better. And he's looking back at me with genuine shock in his eyes, like he can't believe I really just beat the crap out of him. I'm only shocked that I lasted this long.

And this is the exact moment I know everything has changed between us forever. We'll never recover from this.

I shake myself free from my dad's hold and sit down on the floor, resting my back against the sofa. I put my head in my hands. Dad leaves the room, muttering he's going to get the first aid kit.

Sol comes and sits down on the floor next to me. "It'll be okay, Nate, we'll find her." He tries to sound sure but I hear the weakness in his voice.

I move my hands away from my face and stare over at Cal. I'm past fighting, now I'm ready to beg. "Please, Cal, just tell me where she is," I implore him with quiet resignation.

Cal bends his leg up, resting his arm on it. "I don't know where she is. I know you won't believe me but it is the truth, and before you ask, I have no idea where Jake lives - he's the blonde one you mentioned - but even if I did, I doubt he'd take her to his house. He's a smart bloke. I know him from the poker games I go to." He pauses, catching a run of blood from his nose before it trickles into his mouth, and wiping it away with his hand. I watch it run off his finger and drip down to the carpet. I look at my own hands and see Cal's blood all over them. I don't wipe them clean.

"Jake heads up the Vârcolac set in this area," Cal continues. "Last night, when I got home, after we'd talked ... well I was frustrated and I needed the money, desperately." He looks down to the floor. "You wouldn't even consider handing her over to them for a reward."

"Why didn't you just tell me?" I ask, my voice rough. "I'd have given you the money, no questions asked. You know that."

Cal snorts, satirical eyes on me. "What, and hear about my failure for the rest of my life from Nathan the fucking war hero? No thanks."

"So you'd rather sell Alex for money," I blast, "than swallow your pride and ask your brother for a loan?" I narrow my hatred at him. "You fucking disgust me."

My words must have some kind of effect on him because he starts talking quickly. "You don't understand, Nate. I owe a lot of money to people who won't wait to be paid, and they won't just come after me, they'll come after Erin and the baby. I panicked and I rang Jake," he shrugs in a helpless way, "but he wanted to see her for himself before he made a call to the Originals, and when I saw you both this morning, and you said you were taking Alex out, it seemed, well ... ideal."

I hammer my fists into the floor, growling out the rage I want to take out on Cal, silencing the room.

Dad comes back in and sits down beside Cal, opening up the first aid kit.

It's a long moment before Cal speaks again. "After you and Alex left, I rang Jake and told him where you'd be. He said he'd transfer the money into my bank account once he had her. Then he hung up." Dad starts to clean the blood from his face.

"Jake been in touch about your money?" I ask bitterly.

"No."

"Looks like you're not getting it then, doesn't it?" I laugh hollowly. "I hope those people you owe the debt to cut you wide open."

"Nathan!" Dad's head snaps around. "He's still your brother, no matter what."

"No." I look Cal in the eye, shaking my head. "Not anymore, he's not. That ended the moment he made that phone call."

Cal wipes his sleeve across his face, hiding whatever look was on there.

I lay my head back on the sofa and stare blankly up at the ceiling.

How am I going to find Alex now? Cal was the only hope I had. An intense feeling of failure grabs me, stinging straight to the bone. All that training I had in the army and here I sit as useless as fuck.

"You want me to take a look at your face?" Dad asks me from across the room.

"No," I answer stonily, unmoving.

"What are we gonna do?" Sol asks in a small voice from beside me. He sounds like a little kid again.

I turn my head to the side, looking at him. "I don't know," I say honestly. "I don't know where to even start looking."

"What about where Cal plays poker?" Sol suggests, a pitch of hope creeping into his voice. "We could go there, ask around."

Cal mutters a disapproving sound, getting to his feet. "Not a good idea," he murmurs in a voice I don't like, a voice that hints at knowing more than I do.

I let my coarse gaze roam over him. "You got any better ideas?" I snap.

He looks to his feet.

"I didn't think so."

Then an idea filters into my mind. A prickle of hope sparks in me. It's a long shot but worth a try. I sit up straight and pull my phone from my pocket and press speed dial on the number of the only other person in the world I know who might be able to help me find her.

The familiar Mancunian accent bellows down the line at me, the background noisy. "Nate, my man! How the hell are you doing? It's been, what, two months since we last spoke?"

"Three," I say. I take a deep breath. "Sorry to interrupt but I need your help."

"Wait a minute," he says at my serious tone. I hear him moving, the noise disappearing, leaving only silence in the background. "Okay, go on."

"My friend, she's in trouble. She's missing, and I only have a short window to find her before things get a whole lot worse."

"How long?"

I glance down at my watch, thinking quickly. It's quarter past six now, they took her at about, what, three, half-three. That bastard Jake said it'd be fourteen hours before the Originals arrived. If I have any hope of saving her then I need to do it before they get to her. I've got under eleven hours.

"Eleven hours at the most."

"Guess I better get a move on then."

"Craig, this is big what I'm asking you to get involved in. It'll put you in a difficult position and … there might be no coming back from it."

"You need my help?" His question is blunt.

"Yeah," I sigh.

"Then I'll be there in just a little over an hour." And the line goes dead.

Courage is not the absence of fear, but rather the judgement that something else is more important than fear.

Ambrose Redmoon

Chapter 19

Spiders Web

I run my fingertips along the bare brick wall, watching in the dark as a fly struggles in vain to free itself from a spider's web in the far corner of the windowless room. I'm locked in but all the fly manages to do is trap itself further.

We're not so different, the fly and me. We're both trapped, we're both as dumb as hell, selfish (well that's just me not the fly), and we've done absolutely nothing to help ourselves from landing into the situation we now find ourselves in. The only current difference between the fly and me is that I'm in a position to set one of us free.

I drag my weary body off the bed, put my bare feet to the tiled floor and, interfering with nature, drag my fingers through the web, freeing the fly. It zooms off in blind panic and flies straight into the wall, knocking itself out, dropping straight to the floor.

Like I said, dumb.

I sit back down on the bed and rest up against the cold wall. Regret steam rollers over me.

I left Nathan there. I ran and left him to fight my battle like the coward I've always known I am. I know he told me to run but I shouldn't have listened. I should have stayed and fought too.

I just can't get the image of him laid there on the ground, battered and bruised, from out of my head. I did that to him. It might not have been my boot coming down on his face but I was the reason it was happening. I'm the reason all bad things happen. I see that now. People who care about me either die, or end up suffering, and I guess me being here, trapped in this hell, is my penance.

Tears slide down my cheeks, dripping off my chin, but I can't move my hand to wipe them away.

My only hope is that Nathan is okay. I won't blame him if he doesn't try to find me. I just pray to god he will, if only so I can tell him how sorry I am.

But even if he does try, he might not be able to find me. I have absolutely no idea where I am.

I was dumped in the boot of the car they dragged me to, my hands bound behind my back with wrist ties. I listened as hard as I could while they drove for anything to tell me where they were taking me, but after a while things went pretty quiet, and I guessed we were where people don't go. Then the boot was opened and a blanket was thrown over me, covering my head before I could get a glimpse of my surroundings, and I was carried from the car, kicking and screaming, and thrown in this hell hole, and here I've been ever since. While it feels like days, it's probably only been hours.

They're waiting for the Originals to arrive. I wonder just how long I have left.

Without warning, horrific images of what is going to happen to me start flashing through my mind, like they're a graphic trailer to a horror story, the one starring me, the one I am already condemned to live, taunting, torturing footage of the living hell that awaits me probably as early as tomorrow.

My body recoils away from my mind. Bile rises in my throat. My whole body goes numb.

Nathan, please find me. Please.

I let my body fall to the side, my back scraping roughly against the wall, until my head meets with the bare mattress.

I don't know if I fell asleep, or simply passed out, but my mind comes around, alert to the sound of the lock turning on the door. I leap to my feet, swaying unsteadily, press my back up against the wall and dig my toes into the mattress.

Light floods the room and the door swings open, revealing Albino.

My skin crawls at the sight of him. Every muscle in my body is tightening.

"How are you enjoying your stay with us so far, Alex?" His eyes drift idly over my body.

I say nothing. Fear has me choked.

He strolls further into the room and casually leans up against the wall directly across from me. "Didn't anyone ever tell you it's rude to ignore your host?" he chides.

I gulp down. I can literally feel the air around him crackling with its negative charge.

When he realises he's getting nothing from me, irritation flickers over his face and the next thing I know he's standing on the bed in front of me. He leans in, pressing his hard body up against mine, pinning me to the wall.

I can smell his vile, hot breath on my face. Feeling sick, I turn my face away from him.

"Let me make this simple for you." He hooks his fingers around my chin, forcing my face back round to his. "You be nice to me and I'll be nice to you." The instructions are simple and clear, as if he's addressing a child.

My stomach flips upside down and inside out, and I have the distinct feeling of an ice cube slithering down my back. Then, from out of nowhere, I garner some courage. "Fuck you," I say in a low voice.

"Now that's more like." His lips twist into a sick smile. "So, I was thinking … " He casts his gaze downwards, relenting ever so slightly allowing him to explore my body. "We have plenty of time before the Originals arrive…" He runs his fingers intimately down my bare arm. "We could make good of it." He puts his lips against my neck and I feel his tongue brush over my skin. I have to stop myself from throwing up. "You are really beautiful, Alex." His hand moves lower. He runs his fingers along the top of my jeans.

Horror settles itself in the pit of my stomach. I quickly consider my options. There aren't many. Give up, or fight back.

Giving up means, well …

Okay, so I'm going down fighting.

"You touch me," I say quietly, with a discreet undercurrent of menace, "and I guarantee it'll be the last thing you ever do."

He pauses, leaving his hands where they are, still on me, and brings his face close to mine, looking me straight in the eye. "Confident words for a girl in your position," he murmurs. I refuse to blink, holding his stare. He opens the button on my jeans. My heart drops down to zero. Then he presses his disgusting lips to mine and yanks down the zip.

I hold my fear back. "Not confident - true," I get out quickly, muffled by his mouth, before he can attempt to kiss me properly. My lips rub against his. I cringe, holding back the urge to bite them hard. "You lay one finger on me and I'll tell the Originals just exactly what you've done to me, and knowing what I already do about them - what my worth is to them - I'm sure they won't want you getting there first." I take a quick breath. "And I'm guessing this isn't part of the deal and isn't double-crossing them a deal breaker, one that can end only ... well, one way ... " I fight to keep my voice steady, using his own words against him.

He moves back, appraising me. A muscle in his jaw twitches. He scratches his cheek in contemplation and steeples his fingers over his mouth.

It's a long silence while he watches me closely, considering my words. I keep a tight hold of my breath and heart, stilling everything inside me, willing this to work, because if it doesn't, I can't bear to think what's going to happen to me.

"So I brought you a present," he says, moving his hand from his mouth, his voice suddenly bizarrely cheerful.

He jumps down from the bed and strides over to the door.

My legs nearly buckle under the weight of my relief. I grip the wall with my fingertips for support and quickly fasten my jeans.

"I'm guessing you haven't fed in a while," he continues, "so I've brought you something to eat. You can thank me later." He gives me a diffident wave of his hand and I watch as his lips curl up. "Can't have my girl going hungry now, can I?"

I move across the wall, levitating on my fingertips, trying to put more distance between us. "I'm not hungry," I say, keeping my voice even.

I am. I'm starving, but I've got the very distinct feeling the food he'll be putting on offer will not be the same as Nathan's.

"Au contraire, my darling," he winks knowingly at me, "you're very hungry. I can tell. And I also know you've never tasted human blood in your short little life. I can smell that rotting animal blood your shifter's been feeding you on, like you're drenched in it. You can deny your hunger all you want but you won't last another hour, and that works perfectly for me." He pauses, rubbing his index finger over his incisor. He looks like he's trying to sharpen it to his fang. "The Originals will be here in three hours and by then you'll be looking fit and healthy for them." He leans his head out the open door. "Jin, bring Alex her gift now."

I almost know what's coming next and it's confirmed a nanosecond later when I hear the deafening cries of a young girl.

The Asian guy who was with Albino earlier strolls into the room, dragging along a dark-haired girl of about seventeen - eighteen at the most - with him. She looks terrified. Her face is streaked with tears. Jin pushes her forwards, straight in my direction. She stumbles, falling to her knees on the hard floor.

My initial reaction is to go to help her. I'm down and off the bed, pulling her to her feet. "Are you okay? Have they hurt you?" I say quickly.

She shakes her head and I don't know if she means she's not okay or that they haven't hurt her. I don't push it further. I just go with the latter.

"Aww, now would you look at this, Jin. Alex is getting to know her dinner. Sweet, isn't it?"

The girl's confused eyes flicker in my direction. I step back away from her.

"I fucking hate you!" I spit at Albino.

He moves so quickly, and hits me so hard in my face, that it knocks me off my feet, sending me flying backwards. I crash against the wall and nearly bite my tongue in two as my jaw spasms in shock. Blood floods my mouth.

It takes me a moment to find myself. Dazed, I struggle to my feet, using the wall for support. I swallow my blood down.

Albino's calm is long gone. His eyes are flaring and his shoulders are rising and falling with each angry breath he takes. He grabs hold of the girl by her arm and drags her over to me. She cries, struggling, but he's unyielding. Then I see the blade glint in the light as he pulls it out from the back of his trouser pocket and, without flinching, he slices her arm open, cutting clean around it in one fluid movement.

She screams, a gut-wrenching scream. I cover my hand with my mouth, horror-stricken. Her panicked, helpless eyes flick to me, then down at her arm. She passes out. Her body goes slack but he keeps her held up by her arm, showing no effort whatsoever, leaving her limp body hanging in the air like a puppet on a string, her brown hair draped across her young face.

And I can only watch in horror and fascination as her blood trickles to the tiled floor, sitting in a pool by my bare feet.

The second the smell hits me, my fangs are out and I'm consumed.

It's like nothing I have every smelt before. If I thought animal blood smelt good, it's been like having a lifetime of Cava only to discover Dom Perignon.

Albino runs his index finger through the blood on her arm, momentarily breaking its flow, and places it in his mouth. Even the grotesque sucking noise he makes doesn't break my focus.

"Drug free, even better," he says in a sick-sounding voice. "Surprising for a skank like her."

But his words are just a dull buzzing sound. All I can see and smell is her blood. It's my only focus as it runs like strawberry juice down her arm.

I've never wanted anything so badly. I thought I wanted Nathan; that was nothing in comparison.

"It tastes as good as it smells," he tantalises me, his voice soft and silky as he moves the girls arm up closer to me, her body floating like it's somehow detached from her arm. "Why don't you try some?"

The ache in me intensifies. I've never felt this before. It's unyielding, all-controlling, and I'm moving closer to the blood before I know it, my hand itching to reach out and take hold of her arm.

Albino is whispering words I can't hear anymore. The monster is talking to me, ruling my domain, telling me just one little taste won't hurt anyone. The girl is already cut and bleeding, the blood is dripping wastefully onto the floor. It's not like she needs it anymore and all I have to do is reach out and ...

Remember who you are.

Hot unaccountable emotion slaps me hard across the face and, for a split-second, I actually think Nathan's here. My heart searches the room, it wilting when I realise it was all in my mind.

I recoil backwards, covering my mouth with my hands again. "I won't do it," I cry, "I won't be like you!"

His eyes narrow to slits. He releases his hold on the girl, dropping her to the floor before me. He steps over her still body like she's nothing, backing me up to the wall, and puts a hand either side of my head, trapping me.

He leans his face in close. "Yes, you will, Alex." There's no bargaining in his tone. "Play nice with her before you feed on her or don't, I don't give a fuck. But you will feed. You will become a true Vârcolac before the Originals see you, not some animal-fed half-breed. I'll be back in an hour, and if she's still alive, I'll feed her to you myself." He pushes himself off the wall with his hands.

My body is shaking and I can't stop it showing. He turns, walking around the girl, stops and turns back. I see something flicker across his face, like something very significant has just occurred to him. The hairs on my scalp tingle, and a shiver shoots down my spine when I see the smile he gives himself.

He takes a step back toward me. "On second thoughts, don't kill her." He scratches his nose. "Feed, but leave her with enough blood to keep her alive. I'm interested to see if you can change her to be like you. And try your best, Alex, because it'll be real nice for me to have another bargaining chip to play with." He smiles, an oddly pleasant smile, displaying just the level of psycho he truly is.

I wrap my arms protectively around myself, and lowering my trembling voice, say, "Nathan will find me, and when he does, he'll tear you to pieces."

"I look forward to it," he replies, his voice gentle, almost flirtatious, but his eyes are as cold as ice. And with that he breezes out of the door, Jin in tow. The thick metal door closes with a clang. I hear the lock turn, trapping me in here with the girl, the girl who has blood oozing out of her arm.

I run at the door, hammering against it with my fists. "Let me out!" I scream. "Don't do this! Let me out! Please!"

But all I hear is the cackles of their callous laughter as they walk away from the sound of my pointless pleas.

I rest my forehead head against the door, tears rolling down my face, as I continue to bang my hands in vain against it.

Then I hear the girl groan as she starts to come round. The pain must immediately have set into her consciousness because she starts screaming in agony again. "Help me!" she cries out. "I'm bleeding real bad! You gotta help me!"

Slowly I turn to face her. She's sitting on the floor, her arm pressed tightly up against her chest. Her blood is seeping into her white cami. She looks up at my face and in this moment I realise my fangs are still out, but it's too late. I see the horror stretch across her tiny features when she realises what I am, or what she thinks I am, the thing her nightmares are made of.

Only she doesn't realise this nightmare is mine, not hers.

She starts to scream, an ear-piercing scream. She scrabbles backwards across the room, away from me.

I clap my hand over my mouth, pinching my nostrils, cutting off the scent, stopping it flooding in, trying to hide my monstrous fangs. Sinking to the floor, I turn my face toward the door, trying to block her and her blood out.

I won't do this. I won't become one of them. I'm not a monster. I'm not.

But I was wrong earlier. I'm not like that fly at all. I'm not the innocent here. I'm the spider and the girl, well, she's the fly.

Chapter 20

Hold Your Breath

The girl has stopped screaming. It petered out after a few minutes when she realised I wasn't actually intending to kill her. She's been quiet for a while now. I'm still sitting on the floor next to the door, knees up, arms wrapped around them, my nose and mouth buried between my knees as I try to hide from the smell of the girls' blood.

I'm taking small clipped breaths when my lungs force me to, trying to inhale any other smell I can.

I can still smell Nathan on my clothes. He's filling the hollow places inside me. I'm trying to focus on him, on his face, on his dry laugh, on the way he looked right before he kissed me, on the way he kissed me.

But no matter how I try to block it out, the smell of her blood is everywhere and so overpowering I feel like I've showered in it. It's like trying to breathe under water.

My hope for Nathan rescuing me is starting to dwindle. I could be anywhere and, with each ticking minute, the Originals' arrival edges closer, foreshadowing my inevitable fate.

My insides shrivel up at the thought.

"Are you going to kill me?" Her tiny voice carries over from the other side of the room.

It takes all my strength to raise my head and shake it. I look at her from out of the corner of my eye. She doesn't look good. She's lost too much blood. The wound needs sealing and I'm going to have to help her. If I want to staunch the smell of her blood, this is going to be the only way to do it.

Taking a quick breath in, I sit up straight, take hold of the hem of my vest and rip it up the side. Then I tear it all the way around, exposing my stomach and my scar, leaving me with half a vest but freeing a decent piece of black fabric for her to use.

I throw it across the room. It lands on the floor beside her feet. She glances down at it and up at me, her eyes confused. "What do you want me to do with that?" And for the first time I register her accent. It's Teesside. I must be there or somewhere near there.

Pressing my lips together, I motion a tying movement around my own forearm.

"Ahh right." She nods. Leaning forward, she picks the fabric up off the floor and tries to tie it around her arm over the cut, struggling to fasten it with one hand.

"Can you help me?" she asks.

For fuck's sake.

She's obviously past worrying I'm going to hurt her but she needs to be wary of me. I might not want to hurt her, and will do everything in my power to ensure I don't, but soon it might be out of my control.

"I can't," I say quickly.

"Why?"

"You want me to kill you?"

Her eyes widen. "No." She shakes her head vehemently.

I take another quick breath. "If I come near you and your bleeding arm, that could be a big possibility."

"Oh," she says. I see the understanding line her eyes.

She bends her knee up, lays the strip of my vest on it, rests her wounded arm on top, folds one piece over with her hand and slides the other under. She keeps hold of one end and leans forward, taking hold of the other end with her teeth. Then I hear her take a deep breath and count to three between her gritted teeth. She pulls the fabric as tightly as she can. I see her face redden and grimace as she lets out a cry of pain.

She brings her arm up to her chest, holding it with her other hand, breathing heavily. When her breathing finally slows, she simply says, "Thanks."

Keeping my lips pressed tightly together, I force something resembling a smile.

But it hasn't helped. The scent of her blood is still floating all around me. I cover my mouth with my hand again, pinching my nose with my thumb and forefinger, and start to pray for a miracle.

"What's your name?" she asks.

I close my eyes and picture Nathan's face. "Alex," I answer through my hand.

"Mine's Scarlett," she offers when she realises I have no intention of asking.

I remain silent, but I can almost feel the questions she wants to ask me hanging in the air, so I'm not surprised when she asks in a tentative voice, "What ... are ... you?"

I open my eyes and move my hand away from my mouth, exhaling loudly. "You don't want to know."

I see her eyes flicker to the scar on my side, then back to my fangs.

"Are you ... like ... a vampire, or something?"

Before I even get the chance to figure out how to answer that question, I hear a noise, a gunshot. I spin around, pressing my ear up to the door and let my hearing go wide.

"Is someone out there?" Scarlett whispers, hearing it too. She gets to her feet and starts to move across the room toward me.

"Don't come near me!" I order in a quiet voice, holding my hand out to stop her.

"Sorry," she murmurs, backing up. She goes to sit down on the edge of the bed.

I can hear shouting. There's a mixture of male voices and more gun shots. Are the Originals here? But why would they be shooting guns?

Guns. Nathan likes guns. Is he here? Has he found me?

I try to listen again for his voice in the mix, but my pulse is beating so loudly in my ears I can barely focus.

Well whoever it is, and whatever is happening out there, it's not good, and if by a big chance it isn't Nathan, then I need to get out of here, now, and I'm gonna have to take the girl with me.

But the only way out of this room is through this locked metal door.

My eyes start to scan the room looking for something to pry the door open with. The bed's a metal frame. Maybe I could use something off it, one of the legs? I guess it's worth a try.

As I'm about to get up, I hear movement down the end of hall, the sound of footsteps coming downstairs. I hold my breath and listen intently. It's just one person, male, and they're slowly making their way toward us.

Quietly I rise to my feet and start to step back away from the door. My heart is thrumming in my chest. Turning to Scarlett, I put my finger to my lips, indicating for her to be quiet, and motion for her to get up off the bed.

She gets up slowly, her eyes flickering in the direction of the door. "Is someone coming?" she mouths to me.

I nod.

"Alex are you down here?"

My heart leaps up into my throat as I spin around on the spot. "Sol?"

"Alex?"

"I'M IN HERE!" I yell, running to the door, banging my fists against it.

The door rattles from the outside as Sol tries to open it. "NATE, SHE'S DOWN HERE!"

Nathan's here. My heart nearly implodes.

"NATHAN!" I cry.

"He's coming." Sol's warm voice echoes through the metal door. "We're gonna get you out of here. Just try to stay calm. Are you okay?"

"I'm fine ... I just ... "

"Alex." Hearing Nathan's voice causes my throat to thicken with emotion.

"Nathan," I choke as tears of relief spill from my eyes.

"Are you okay?" he asks, voice soft. I can almost envision his hand on the door, his nose touching the metal as he speaks to me through it.

"I'm okay," I wipe my runny nose on the back of my hand, "but I'm not alone, There's a girl in here with me and he cut her. She's bleeding, Nathan, and she needs help." The words are tumbling out of my mouth.

"He was trying to make me feed on her but I haven't, I swear. But please, Nathan, you've got to get me out."

"It's okay," he soothes. I can feel his heat and strength, and silent power radiating through the door. "I'm gonna get you out. Sol, you got anything with you that I can use to pick this lock 'cause I can't see us getting through this door any other way, not unless you've got a stick of dynamite, that is?" I hear Nathan's hand tap against the dense metal door and the almost-humour in his voice.

"This do you?" Sol replies. I can practically hear his smile.

There's an approving chuckle from Nathan. It coats my insides, warming them. The desire to be near him is overwhelming.

"I don't even wanna know why you've got one of these." Nathan chuckles again, then says to me, "I'll have you out in a sec."

I step back away from the door as I hear Nathan start to fiddle with the lock.

"Don't worry," I say, turning to Scarlett. "Nathan's gonna get us out."

"Your boyfriend?" she asks, moving a touch closer to me.

I cast a surprised glance her way, feeling a lurch in my stomach.

I stare back at the door, wrapping my arms around myself, well aware that Nathan is on the other side listening, and just shrug a response. I can't answer because Nathan and I haven't got that far, yet.

Chapter 21

Who Knew

The lock clicks open less than a minute later. Relief overwhelms me at the sight of Nathan.

He closes the distance between us in a few strides, and just when I think he's going to pull me into his arms and take me away from all of this, his eyes flicker down to my torn vest, my dirty jeans, my bare feet, and to the blood that is laying in small pools all over the floor.

He stops, holding himself in check. His eyes come back to mine, afraid, and I see the grotesque image flicker through them.

"Did they … " his voice is rough, affected, " … hurt you?" He's deathly still except for the tremble of emotion I see rippling under his skin.

My eyes fill with tears. "He tried," I wrap my arms around myself. Nathan's face hardens with anger. "But I talked my way out of it," I add, my voice quiet. "He didn't. No one has." I shake my head again as I rub away my salty tears and gulp down.

Nathan steps close to me, his boots flush with my bare toes. He lifts his hand slowly to my face and cups my chin. His touch so light, it's like he's afraid to touch me.

"I'm so sorry," he murmurs. Tilting his forehead against mine, he looks deep into my eyes.

I breathe him in. "You've nothing to be sorry for. I'm the one who should be sor … " He cuts me off with a kiss.

I crumble into him, wrapping my arms around his neck. The warmth of his body casts away any lingering chill I had. His arms go around me and he lifts me off my feet, holding me tight to him. But the kiss is far too brief and he rests me back down, moving his lips from mine. "You should feed," he says, almost as if he can taste my hunger.

"There's no animal blood here. Only human." I cast a glance back at Scarlett and see Sol is standing with her examining the wound on her arm. I was so caught up in Nathan momentarily, I forgot they were even here.

A smile lilts Nathan's face like a tune as he slips his hand into the inside of his jacket and pulls out a small flask filled with blood.

I breathe a sigh of relief, feeling my quivering lips crack into a smile. I'm so torn between laughing and crying right now.

Taking the flask from his hands, I can't drink its contents quickly enough. But I instantly know something's wrong. It's not working like it normally does. It hasn't satisfied my hunger at all. I run my tongue around my mouth, trying to savour the taste, but it makes no difference.

What's going on?

My mind whirs. Then a thought clicks. I've been exposed to human blood, I'm still exposed to it, and now it seems, animal blood isn't quite enough to curb my appetite.

This is bad. I can't let Nathan know.

Maybe once I'm away from here, away from Scarlett's blood, I'll feel better. It's not like I've tasted any human blood, so I'll be fine. I know I will.

"How bad is the girl's cut?" Nathan asks Sol.

I hand the empty flask back to Nathan and turn around to them.

"She's gonna need stitches," Sol answers.

I look at Sol, smiling appreciatively, glad that he's here. But he meets my eyes with a hardness in his and it shocks me. I stare at him, confused, but now he won't look at me. I want to ask him if he's okay, ask him what's wrong, but something stops me.

"We can't take you to the hospital," Nathan tells Scarlett, his deep voice rumbling over me. "There'd be too many questions that we can't answer. I'll have to fix you up myself when we get back home."

"You're taking me with you?" she sounds surprised. I'm not. I think Nathan's set on turning the farm into a halfway house for Vârcolac refugees.

"Well, we're not gonna leave you here," Nathan says stonily.

Taking hold of me by my hand, he leads me out of my prison, Sol and Scarlett following behind, into the darkened hallway.

The four of us move quickly down the hall and up the stairs. The door at the top is wide open, letting in a stream of light. Nathan goes through first, me behind, and I find myself in another hallway. This one is much nicer.

The marble floor is freezing cold beneath my feet, and for the first time I realise I'm in a house, a big house, a mansion if the length and swankiness of this hallway is anything to go by.

We all continue down the hallway in silence, passing by old looking paintings that look like they belong in a museum.

As we near the end of the hall, Nathan slows me to a stop. Sol carries on, leading Scarlett past us.

I watch them go, puzzled, then bring my eyes back to Nathan.

"There's something you need to know," he says. Worry trickles down my spine. "Cal is here."

His words drop with a loud thud into my head. I take a step back from him, pulling my hand free. "What?" The word trembles out.

"I didn't want him here either but we needed the numbers. He wanted to help and it made sense." Nathan moves closer to me and tries to take hold of my hand again, but I snatch it away.

"And you trusted him?!"

He nods, not moving his eyes from mine.

"Then you're an idiot!" I start to back away from him. "How could you bring him here?" My look is incredulous but my tone is pure hurt. "He's the reason I'm here, the reason that I was nearly raped by that bastard!"

Nathan looks like I've just hit him.

Then the need to get out of here, and far away from Cal, becomes urgent. I turn to bolt but Nathan's quick and he grabs hold of me from behind, hooking his arm around my stomach, lifting me off the floor, holding me tightly to him.

"I'm sorry," he says urgently into my ear. His other arm goes around me, holding me tighter. "Alex, everything I've done, every decision I've made in the last ten hours, I've done with the sole intention of getting you out of here." His tone is suddenly all military. "And I don't regret one decision I've made because I've got you here with me, safe and in one piece. And, honestly, it's a good job Cal was with us because there were ten of them and five of us. Any less and we might not have made it."

"Five?" I do a quick mental count: Nathan, Sol, Cal, and Jack, I'm guessing. So, who's number five? "Who else did you bring - Eddie?" I smart, yanking his arms off me. Dropping lithely to my feet, I turn around to face him.

He gives me a look. "Craig."

"Craig - your army friend? The one whose life you saved?"

He nods. "He's the reason I was able to find you." He rakes his fingers through his hair and sighs, a tired sound. Then he moves in, taking my face in his hands. "I'm sorry it had to be this way, really I am." His apology blows over my skin. "But don't mistake this and think I'm okay with Cal, because I'm not. We're done." I close my eyes into a long blink and I feel Nathan's lips against mine. "Are we okay?" he murmurs.

All my anger just dissipates. "Yes," I breathe. And I'm just about to indulge in him when he moves away, my hand in his, him leading me forward.

Rounding the corner I find myself in huge entrance hall. There's a double sweeping staircase opening up to my immediate right and a chandelier hanging from the high ceiling above.

Cal turns as we approach. I can't even bring myself to look at him. Sol and Scarlett are with him, then I see Craig.

He looks nothing like I expected. He has short mousy brown hair that has a natural curl to it that he clearly tries to hide with the cut. He's about 6'4" and wide, built of pure muscle. And I instantly know he isn't a shapeshifter, which surprises me. Nathan never said either way, I just assumed. But I do know what he is - natural instinct, I guess, and that's what surprises me most - that he's here helping me escape.

Craig walks toward us. "I'm real glad to see you're okay, Alex." He smiles broadly at me, showing a set of perfectly lined teeth any movie star would kill for.

"Thanks." Then the words are out of my mouth before my brain has a chance to consider them. "You're a werewolf." My voice comes out in a wisp, like a gasp.

I move closer to Craig, leaving Nathan's side, and I can't explain it, but I have this inexplicable sensation inside of me which is drawing me to him, and it's not just simple curiosity. I feel like I already know him, like I've already met him, it's the weirdest thing.

A light smile crinkles up the corners of his eyes. "And you're wondering why I'm here."

I nod slowly, remembering it was the werewolves who saved the Originals. They were the ones who raised them after the vampires had killed their parents and, from the story Nathan told me, I got the distinct impression there is still a strong allegiance there. I wonder if Craig's the reason Nathan knows so much about Vârcolacs.

Craig scratches the back of his head, casting a brief glance at Nathan behind me. "Let's just say we don't all agree with the Originals idea of a better world and how to achieve it. And, of course, I owe this one here, big time." He nods in Nathan's direction.

I know there's something he's not telling me and that Nathan knows exactly what that is.

"Well, thank you," I say, "for helping Nathan find me."

He smiles warmly. It's so warm I can almost feel the heat radiating off him.

"My dad not back with the car yet?" Nathan asks. I can hear the edge of urgency in his voice

"No." Craig shakes his head, glancing at his watch.

I turn to Nathan. "Where is Jack?"

"He went to get the car. We couldn't drive up to the house 'cause they would have heard us, so we had to leave it about half a mile back. We came in through the woods up back on foot."

"Maybe we should start on foot?" Sol suggests. "Meet Dad coming."

Nathan nods. Looking back at me, he says, "You go with Sol and the girl. I'll follow soon, I just need to torch this place."

"Why?" I ask, puzzled.

"Because we need to rid the house of your scent so the Originals have nothing to track you on, and it'll get rid of the bodies."

I glance around but can't see any bodies and, wouldn't you know it, just as I think it, I catch sight of a boot sticking out from behind a door over to my right. Attached to the boot, a leg. Oh God. I've never seen a dead body before. The hairs on my scalp prickle, causing a chill to slowly tiptoe its way down my back.

No, actually, I'm glad, and I hope its Albino's dead body that is attached to the rest of that dead leg.

"Are they all dead?" I ask, needing the reassurance from him that Albino is really dead.

"If you're referring to our blonde friend," he says knowingly, "then yeah, I pulled the trigger myself."

Relief swims into me, coating my insides. Then out of nowhere I get this weird sense of foreboding. Panic slides down my spine, trickling its chill into my stomach, and all I'm left with is a feeling of impending doom.

I look at Nathan, wide eyed.

"Hey, it's okay," he soothes, mistaking my panic for fear over the dead bodies. He takes me by the shoulders, levelling our eyes. "Get out of here, go with Sol and the girl, and meet Dad. Me, Craig and Cal, will light this place up and then I'll be with you."

Something's deep inside is telling me I shouldn't leave him. "No I want to stay with you."

He shakes his head. "And I want you out of here. Go with Sol and I promise I'll be with you in five." He brushes stray tendrils of my hair off my forehead.

Even though everything inside me is telling otherwise, I find myself making a noise of consent.

Nathan leans forward and presses his lips to my forehead. Something about the way he kisses me gives off an air of finality. I try to reassure myself he'll be fine, it'll all be fine. He'll be out of here in five minutes and we'll be together. But try as I might, I can't free myself from the worry gripping me.

He tries to move away but I cling onto his jacket with my fingertips, keeping him close. He kisses my forehead one more time, looks down at me and gives me a heartbreaking smile. "Five minutes. Now go," he orders, flicking his eyes in the direction of the open front door.

Reluctantly, I break away, turning for the door, and I catch Sol's eyes on us. They clear the instant mine meet with his, but it's too late. I saw it. I saw the longing. And then it all suddenly makes sense. It's like someone's just switched all the lights on, and I wonder how I never realised before.

I open my mouth to speak but Sol shakes his head gently. His disconcerted eyes flicker to Nathan and back to me. Swallowing against my words, I close my mouth, pressing my lips together in a tight line.

Sol ushers Scarlett toward the door. I move quickly, following behind. I catch hold of his arm. "Sol ... "

He turns, his face blank, but his eyes tell a different story. "What?"

"Are you okay?"

"I'm fine."

Lowering my voice to a whisper, I say, "We should ... talk." I glance around but Nathan, Craig and Cal have already disappeared somewhere into the house. There's only me, Sol and Scarlett left, and she's hanging back, pretending she hasn't a clue what's going on, and after what's she's witnessed tonight, I could almost believe it to be true.

"Why?" He lifts his voice, trying to look confused, like he doesn't know what I'm talking about, but I know better.

"Sol, don't ... "

He sighs. Putting his hand up to his head he ruffles his hair, keeping his eyes fixed on mine. He looks almost angry and I'm not sure if it's with me or himself. "It doesn't matter," he says, deep and coarse.

I look at him, stunned. "Of course it matters." Does he think I can carry on and pretend I don't know how he feels about me?

"No, it doesn't. Nathan's my brother and that's all that matters."

"I know but we can't just ignore this." How is he going to feel when he sees me and Nathan together? How am I going to feel knowing what I know?

"That's exactly what we're gonna do," he says low, eyes deep with meaning, "because whatever I might feel for you is nothing in comparison to how much I love my brother."

Something like grief catches in my throat. I try to swallow past it but it won't go. I open my mouth to speak but he's already turned from me and is walking out of the door, down the steps and into the night.

I follow him out, not ready to let this go yet. There's more I need to say. Then I see the blur move from out of the shadows. I cry out his name but I'm too late.

And I can only watch in complete horror as Jin sinks his teeth deep into Sol's neck, tearing out his throat.

Chapter 22

The Lost One

"NO!" I scream.

Sol drops to his knees as Jin releases his hold on him, blood gushing out of his neck, running everywhere, soaking into his clothes. He looks at me, panic and confusion swilling around his eyes. Then something in them fades and he drops to the floor.

"SOL!"

Scarlett grabs my arm from behind and tries to pull me towards the house. I stagger back, tripping on my own feet, unable to move my eyes away from Sol.

Jin steps over Sol. I lift my eyes to him to see his sinister ones chasing us down, his sights clearly set on Scarlett.

"GO!" I yell. Turning, I push Scarlett into the house. Then I hear the gunshot.

I spin around.

I see a hole in Jin's chest where his heart used to be. The gun goes off again. Jin's body jolts like he's being electrocuted and I see Nathan striding toward him, gun held high and aimed straight as he empties the clip into Jin's chest until he drops to the floor with a thud.

Everything pauses to catch its breath. The gun in Nathan's hand drops, clattering to the floor, then we're both running to Sol.

I drop to my knees beside them. Sol's alive. I can hear his weak heart beating but he's struggling to breathe. I can hear the gargle in his throat as his own blood chokes him. He's drowning in it. *Oh God, no.*

"Sol." Nathan turns his face carefully round to us. I gasp, choking on tears at the gaping hole in his neck. Nathan puts his hands over the wound, trying to stem the blood flow. "HELP!" Nathan cries, desperation and panic overtaking his voice. "HELP US!" Lowering his voice, he moves closer to Sol, "Come on, wake up. You need to wake up."

Cal and Craig come running out of the house seconds later.

"Oh God!" Cal cries, dropping down beside him. "What happened?"

"Jin," I say sobbing, "he came out of nowhere."

Craig reaches down and pries Nathan's bloody hands off Sol's neck. The look on his face says it all.

Sol coughs, coming round. "Nate," he groans.

"I'm here, I got you." Nathan holds him closer.

Cal's hands are hovering over Sol like he doesn't know which part of him to touch first.

Tears drip down from my chin.

Sol coughs again, choking. Blood trickles out of his mouth. His heart rapidly slows, beating intermittently. "Oh no, no!" Nathan grips hold of Sol's face with his hand, trying to hold him here with his eyes alone. "You stay with me, you hear? You're not leaving me, you hear me?" A sob breaks somewhere deep inside of Nathan.

Sol's eyes focus in on him, "Tell Dad ... " but the words never come. And I watch as the life in Sol's eyes fades, the exact moment I hear his heart stop beating.

Chapter 23

I Am Not There

You would think with the loss I have endured in my life that it would have prepared me for when it happens again. It hasn't.

Losing Sol hasn't even broken through my consciousness yet, and still it's complete and utter agony.

And to have to watch on the sidelines as Nathan suffers in the worst kind of way is crippling me. He won't let me help me. He blames me for Sol's death. He's hasn't said this exactly, he hasn't said anything to me at all. He's cut me off. It seems to him I no longer exist.

I wish he'd shout at me, blame me. He'd be right to. Sol is dead because of me, another casualty of my existence, like Carrie.

These words are fast becoming an echo of mine. An echo I have to silence.

I wish I could rewind to that moment. I'd tell Sol what he means to me. I may not have felt exactly for him what he felt for me, but it was somewhere close. He was my friend. I loved him. And now he's gone.

If I could change everything, I would. I'd go back to the beginning. I'd trade places with Sol and Carrie, whatever it would take to bring them both back here as they're meant to be.

Scarlett draws in a sharp breath, catching my attention. I glance up to see Craig pushing a sewing needle into her skin. He's stitching up her wound. There's no anaesthetic except for the large glass of whiskey he gave her which she downed the moment her fingers curled around it.

We're in the living room at home, Scarlett, Craig and I. Scarlett and Craig are sitting on the sofa while he stitches her up. I'm perched on the edge of the chair at the other side of the room, keeping a safe distance from them both, well a safe distance from Scarlett's blood. The smell is intense. And my hunger, for the moment it seems, isn't ready to wane.

Craig has suggested I go upstairs, take a break, while he stitches Scarlett up. I declined. I don't think he trusts me around her. So far, I'd say she is the only thing he can trust me with. I was locked in a room with Scarlett and I didn't touch her or her blood once.

I need to be here. I need to remind myself human blood is off limits, no matter what. If I hide from it, it will only weaken me to future exposure. The more exposure the better until I have dulled this ache into indifference.

And, really, I don't want to be any further away from Nathan or Sol than necessary. I'm not ready. Not yet.

Nathan's in the kitchen with Jack and Cal. Sol's body is resting on the table.

Nothing feels real anymore. My head hurts. It's filled with too much noise. Thoughts are whizzing past but I have no wish to pin any of them down. And I can feel Nathan's grief and anger emanating through the wall that separates us as clear as if we were in the same room.

Craig's finished with Scarlett. I see her arm is now covered up with a bandage and she sits quietly staring off into space. I feel a powerful wave of sympathy for her. She's just a young girl thrown into a situation she didn't ask to be in. We're not so dissimilar in that respect.

Craig is tidying up around her. None of us is speaking. There's nothing to be said. But the silence is blistering, almost as blistering as the heat that poured from the mansion when Craig threw the match that lit it up like an inferno. I only wish I'd been there to see it burn down to the ground.

I look at Scarlett again. She's so weak and vulnerable. I feel like she's my responsibility now but, honestly, I can't even look after myself let alone a severely distressed, potentially damaged-for-life teenage girl. I don't think I can take on that responsibility.

I hear movement in the kitchen. My whole body tenses. I grip the chair edge with my hands. The door opens and Nathan comes into the living room. I catch sight of Jack sitting beside Sol's body. The sight will haunt me forever.

Nathan quietly pushes the door to a close. His hair hanging across his face, he wraps his arms around his chest. The longing I feel for him is unbearable.

"We're going to bury Sol here," he says quietly, not addressing any of us in particular, "out back in the forest. He loved it there so … " His voice breaks. He rubs both hands over his face roughly, pressing his palms into his eyes and blows out a breath.

Without thinking, I get to my feet, wanting to go to him, but stop, holding myself in check.

Nathan drops his hands by his sides and clears his throat, almost self-consciously, like he's embarrassed to have shown emotion in front of us. "I'm going to dig a grave now." His voice is suddenly business-like, hard, and he starts backing away, heading for the door.

I feel a rush of panic. I don't want him to go. I want to fix this. Fix him.

"No, mate, you don't want to be doing that," Craig says, stopping

Nathan in his tracks. "I'll do it."

Nathan looks at him, gratefully. "You're sure?"

Craig nods.

"There's a big oak tree just up the front of the forest. It's got an open clearing right behind it. That's where Dad wants it."

"I know where you mean. I got it, mate." Craig pats him on the shoulder as he passes by, leaving the room.

I expect Nathan to follow but he stays put, his eyes fixed firmly on the floor.

My eyes search over Nathan with utter desperation. You could hear a pin drop in here. The air is thick with unsaid words, mainly mine. I'm afraid to speak and say the wrong thing. If I do, I could push him even further away than he already is.

Scarlett clears her throat. I've forgotten she is here. "Sorry, but I erm ... I need to use the bathroom."

"Upstairs, second on your left," Nathan says flatly.

Scarlett stops by the door. "I'm real sorry about your brother."

He looks up at her, and nods.

Scarlett has just said the one thing I've been terrified of saying for the last two hours. I'm sorry. Just as easy as that. But then she stands to lose nothing.

And now it's just me and Nathan, and a thick wall of silence.

My whole body is shaking with nerves. "Nathan ... " my voice breaks. He brings cold eyes to meet mine. I wrap my arms around myself, trying to hold off the chill. "I'm so sorry," A tear trickles down my face. I wipe it away with my wrist. "I wish more than anything it was me in there and not..."

"Pack your stuff," he cuts me off, voice emotionless. "We're leaving straight after the funeral." He slams the door so hard it rattles everything in here, including me.

I stay still for a long moment then I hear Erin arrive. Her cries ring painfully in my ears.

With wretchedness crushing my chest, I force myself to move. I go upstairs, into my bedroom for the last time, and begin packing my things.

* * *

It's dawn and a fog is laid thin over the ground like rising ghosts. I'm stood at the edge of Sol's open grave with the others. My throat is thick and I'm striving to fight the tears, not feeling I have the right to cry.

Jack clears his rough throat. "Do not stand at my grave and weep." His voice is as still as a break in the breeze. "I am not there. I do not sleep. I am a thousand winds that blow. I am the diamond glints on snow. I am the sunlight on ripened grain. I am the gentle autumn rain. When you awaken in the morning's hush, I am the swift uplifting rush of quiet birds in circled flight. I am the soft stars that shine at night. Do not stand at my grave and cry. I am not there. I did not die."

Unable to hold the tears back anymore, I let them go. Then I sense Nathan's stare on me. Looking up through my damp eyes, I let them meet with his.

His stare slices into me, through flesh and bone, straight to my heart. I hold myself still as the pain rolls in sharp waves over my skin, covering every inch of me. I see the resentment clear in his eyes and know unequivocally he wishes it was me down there in that grave.

And I can't say I disagree with him.

Chapter 24

The Unknown

That was the second funeral I've ever been to. I don't intend to go to another.

I've put my things into Nathan's Range Rover and I am standing outside it waiting for him. He's still with Jack and Cal at Sol's grave, saying their final goodbyes. Craig and Erin are inside the house.

When I first arrived back, I went in to collect my things and to check on Scarlett. She was sleeping. After I had cleared my room out, I put her in my bed to sleep. She was exhausted and I guess for as long as she's staying here, it should be her room. I no longer need it.

I hear the back door open and look up to see Craig coming over to me.

"You okay?" he asks.

"Yeah." I twist my hands together in front of me.

"Do you know where you're going?"

"No." I shake my head.

It's only me and Nathan leaving. Everyone else is staying put. Craig told me. He thought I already knew. I pretended to, but I know he could see right through me. I'd just assumed we would all be leaving. It was dumb of me. They don't need to leave. The Originals aren't looking for them. They're looking for me. The Originals know nothing of their involvement. Anyone who could have led them here is dead. But still, it's not safe for them if I stay. If I leave, they're all safe.

Nathan's only coming with me because he feels I'm his responsibility.

And I'm letting him because I'm weak. I'm well aware I'm no longer his preferred travelling partner. He just wants to get me as far away as possible from what's left of his family. He's right. He's doing what I should have done a long time ago. And I assume once Nathan has me settled somewhere, he'll come back home and get on with his life. But I can't think about that, not yet.

I sense Nathan and look over to see him coming toward us with purpose in his stride.

"Time for me to go." I offer a weak smile to Craig.

"Did you get your cooler bag with your blood in?" Craig asks.

"Oh, no, I forgot."

"I'll go get you it." He smiles.

"Thanks," I say after him.

Without a word or a glance, Nathan walks straight past me and goes into the house. Getting his things, I assume.

I hear the back door open and look up, expecting to see Craig, but instead seeing Erin.

She comes over to me, not meeting my eye. I'm not sure what to expect. We haven't spoken once since she arrived. She knows everything that happened. Cal told her. I guess he had no choice.

Without a word, she wraps her arms around me, hugging me to her. I have to choke back a sob.

"I'll miss you." Her words are muffled by my hair. "And I'm so sorry about Cal, about everything he did, I wish ... I ... " She stops, her voice breaking.

I lean away from her so I can see her face. Her eyes are so wide and sombre it's a punch in the gut to see them. "You have nothing to be sorry for. Everything that happened, happened because of me, because of what I am." My voice wavers, all my pain and regret bubbling up to the surface.

"That is not true and you know it." Her brown eyes turn serious on me.

The back door bangs. Nathan and Craig are coming toward us.

"Take good care of Nate for me." She kisses my cheek and lets me go, heading straight for Nathan.

He stops, putting his bags down at her approach. Craig picks them up and continues to the car, heading for the boot.

I look away and turn my hearing off as Erin hugs Nathan. They've probably got things to say that I don't want to hear.

I go to the back of the car just as Craig is shutting the boot closed. I have a favour to ask him. "Craig, I need to ask something ... " He gives me a curious look. "Would you mind ... helping Scarlett? I know I should be the one to help her but ... " I shake my head disconsolately., "I can't stay. And I can't take her with me, and she's just a kid ... "

"I got it." He cuts me off, giving me a small smile. "I'll be staying here for a while anyway. I'll make sure she's okay."

I smile gratefully at him. "Thank you."

He reaches in his back pocket, pulls out a business card and hands it to me. "If you or Nate get into any trouble, ring me straight away on that number."

I take a quick glance at the card.

'Craig Brigham, Criminal Lawyer, Bennetts, Hamble & Parsons. Criminal Defence Lawyers.'

He's a lawyer? I look at him surprised. This huge guy who was in the army and happens to turn into a wolf a few nights a month is a lawyer? He really doesn't look like a lawyer, not that I know many lawyers to know how one should look, but you know what I mean.

"Don't look so surprised." He chides, chucking.

"Sorry I just ... "

"Don't worry, you're not the first, won't be the last." He waves me away with a smile. "I qualified before I joined the forces. After I got injured in the blast, I came back home and wallowed in self pity for a while. It didn't really fit so I decided to finally put my degree to good use." He leans close and whispers conspiratorially, "I deal with ... special clients." He winks. "It was one of them who helped me find you." His tone leaves me wondering whether I should be feeling gratitude or a little fear.

Nathan climbs into the car, slams the door shut and switches the engine on.

"My cue," I say.

I make my way down the side of the car and climb into the passenger side. Craig shuts the door behind me. I wind the window down.

"Stay safe," Craig says to Nate.

Nathan gives him a nod and slowly pulls the car forward. Craig steps back, moving out the way. Erin waves from where she stands. I force a smile and wave to her. Then I realise I haven't said goodbye to Honor and Hope. I open my mouth to say as much to Nathan, desperately wanting to go back and see them one last time, but think better of it. So, instead, I just wind the window up and steal a quick glance at the house before it disappears out of my sight.

* * *

We've been driving for thirty minutes in absolute silence, not even the radio for company, and it's taken me this long to finally pluck up the courage to speak.

"Where are we going?" I edge out tentatively, fiddling with the metal button on my denim jacket.

"Scotland."

I let me eyes slide sideways to look at Nathan. He's focussed on the road ahead, frown lines etched deep into his forehead. "Any particular reason ... Scotland?"

He takes his eyes off the road for a moment to give me a hard stare. The disdain in them is like razor blades against my skin. He looks back out through the windscreen. I practically sigh with relief when he does. "You need to get as far away from here as possible. The Originals are in the UK and they are looking for you." His voice is cold. A shiver of absolute terror runs down my spine. "And as you can't currently leave the country, Scotland is as good an option as any. It's big and we should be able to move around pretty much unnoticed."

He reaches over to my side, opens up the glove box and pulls out a baseball cap. He drops it onto my lap. "Put this on," he orders. "I need to make a stop in the next village."

I pick the baseball cap up and run my finger over the motif. It's the cap he was wearing the day he came to see me when I was cleaning out Honor's stable with Sol, the day which started the change of everything between us.

Feeling a lump in my throat, I gather up my long blonde hair and twist it up to sit on the top of my head, and pull the cap on.

We enter the village a few minutes later. It's quiet. There's not a soul around.

Nathan parks the car up on the roadside by the local shop. "Keep your head down. I'll only be a few minutes," he says, switching off the engine and getting out of the car.

I slouch down in my seat, hiding my face under the peak of the cap. I watch him go into the shop. He comes out less than a minute later and walks a bit further down the street and goes into what looks to be a chemist. I wonder what he's buying.

The sky suddenly rolls in dark, and from out of nowhere the heavens open. The rain beats down hard on the car. Moving forward, I peer out through the windscreen just in time to see a blue flash of lightening. Keeping my face close to the windscreen, I count out loud, my breath fogging up the glass, "One Mississippi ... two Mississippi ... three ... "

The thunder crack is so loud that I nearly jump out of my skin even though I am expecting it. Wrapping my thin jacket around me, I shrink back into my seat.

A minute later, through the haze of rain, I see Nathan jogging quickly down the street toward the car. He's getting soaked. His leather jacket is doing little to keep him dry. And suddenly, from out of nowhere, I feel a longing for him inside so strong that it nearly chokes me.

He climbs into the car, bringing the damp in with him. His face is glistening from the rain. He runs a hand over his hair, freeing the settled raindrops, unknowingly showering me with a fine mist. I say nothing. He turns the engine on, cranking the air con up to hot, unzips his coat and pulls out from inside it a small plastic carrier bag. He hands it to me without a word.

Taking it curiously, I open it up and peer inside. There's a pair of scissors and a dark brown hair dye.

I look from the bag to him, a sudden sense of dread filling me. "Hair dye?" I question in a tight voice.

He pulls off his wet coat and throws it onto the back seat. "You need to change your appearance. It'll help us move around a lot easier if you're not so easily recognisable to people. It's not gonna help with the Originals knowing you exist, but if Joe Public recognise you from your picture in the paper, we're basically fucked." He shifts the car into gear and drives forward.

"And the scissors, what are they for?" It's a stupid question, I know. But still, I have to ask.

"What do you think they're for?" His tone is hard.

"You want to cut my hair?" I swallow.

"No, Alex, I want *you* to cut your hair."

"But I don't want to cut my hair." I shy away, putting a protective hand to my head.

"I don't give a fuck what you want!" he suddenly roars, slamming the breaks on. I jolt forward. The bag flies out of my hand. The seat belt tightens, digging me hard in the ribs, knocking the wind out of me.

Easing the seatbelt off, I put a shaky hand to my sore ribs, trying to catch my breath. From out of the corner of my eye I can see Nathan's shoulders rising and falling with each angry breath he takes, his hands gripping the steering wheel.

A second later, without another word, he shifts the car into drive and pulls forward.

Tears have formed in my eyes. I blink them back and turn away, looking out of the window as Nathan drives us into the unknown.

Chapter 25

Ipseity

The next few hours in the car are painful.

I'm relieved when the weather worsens and Nathan finally relents, pulling into the next services to get us a hotel room for the night.

"I got us an adjoining room," he says coming to a stop outside room six-two-nine. He slots the key card into the lock, opens the door for me and hands me the key.

He stands aside.

I walk past him into the room and drop my bags down on the double bed. "Thanks," I say, turning back. He's leaning up against the door jamb, his own bag still in his hand. There's a brief but awkward silence. I wrap my arms around my chest for something to do with them.

"I'm going to get some sleep." He reaches in and closes my door. Seconds later I hear the click of the next door room.

I'm all alone.

I grab the remote control off the desk and turn on the TV. I sit down on the edge of the bed and start flicking through the channels.

My eyes drift around the room. There's a small fridge. Nathan must have requested a room with one so I can keep my limited supply of blood fresh.

I wonder what I'll do when it runs out; hunt for myself, I guess. I wish I'd taken Nathan up on his offer to teach me now. Maybe I'll ask him to teach me before he leaves.

A tightness settles itself into my chest.

I put the remote down on the bed, open up the cooler bag, take a bottle of blood out, put it on the bedside table, and go and put the rest in the fridge. I don't bother unpacking my clothes, figuring I won't be here long enough to warrant it, so I just store my bag in the bottom of the wardrobe.

I sit back on the bed, pick my bottle of blood up and immerse myself in other people's lives on the TV, desperately trying to forget my own.

After an hour, I finally bite the bullet, knowing I can't put it off forever, and pick the plastic bag up and take it to the bathroom with me.

Standing over the sink, I empty the contents of the bag into it.

I stare at myself in the bathroom mirror. I don't know who I am anymore. I'm a ghost. I'm nobody. I don't matter to anyone.

So then, I guess, it shouldn't matter what I look like anymore either.

Without allowing a second thought, I pick the scissors up, pull my hair to the nape of my neck and start cutting.

My blonde hair litters the floor. I glance down at it. Stupid tears leak from my eyes. Sucking it up, I dry my face on my arm, pinch my lower lip between my teeth and continue to cut.

When I'm finished, I have a chin-length bob. I don't know how short Nathan wanted it, but I thought it best to at least have some hair left to hide behind.

Collecting my old hair up from the floor, I dump it in the bin and open up the box of hair dye. I read the instructions, mix up the dye and lather it all over my light hair. Then I pull the toilet seat down, sit quietly and untangle painful thoughts in my mind while waiting the long fifteen minutes for the dye to do its job.

When my fifteen minutes are up, I peel my clothes off and get in the shower.   Soon enough the water is running clear of the dye, so I get out and wrap my hair and body up in the hotel provided towels.

I pad my way back into the room, go to the wardrobe and get a pair of my pyjamas out of my bag.

There's a knock at my door. I look at it surprised. I thought Nathan would still be sleeping.

I drop my pyjamas onto the bed and go to look through the peep hole, checking it is him. It is.

I open up the door.

I smell the alcohol on him instantly. He hasn't slept at all. He must have gone down to the hotel bar. This isn't good, but understandable.

His eyes do a quick sweep of my body. Feeling self-conscious, I tighten the towel around me.

"I brought you some food." He holds out a pre-packed sandwich. "It was all they had."

"Thanks." I reach out and take it from him. My fingers graze his hand. He shoves his hands in his pockets. Lingering, he looks at anything but me.

"Do you wanna come in and have a coffee?" I ask and wait for the rebuff.

"Sure." He nods.

Hiding my surprise, I step back, allowing him space to pass by. His nearness makes my heart and head hurt.

I put the sandwich down on the desk, go over to the kettle and switch it on.

"I'll go get changed," I say, picking up my pyjamas and heading for the bathroom, desperately trying not to hope on the fact he's actually here with me.

When I'm dressed, I stand in front of the mirror trying to pluck up the courage to look at my hair.

Stop being stupid, Alex, it's just hair. It's done now, there's no changing it. Come on, deep breath, and on the count of three.

One... two... three.

I whip the towel from my hair.

Okay, so dark hair does not suit me, at all. Seriously, if Carrie were here she would be taking the piss. Come to think of it, so would Sol. A painful smile forces its way onto my lips.

I tidy my damp towels onto the rails and go out to make Nathan's coffee. He's sitting in the armchair in the corner of the room.

In the silence I make us both a coffee. I carry Nathan's over to him. He takes it without a word. I sit myself down on the bed, cradling my own cup in my hands.

"You look different," he observes.

"Wasn't that the point?" There's an edge to my voice I didn't intend.

He sets his cup down on the floor. "Have you had some blood?"

"When we first arrived." I sip my coffee.

He leans forward in his seat, resting his forearms on his thighs, hands clasped together. He looks down.

"Have you eaten?" I ask him, indicating the sandwich on the desk.

He shakes his head.

"You really should eat something," I urge gently.

His eyes snap up at me. "When I need your concern, I'll ask for it. Until that time, back the fuck off."

The atmosphere disintegrates to something near horrendous. My eyes are wide with surprise, hot tears pricking the back of them. Nathan abruptly stands and strides toward the interconnecting door.

"You're going?" I ask. My tone comes out needy.

"Looks that way." His is detached.

"But your coffee, you haven't touched it."

"I changed my mind."

I get the distinct impression he's referring to something altogether different than the coffee. He opens the door connecting our rooms. "Be ready to leave at six in the morning. We'll get on the road again while it's quiet."

And the last thing I hear from him is the cold hard click of the lock as he locks me out, permanently.

Chapter 26

Imputed

I open my eyes up to the white ceiling in yet another hotel room in another part of Scotland. The silence is all around me as I breathe in the stale, warm reproduced air the air conditioning system is funnelling out.

This is how it's been for the last week, Nathan and I staying in hotels night after night, big enough and generic enough so we go relatively unnoticed as we move around Scotland, going to places I've never even heard of before where the accents are so thick I struggle to understand what people are saying. Not that I actually have any interaction with people, or Nathan, for that matter.

He still barely talks to me. He never talks about Sol and he drinks, a lot. Nathan has always liked drinking but this is something else entirely. He's not drinking for enjoyment now, he's drinking to forget. And I wonder for just how much longer we can both continue this way.

I rub the sleep from my eyes and sit up in bed, resting my back against the wall. The TV is still on from earlier; I must have fallen asleep watching it.

The TV is always on. I can't bear to sit in silence. If I do, I start to think about the things I want to forget, and the TV is the only real company I have nowadays.

I pick the remote up and turn it over to the music channel. Glancing in the direction of the window, I see it's getting dark outside. I look at the clock - its 7pm. The last time I saw Nathan was at lunchtime when he brought me some food.

I'm surprised we're still here. We're usually out of the hotel and moving onto the next one by now.

I listen into Nathan's room. Nothing. Maybe he's in the bar. That's not unusual, but this is, being here this long.

I start to get an uneasy feeling in my stomach.

What if he's drunk too much and passed out somewhere? No, that's not Nathan, he can hold his drink. What if something worse has happened? What if the Originals are here and they've somehow figured out he's with me. What if they've taken him to get to me?

I sit up on my haunches.

My stomach is rolling with unease. What should I do? I should go look for him. No, Nathan will be mad if he knows I've left my room. Well, he won't be mad if he's in trouble and needs my help, will he?

I jump up and pull my hooded sweatshirt on over my T-shirt. I'm just about to put my trainers on when I hear Nathan's door open. He's back. *Thank god.*

Relieved, I sit down on the bed and remove my sweatshirt again.

Realising I haven't fed for a long while, I go get some blood out of the fridge. I look at the fridge contents. I haven't got much left - a couple of days' worth, max. I've been trying to limit my intake. It's not easy. I still have a nagging ache inside me for something a little better, a little stronger.

I've just unscrewed the cap when Nathan walks into my room through the interconnecting door without knocking.

We always stay in rooms with connecting doors. I don't know why. I like to think it's because he wants to be close to me, to be still connected to me in some way, but in reality I think it's just so he can have easy access to me if he needs to, you know, in case the Originals find me.

Actually, I'm a bit annoyed he's just walked into my room without knocking. I could have being changing my clothes for all he knows. He doesn't usually just walk in, though. He always knocks. Something's different.

I watch him with interest as he crosses my room and sits down on the bed, facing me. He reeks of alcohol. Well, he does to me. A normal person probably wouldn't be able to smell it, but to me he smells like an old drunk who's just had the time of this life with a bottle of cheap whiskey.

He runs his hand through his hair. "You're leaving the country," he states. Pulling a passport out of his pocket, he drops it on the bed.

"What?" I look at him aghast.

"It's necessary for your safety. The sooner you're out of here the better."

My insides take a steep dive. I don't want to go but I know it's pointless arguing. This isn't debatable; I can tell by the set of his jaw and the low tilt of his eyebrows.

My eyes drift to the passport. "When?"

"Tomorrow. I've just been waiting for Craig to sort you out a fake passport. He sent it out yesterday and I just picked it up earlier today."

"And you're only telling me this now?"

"I was busy." There's a gravelly edge to his voice.

"Yeah, busy getting drunk," I say derisively, the words out before I can stop them.

He gives me such a hate-filled look that I may as well be something he's just scraped off the bottom of his shoe.

I look to the floor, ignoring the ache it creates in me. You think I'd be used to it by now.

So this is it. This it when I go it alone. Tomorrow he's going to put me on a plane and walk away. Can't say I blame him but the thought of being without him is doing all kinds of awful things to my heart.

I put my bottle down on the bedside table and go and sit next to him. I feel his body tense up at my nearness. It makes everything hurt just that little bit more.

"Where am I going?" I ask, unable to keep the sadness from my voice.

"France, to start with," he says to the wall. "We're gonna take the ferry over. We'll drive down to Dover first thing … "

But I'm not listening anymore. He said 'We're'.

"You're coming with me?" My words come out a mess, all tangled and stuttery.

He gives me a look. "What? You thought I was gonna stick you on a boat and just ship you off?"

Well aeroplane, actually, but …

I look at my feet.

"Is that what kind of bastard you think I am?"

He's trying to pick a fight with me. I figured that from the moment he walked through the door. I know it's just the alcohol. Well, for the most part it is, anyway.

I look up at him, meeting his eye. "I don't think you're a bastard. Far from it. I just think … look, I don't know what I think." I shake my head. "I just didn't expect you'd give your life up for me."

"Haven't I already?"

Yes, and that's the problem. I've been trying to ignore the voice in my head telling me what I needed to do, what the right thing to do is, but now I don't think I can ignore it anymore.

I stare at the wall ahead. I can't look at him when I say this. I take a deep breath and let the words out. "I don't want you to put your life on hold for me anymore."

"What are you saying?" His words come out edgy.

I turn to look at him. There's no expression on his face, just a whole lot of anger in his eyes.

"I'm saying I want to go to France alone."

I've finally said it. I can't believe how strong I'm being but it's conflicting. I know it's the right thing to do but that doesn't stop it from hurting in the worst possible way.

He stares at me for a long, cold moment, then gets up and walks over to the desk. Leaning forward, he rests his hands on it and looks out of the window.

I stare at his back, troubled. "Say something."

"What do you want me to say?" His response is icy.

"Anything." *Stay.* "Talk to me, about ... Sol."

"Don't," he warns, turning to face me. His body rigid.

"Why won't you talk about what happened that night?"

"Why do you want to talk about it?"

"Because it'll help." My words come out sounding as weak and inefficient as they truly are.

"Will it?" He grips the edge of the desk with his hands. "I don't see all the talking you've done since Carrie died doing you any good. You're still as fucked up about it as you were the day it happened."

He might as well of just punched me hard in the stomach. Angry and disappointed I get up from the bed and start to walk away from him with absolutely no idea as to where I'm going. "You're drunk," I mutter.

"I might have had a drink but I'm far from drunk. You just don't like the truth because it hurts."

I turn around, resigned. "No, Nathan, you do. All the time."

He looks confused. I can see him quickly trying to work through my words. His expression clears. "Problem is, Alex, you expect too much from me." He sounds bitter. He's every right to. "You always have. You want what I can't give you." He rubs his hand over his face, hard, like he hopes it will erase me from his memory. "What I'm not willing to give you."

That hurts. "I've never asked for anything from you!" Okay, so that's not strictly true.

Anger overpowers his features, distorting them. "No? *Be nice to me, Nathan!*" he mimics, gesticulating angrily. "*Like me, Nathan! Be with me! Take care of me! Save me from the bastards that killed Sol!* He would still be alive if it wasn't for ... " he cuts off abruptly, his breathing coming in hard.

"If it wasn't for what?" I demand. I need to hear him say it.

He looks at me defiantly. "You," he simply utters, "you."

And there it is. But still, the words cut into me so deeply I'm sure I must be bleeding out right now. I grip a hand to my stomach, resting my back against the wall for support.

Then, without warning, Nathan picks the TV up off the stand and hurls it clear across the room. It smashes into the wall, dropping to the floor with a loud thud.

I stare at him, shocked.

Without a word or a glance, he storms out the room, slamming the door behind him, heading down the hall and far, far away from me.

I sink down to the carpet and bury my head in my hands.

A minute later the room phone starts to ring. I nearly jump out of my skin. I leap over the bed in my haste to answer it. "Nathan?" I say, breathless.

"No, madam, it's reception," comes a deep Scottish male voice down the line. "I'm just calling to check that everything is okay."

"Oh, erm, yeah everything's fine."

"It's just ... we, er, received a call saying there were loud noises coming from your room."

"Oh," I fiddle with the phone wire, "I must have had the TV on too loud."

"No, madam, they said there's was, erm ... shouting and loud banging noises."

"Oh, sorry." I think fast on my feet. "I er, fell off the bed. The bang was me. I'm sorry I didn't mean to be noisy."

"No, madam, of course. Are you okay? Do you need to see a doctor? I can call one for you now ... "

"No," I say quickly, cutting him dead, "I'm fine. No need for a doctor."

"You're sure?"

"Yes."

"Okay ... well if you change your mind, or need anything at all, please do call reception, won't you?"

"I will. Thank you." I hang up the phone and go over and pick the TV up off the floor, putting its broken shell back on the stand.

I trace my finger around the dent it has left in the wall. Nathan has a temper but this is something else entirely. We can't go on like this. It's tearing him apart being here with me. I'm destroying him. I need to let go of him once and for all, let him finally be free of me so he can have the life he deserves.

Pushing all my fear and reservations aside, I reach for my bag and start to fill it with my things. One of the first is the passport.

Chapter 27

You and I

I can hear the sound of Nathan's footsteps as he makes his way back down the hall toward our rooms. My heart starts to thud in my chest.

He's been gone for half an hour and it's been the longest thirty minutes of my life. My bag was packed and ready to go within five minutes. For the remainder of the time I've been sitting here chewing my nails to oblivion, waiting for him to return.

I couldn't leave without saying goodbye. He deserves more than that from me. And I had to see him, just one last time.

I'm not sure if he'll just go straight to his room, though. He may still be pretty pissed off, so it is quite likely. If he does, I'll go and see him.

He's stopped outside my door. I hear his gentle knock. My pulse quickens. Taking a deep breath, I get up, and go and open the door.

He looks at me. His expression is so pained that my insides start to ache and I almost break all of my resolve and change my mind about leaving.

Almost.

Silently I turn away and walk back into my room, leaving the door open with the invitation for him to follow. I lean up against the far wall and watch him as he slowly makes his way toward me.

He stops just past the bathroom door and leans his shoulder up against the wall, leaving the bed between us. My eyes flick to my packed bag. It's sitting there like a hot potato.

And then I'm all kinds of uncomfortable and everything in-between.

"I'm so sorry," he starts, lifting apologetic hands, his voice rough. "I shouldn't have behaved like that, I've never in all my life ... " He fixes his gaze on me. "I would never hurt you, Alex, never."

I want to laugh, a nervous, slightly hysterical laugh, but I don't think it would go down well. He's trying to apologise, and all I can think about is what he's going to say when he realises I am actually leaving. He'll probably be relieved.

And all that thought proceeds to do is to drive all the air out of my lungs and to start my head clicking over like a car with a dead battery.

Nathan takes a deep breath. "I need you to know, what I said about Sol, I didn't mean ... " He cuts off mid-sentence, his eyes finally landing on my bag.

I see it pass over his face, the glimmer of confusion, quickly clicking into understanding.

My body starts to tremble so hard that my knees knock together. I cross one leg over the other, pressing them together, stopping the shake.

"So you were serious." He hasn't taken his eyes off my bag yet and I'm getting nothing from his even tone.

"Yes." My voice cracks. I clear my throat. "This isn't healthy - the fighting, the animosity. You can't spend the rest of your life evading the Originals with me, trying to keep me safe." I rub my face.

He lifts determined eyes to mine. "I disagree."

I'm half-relieved, half pissed-off. Nathan has this way of tying me up into all kinds of tangled knots, to the point where I barely know my left hand from my right.

"It doesn't change anything."

He folds his arms across his broad chest. For a fleeting second I remember what it felt like to be held by them, back when he wanted me. "Where will you go?" he asks, not a trace of emotion in his voice.

I shrug uncomfortably, running a nervous finger down the wall, picking at the paintwork.

I hadn't gotten that far. I'd got as far as getting myself out of this room, down the hall and into the lift. In my mind, the rest, in comparison to walking away and leaving Nathan behind, is easy.

"Come on, you must have an idea." His tone is coaxing, bordering on patronising.

"I don't, yet, but I will ... soon." My face flushes as he shakes his head disparagingly at me.

Unfolding his arms, he stands up straight. "Well you don't have any money and it's not like you can go to anyone you know - family, friends, your ex-boyfriend. You're supposed to be dead, remember? But then it's not like you have any family left to go to, is it?"

My body freezes cold.

I know he can be callous but even that has surpassed my expectation of him. He really and truly meant that. He meant to hurt me.

I cast a brief glance at him. "That was a shitty thing to say." I go over and pick my jacket up and pull it on. "Why do you even want to be here with me?" I challenge. "You can barely stand to look at me for the most part, let alone be around me. I'm doing you a favour here, Nathan. I'm freeing you of me."

I get nothing back.

Frustrated, I swing my bag over my shoulder and head for the door.

"Wait ... " I can tell how hard it was for him to say that. He's behind me now. "Stay."

I hold my resolve. "No."

"I'm not asking." He's closer now, too close. I can't catch a breath.

I turn to face him. His stare is intense. I feel like he can see inside me, that he knows every single thought possessing me.

"I thought we were done." I can barely get the words out.

He takes a step closer, putting his boots flush with my ballet pumps. My heart does a nervous flip. "We'll never be done."

My bag slides off my shoulder, dropping to the floor with a thud. Then he leans in and puts his mouth on mine and everything else just fades away.

I kiss him back feverishly. Even the strong taste of whiskey on his tongue can't detract from this moment. If anything, it only makes me want him more.

He runs his impatient hands down my back and, gripping my clothes, he lifts me up off the floor. I wrap my legs around his waist. He presses me hard against the door. All of him is on me.

"I need you," he says into my mouth. His deep voice vibrates through me, touching me in all the right places, and I have to remind myself just to breathe.

He peels me off the door and carries me over to the bed. He sits me down on the edge of it and kneels between my legs. Taking my face in his hands, his fingers buried deep in my short dark hair, he picks his kissing up from right where he left it.

My pulse is pounding. I feel like I'm on the edge of bursting out of my skin.

Impatient, I yank his T-shirt up. I need his clothes gone. Now. Nathan lifts his arms, allowing me to pull it over his head.

I drop it to the floor and trail my hand down the base of his neck, running my fingers along his dog tags, then slide my hand downwards, feeling over the hard ridges of the muscles on his chest.

His eyes are fixed on mine as he presses his hand to my cheek and runs his thumb over my lips. I part them, letting it slide inside. I run my tongue over it, tasting him. There's a look in his eyes that's discernible and I know just exactly what he's thinking. A bolt of lust shoots through me and I'm sure I'm going to explode from the sheer force alone.

I lean in to kiss him, lips barely touching. He moves in closer, trying to kiss me back harder, but I move away. Grinning, I lick my lips and lean down and kiss his chest, running my tongue over his tattoo, lower and lower, until I reach the waistband of his jeans. Running my fingers inside, I feel him shudder beneath my touch. It sends a huge wave of pleasure rippling through me.

He pushes my jacket off my shoulders, kissing wherever my bare skin is. Then the rest of my clothes are off so quickly I barely register it happening. All the time his eyes never leave mine and I don't feel as naked as I actually am.

My hands are shaking so badly with desire that I'm struggling to undo his belt buckle. He laughs with a low, certain desire. It's deep and sexy, and it sets off fires at key locations on my body.

He takes over, releasing his belt in one fluid movement. My face flushes. Then one-by-one, I pull down the buttons on his jeans.

I slip my hand inside, working my way past his boxer shorts. His lips are back on mine but this time he kisses me gently, tenderly. He parts my lips with his, slipping his warm tongue inside my mouth. But now I don't want gentle. I just want him.

I touch him urgently and he quickly lets go of whatever control he was trying to maintain. He yanks his jeans and boxer shorts off, and pushes me back onto the bed. He climbs on top of me. And now all that separates us is the flimsy cotton of my knickers.

He kisses my neck, letting his tongue roam my skin, his hands everywhere. He moves lower, kissing his way downwards. When he reaches my stomach, I instinctively put my hand up to my scar, covering it, self-conscious of the permanent reminder of what I really am.

Nathan lifts his head, looking up at me through his long lashes. He takes hold of my hand and moves it away. Pinning one arm to the bed, then the other, he presses his lips to my scar.

Something dances behind my naval then waltzes lower.

He releases my arms. With his eyes fixed on mine, he hooks a finger under my knickers and slides them off.

Not willing to wait any longer, I reach down and take hold of his dog tags, leading him back up to me.

We're touching at all the strategic points on our bodies but he pauses, hovering his face over mine. I can barely contain myself, and here he is pausing.

"I love you," he says, deep and sure.

Pleasure and pain shoot simultaneously through me. I lift my mouth up to his and kiss him. "I love you," I murmur.

He sinks into me, his hard body against mine. And when he moves inside me, and we become an entanglement among the bed sheets, for the first time in a long time the demons in my head are silenced.

Chapter 28

Without You

The hotel room is shrouded in darkness. There's a faint glow from the street lamp outside that is shimmering its way across the space, lighting Nathan's perfect form. He's laid on his stomach, sleeping, shallow breaths emitting from him. He looks so peaceful, so incredibly beautiful.

I'll never love anyone like I love him, and I'll always be his whether I'm with him or not.

I reach down and pick up my bag.

I was always leaving. Having sex with Nathan was the only real and good thing that has happened to me in a long time and now I have that memory forever. But it doesn't change anything. I was only allowing myself to delay the inevitable.

You're probably wondering why I'm leaving. You think I'm crazy. I'm not. This is actually the sanest thing I've done since I was turned into this monster.

And, trust me, if I could, I would climb back into that bed and curl up against his warm, hard body and stay there forever.

But I have to do this, for him. Because I love him. Nathan will never be safe, or truly happy, while he's with me. He can't see it now, but he will, soon.

I can't allow him to continue risking his life for me. If anything ever happened to him, well, I can just about cope with the thought of living without him so long as I know he's alive and safe. I couldn't live without him permanently.

I didn't want to leave like this, slipping away into the night without a word but, as I've discovered, Nathan's not willing to let me go without a fight. He's left me no other choice.

I pick his jeans up off the floor, snake his wallet out of the pocket, remove a wad of notes and slip it in my own pocket. I don't like to do it - I feel like a thief - but if I'm going to get far enough away from Nathan so that he can't find me, I'm going to need a good head start. I know he won't let me go easily, he'll look for me, so I need to ensure I'm not easily findable, by him or by the Originals. I will send the money back to him as soon as I'm on my feet.

I resist the urge to touch him one last time, afraid I'll wake him. Silent tears trickle down my cheeks. I don't bother to wipe them away.

I take one last look at him, ingraining him onto my memory. Then, using every ounce of strength I have, I turn and move silently through the room.

With a quiet click of the door I let myself out into the well-lit hallway.

And then I run.

Acknowledgements

I'll try to keep it short... well as short as I can.

Thank you so, so much to every single one of you who read 'The Bringer'. You're kind words and reviews have meant the world to me.

I want to say big thank you to Poppet. Thank you for the edits, for loving Nathan as much as I do and for always been there when I go into writer's meltdown. Also, thank you to all my 'FB and Night' writer buddies - Catherine, Drew, Reg, Mike, Jessica, Chris, Hannah, Johanna, Shalini and Suzy. I have the best time chatting with you guys, and it's so great to know I can always log on and talk to one of you when I'm stuck on a plot line or just need some advice. God bless the Internet!

Thank you to all my friends and family – especially my mum, Carol Towse, and my in-laws, Mally and Sue Towle. Big thanks to Miss Oliver, my friend and cousin in-law. You're the best friend a girl could ask for.

Thank you to my publisher Tim Roux, what you have done, and continue to do with Night Publishing is amazing. We all love and appreciate all the hard work you put it. And I for one couldn't do this without you. Now go take a holiday!

And thank you to my gorgeous husband Craig and my two beautiful children, Riley and Isabella. We had quite a 2011 together and I for one can't wait to see what 2012 has in store for us. I love you all so very much.

Printed in Great Britain
by Amazon